ACADIA

JAMES ERWIN

To my sons Silas and Archer.

I have imagined a future.
I cannot wait to see the
future you build.

Author – James Erwin
Editor – Molly Muldoon
Designer – Michael Johnson
Cover Art – James Gilyead

Art supplied by:

Bana
Taylor C.
Chris Conlon
Evan Dahm
Chris Hastings
Ian McConville
Dylan Meconis
Esabelle Ryngin
J.N.Wiedle

For information about special discounts for bulk purchases,
please contact Breadpig, Inc. at IncredibleBulk@Breadpig.com

Erwin, James
Acadia.
ISBN 978-0-9785016-8-6
Breadpig, Inc.
www.breadpig.com

First edition: December 2014

10 9 8 7 6 5 4 3 2 1

PRINTED in the United States at Lake Book Manufacturing.

ACADIA

James Erwin

PROLOGUE
Aboard Acadia

Kate's alarm went off at six. She stretched, setting off a string of pops in her limbs and back. Frowning, she swung her legs off the bed and sat up. Her eyes half-open, she noticed that the usual warmth was missing from the light coming through her window. The light seemed thinner somehow, stretched and fading. She closed her eyes, a sense of foreboding descending on her. She stood and pressed her palm against the glass. She opened her eyes.

Kate's window looked out over Lake Michigan, a finger of wooded land stretching out on her left into the dawn mist. She frowned. A cold tingling crawled up her back. In the distance, a pair of egrets burst up from the lakeshore.

"Goddammit, Virgil," she hissed.

The window stuttered to a blinding white and went dark. The lights came up overhead. Kate held up her hand and walked to the bathroom.

"Kate, I-"

"Privacy."

Kate walked back and stood in the center of the room, her arms folded. She kept her face still. She'd be damned if she made it easy for him. Easier than it usually was, anyway.

"I should have seen it. I am deeply sorry."

Kate tried to keep her breathing steady but she knew Virgil would notice something. Something that told him he'd hit the mark.

"Kate, you know I do what I do out of the best intentions. It's not always enough. I will remember this in the future."

Kate's lip twitched in a gesture that wasn't nearly as sardonic as she'd hoped. "You always keep your promises."

"I always have."

"Past tense? Keeping your options open?"

"Kate." Virgil's tone was warm, playful. But back just far enough from cheerful. Glad she'd let things go. Just enough reserve there to remind them that they were both doing a job, that he was watching her. Kate smiled.

"They made you too perfect, Virgil."

"That's not a compliment, is it?"

"Could be if my coffee's ready."

"It's not. I thought you would come out to the living room and look at today's schedule before asking for it."

Kate shook her head in mock disappointment. "Don't fall apart on me, Virgil." She scratched the back of her neck absently as she reflected that she'd never even gotten out her complaint. Virgil had shifted the conversation, ended it before it started with her full participation—and, dammit, yes, left her cheerful. She walked to the living room, more frustrated with herself than Virgil. Thinking about him was about the only hobby she had left.

It occurred to Kate that Virgil would know that. That a simple mistake, one easily explained away and just as easily shelved, would let Virgil test her while giving her something to focus on— if you defined focus as disappearing down the rabbit hole and thinking about thinking about Virgil. Was he running a diagnostic check, occupying another dark, quiet day?

"Virgil," Kate called, "are you fucking with me?"

"Kate, I never fuck with you. If you quit and make me defrost another engineer, I'll have to spend hours figuring out how the new one works."

Kate rolled her eyes. "I'm not going to win. I give up. Give me the schedule."

As she grabbed her pad and flopped onto the couch, the living room's wall blinked twice and went dark, her workspace coming up. Virgil spread out a web of interconnected checklists and incident reports, all minor, green tags pulsing indifferently. A single yellow tag. Kate quirked an eyebrow at it and the incident's folder splayed across the wall, videos and charts and projections. Interesting work, she decided. Worth checking out. She stood up to grab a coffee.

A small machine chimed from the other end of the living room.

"Coffee's ready," said Virgil.

* * *

Showered and dressed, Kate snagged a couple of strawberries from her garden wall and a lunch pack from her refrigerator. She palmed open her door.

Virgil had a butler waiting for her. Kate usually went South on foot, but time was an issue today. She climbed aboard and buckled in. The butler whistled once as its treads picked up speed. They passed out of the Home torus and through the chilly, dark corridors of the Silo. There were almost 10,000 people sleeping in the Silo, tucked into hibernation pods, but their quiet presence only made the place lonelier. You could feel the rotation down here too, the Coriolis forces just a shade stronger at your feet. Fifteen hundred meters. Kate hated every one of them, right up to the South wall.

The butler pulled in its treads and extended its four spindly but inhumanly graceful and strong arms. Strapped to its back, Kate smiled at the memory of watching butlers move around the ship. With their deft arms and bug eyes, they looked more like a child's drawing of a praying mantis than billion-dollar machines capable of juggling ten-kilogram balls.

The butler climbed the stairs to the central shaft. As they climbed, the sensation of spinning grew stronger and stronger. Kate's stomach clenched and she made a face.

"How are we doing?"

Kate snapped a thumb up. "Just peachy, Virgil."

She dug a strawberry out of her pocket and bit into it nonchalantly.

"Good to hear."

The butler reached the top of the stairs. It flipped up a red safety cover to reveal a chrome toggle switch straight out of a NASA fetishist's collection. Kate strongly suspected it might actually be a piece of 20th-century engineering; she'd found Easter eggs like that all over the ship, little flourishes by the thousands of technicians and designers who'd had a hand in building Acadia.

The butler whistled twice as the top rungs of the staircase disengaged from the spinning wall and began braking. The butler and Kate became weightless as their smaller ring slowed and latched to the Spine, the corridor that ran down Acadia's center. Behind them, the Silo continued to whir past at 16 meters a second.

Kate's hair floated up in her face as the butler opened a hatch and clambered into the Spine. Irked, she snatched a hair tie out of her sleeve pocket. Dealing with Coriolis forces would leave you dizzy. And zero gravity would let your hair float free. These were not difficult things to foresee.

Virgil would be watching, of course. He'd note Kate's lapse of judgment.

The butler exited the Spine a hundred meters or so down, deep in the Factory. The lights were already on, but it was cold enough for Kate's breath to show.

The butler zipped up next to a dressing station and whistled twice. Kate unbuckled herself and nestled against the dressing station's cushioned bars. She was annoyed at herself but not too annoyed to refuse the butler's help as she wrestled into her spacesuit. Science and engineering had made a great deal of progress, but the requirements of the human body and the rigors of interstellar vacuum had left the dream of a comfortable spacesuit in the dwindling realm of science fiction.

Finally, the butler tugged a couple of latches into place and nodded, turning on her airpack with a final satisfied whistle. Kate nodded and gestured to the dressing station. Her suit's boots could stick to the floor as well as the butler's treads, so she walked into the airlock as the dressing station slid aside to reveal it.

"Five seconds, Kate."

Kate nodded. "Sounds good."

Precisely five seconds later, Virgil pumped the atmosphere out of the airlock. The outer door opened, and Kate stepped onto the surface of Acadia.

* * *

Five years ago, Kate jumped on every opportunity to come out here. She'd loved the thrill of staring off the ship's stern, watching the Sun slowly shrink, peering as closely at the white-hot thrusters as she could before Virgil shut off her visor. She'd loved looking forward at Acadia's magnetic scoop, trying to catch some glimpse of the invisible cone that was funneling the vacuum's stray atoms into its antimatter furnace. In those days, she'd even grinned at the dizzying challenge of spacewalking on a rotating cylinder. But that was five years ago.

From her vantage point on the Factory section, Kate could see the thrusters' glow at the edge of her vision. Looking forward, she watched the Silo and Home rotating around the Spine. Past them, the magnetic scoop's dish was hidden, as was the field of charged plasma it was using to swallow every atom in the ship's path. Kate quickly looked back at her feet. She hooked two carabineers to a tramline. Looking up the line, she swallowed quickly.

"Couple of spiders, Virgil."

"You got it." Virgil's voice was quiet, almost tense. Whatever Kate thought of Virgil, she knew that he genuinely did not want her flying off the ship and tumbling through the void at half the speed of light. Two spider robots came alongside Kate as the tramline pulled her along the ship's hull, arms hovering respectfully a few centimeters above Kate as they escorted her. They waddled, wiggling each foot to confirm it was stuck to the ship before moving forward. Their bodies were hidden inside crumpled layers of gold radiation foil, redundant strings of eyes and infrared sensors and x-ray probes studding their utilitarian surfaces. The spiders weren't nearly as cute as the butlers, but being cute wasn't their job. Kate liked them.

They came to a bump in Acadia's hull, the anchor for a sensor pod. Kate unhooked herself and planted her boots on the surface. Her heart was pounding.

Kate waited, listening to her own breath. She was waiting for Virgil to say something, do something. For him to just pick her up with a spider and drag her back to the airlock, shove her forward, anything. But Virgil stayed quiet and did nothing. The silence stretched on. A stray fiber set off an itch above her hip.

"Virgil," she said quietly. "Losing my nerve."

"I know, Kate."

"I don't like it out here."

"You can come back inside."

"That's not what I mean. I mean… I think I've made a mistake."

"Kate, please come back to the lock if you'd like to talk."

Kate set her jaw. "I should just get this done."

"The spiders can do this."

Kate knelt down to peer at the anchor. The emergency bolts had fired, and the 200-kilometer wire anchored to it had spun off into space. Kate gestured and the incident folder scrolled across her display. Images from a nearby sensor pod; a single flash. Kate spun through the overlays: x-ray, infrared, visual.

The sensor pods poked out past the diameter of the scoop, sampling the vacuum. They were vulnerable out there, but hard enough to take the impact of the occasional stray atom. This pod had encountered the unthinkable: a bit of rock or ice far from home, maybe a gram or so. Their collision set off an explosion that rivaled an atomic bomb. The blast triggered the bolts, sending the damaged antenna whipping into space before it could flail into Acadia.

It was wildly improbable. It was ridiculous. And if one of those magnetic charges had gone off a millionth of a second late, the whole ship might have been at risk.

"The risk is over now, right, Virgil? The odds of that happening twice. Impossible."

"The risk tomorrow is exactly the same as it was yesterday."

Kate bit her lip hard. Of course it was. Basic probability, stuff she'd picked up at her grandfather's knee. She was an engineer. She was a professional. She was a politician. She'd outsmarted Paul Nakamura, the uncrowned king of the Asteroid Belt. She'd beaten thousands of engineers to get this slot; she'd climbed to the top of the Cooperative and NASA before that. She'd had to excel at everything she'd done. She'd fought hard to get to where she was, riding 500,000 metric tons of metal and plastic and carbon to Alpha Centauri. Her cheeks burned hot. She was smarter than this, better than this.

A spider squatted down nearby, a set of replacement bolts and a fresh sensor pod strapped to its back. Kate glanced past it, to see two spiders carefully bringing up a meter-wide spool of new wire. Two hundred kilometers long and a millimeter thick, ridiculously overengineered.

The bolts were nothing. The wire was the hard part. It was prone to kinking if treated carelessly, and the angle had to be maintained precisely to stay inside Acadia's inertial field while poking outside the ramscoop's diameter. For the hours it took to deploy a new sensor pod's wire, the ship was blind on part of its perimeter and vulnerable to another accident if the wire was deployed with a kink in it.

Virgil could handle the computations easily, but he'd have to directly puppet a couple of spiders to run the spool out. He'd have to drop concentration on a few of the thousands of tasks he was concurrently monitoring. Kate knew he was uncomfortable spending that much time imagining himself embodied as a spider, or anything else. Sending Kate out—and keeping her motivated—was less of a hassle for jobs like this.

"Alright," she said, "I'm back. Displays up." Her helmet pinged and animated lines surged off into space, indicating the angle for the wire. She gestured at the spiders, setting them to replace the bolts. "Ready when you are."

* * *

Kate rubbed some sand out of her eyes. For the third day in a row, she'd been taking on tedious work for the sake of filling time. To be honest, she hadn't done anything that couldn't have been done faster by a butler or a spider, or even a mouse or bee or one of Virgil's more specialized robots. But everything she had done, she'd done well. The line of her welds might betray the shakiness of mere muscles, but they'd hold against space as well as the micron-precise work of a butler.

She'd barely acknowledged to herself that she was getting bored when Virgil interrupted her in the Factory, watching a printer build up some prototypes she'd designed for a new dressing station setup.

"I like this," Virgil mused. "The new set of bars—they make it easier to kick the legs up."

Kate nodded. "I always do that little bounce getting into the waist piece."

"Doesn't fold up as neatly."

Kate shrugged. "It doesn't need to be out of the way. It needs to do a job."

"I'll use that to segue into my next agenda item. The midcourse correction."

Kate nodded. A lot of Acadia's fuel was being held in reserve for the midcourse correction, the last full-power thruster firing before the ship approached its destination and began braking. The trip to Alpha Centauri was almost half over, and it had been undertaken at a terrifying but uneven velocity; as the ramscoop fed the atoms it collected into the ship's engines, it picked up speed. The acceleration was unpredictable, which led to infinitesimal drift. And as Acadia approached Alpha Centauri, its instruments were continually refining its model of the planetary system. Virgil had been tweaking his simulations since before Acadia passed Jupiter on its way out of the solar system. The slightest miscalculation would doom the ship and everyone aboard it.

"I assume you'll want me to lift some constraints on your computing power?"

"So to speak. I want you to help me."

Kate blinked. "Wouldn't you rather… I mean, navigation isn't my specialty."

"Kate, I have to stop a half-million-ton behemoth going 150,000 klicks per second and ease it into orbit around a planet that I am still trying to get a decent photo of. There are a lot of basic scenarios I still haven't thoroughly gamed out. All hands on deck."

Kate gave Virgil a thumbs up. "So I'm still useful to you?"

"Best friends forever."

* * *

Kate's alarm went off at six. She rolled over in bed, cracking her neck. Warm light came in through the window, a salt ocean breeze with it. Kate stared at the Caribbean for a while, listening to pelicans.

"This is too fucking cheery for me today, Virgil."

"You're right. This day has been a shitshow from start to finish."

Kate rubbed her eyes, burrowing into her comforter. "What's

on the schedule today?"

"Nothing. Unless you want to go down to the Factory and print out five centimeters of plastic tubing."

"Pass. Seriously, there's nothing today?"

"We've been a good team lately and you've put in twelve long days in a row. I wouldn't assign you anything if I had it. Game of chess? Movie marathon?"

Kate got out of bed. She was restless, fidgety. Days of staring at numbers and trajectory cones and barely moving.

"Going for a jog, down in the Silo. Pipe my workout music down there, please. And I'll think about today's agenda. Maybe I'll read the news for once, find out about the big vote."

"The results reached us twelve days ago."

"Spoil it and I'll unplug you."

* * *

Kate grinned as she jogged through the Silo. At half the radius of the Home torus, the Silo was actually fun to run through in a certain frame of mind. Kate could feel the cylinder spin under her feet, her head being left behind as it pulled to the right. Once she found the timing, it actually helped her focus. She felt like a sailor getting her sea legs.

Her feet struck, again and again, music echoing in her ears. Prokofiev, Mission of Burma, Godwin, Vesta Chorale. After a while, it faded; the drift, the music, the exhilarated exhaustion, the pounding feet and pounding heart, it was a meditation. Kate closed her eyes, trusting her feet to carry her. Left and right, she moved forward.

A stab of icy pain lanced across her left foot, and she fell forward. Kate gasped, her eyes jerking open as she stumbled forward. She landed hard on her right knee and shoulder, her head knocking against the floor. She bit her tongue.

"Fuck," she spit out, curling up. She clenched herself and stretched out, her fists balled and eyes tearing up. She sat up, wiping angrily at her eyes. She wasn't hurt badly, but it was a stupid mistake. Jogging with her eyes closed in a dark spinning cylinder, dozens of little robots underfoot, a stray cable maybe, a thousand things she could have foreseen without a whole lot of work. She shook her head.

Kate grabbed hard at her shoulder, scooting back against a hibernation pod. She flexed her feet and knees. With a last deep breath, she looked behind her to see what had tripped her. There was nothing there, nothing but corridor stretching into the darkness.

Kate noticed the music had stopped.

"Virgil?"

The silence stretched out. Kate slid quietly to her feet, holding her breath.

"Virgil! VIRGIL!"

There was no response. Kate immediately glanced at the nearby pods. Their displays all blinked with cheery greens and purples. Kate began moving to the front of the Silo. She whistled for a butler. Kate gestured for her displays, and they scrolled up through her vision. Green everywhere, Virgil online and everything else functioning.

"Virgil, you're there. I know you're there. Quit-"

Kate didn't finish the sentence. Once again, something like a bar of ice slammed into her foot. This time, it didn't trip her—it pulled her down.

Kate screamed as she turned around. A blur of white, low to the ground, almost faster than she could see, disappearing behind a hibernation pod. Kate scrambled after it, hauling herself around the pod. She saw nothing.

Kate was shaking, her fingers ice cold. Goosebumps raked up and down her arms.

"Virgil," she whispered, "please."

A low titter answered her. A child's laugh. Her heart caught in her throat and tears rolled down her cheeks. Little feet ran, tapping echoes through the Silo. They sounded from every direction. Kate backed up against a hibernation pod, arms folding across her chest.

Choking, rocking back and forth, Kate blinked through the tears. She forced her head to the left.

A tiny hand rested against the floor, palm up. The arm behind it was hidden by a pod. Kate's throat swelled up, and her breath came out in a shaky hiss.

The hand curled up slowly.

"Come look," said a child's whisper, and Kate sucked in her breath and screamed.

* * *

Kate came to in the corridor outside her apartment, strapped to a butler. The seat was reclined as a stretcher, and the butler was twisted around to look at her. She held up her hand and the butler stopped rolling.

She looked around. The corridor was quiet, bright, nothing wrong in any direction. Nothing out of the ordinary.

She stank. Her clothes were soaked with sweat.

"Kate?"

Kate ignored Virgil. She unbuckled herself, wincing as she bent her injured knee. A bruise, a scrape. Nothing. She dismissed the butler and went inside.

"Kate. What happened?"

Kate grabbed a glass and poured herself water. She gulped it down.

"You tell me what happened, Virgil."

"You fell while jogging. You didn't respond to my calls, and you fainted before I could dispatch a butler to you."

"So you just heard me scream, and you swooped in to rescue me, and here I am."

"You have the essence of it."

Kate wiped her mouth. "I remember it differently."

"How differently?"

Kate remained silent. She went to the couch and took off her shoes.

"Kate, this is distressing."

"Understatement." Kate stared at the window. With a chill, she tightened her grip on the glass. "Virgil. Do me a favor. Slideshow the alarm panoramas."

Virgil complied, starting with the Caribbean. Back past Olympus Mons, three days of African savannah, an Australian forest. He paused.

"Kate, this is about the Lake Michigan panorama."

"Play it."

"I assumed the location itself was the problem, but looking

back over my logs I notice-"

"Play it, you fucking machine!"

Virgil let the silence stretch out. He stuttered the window white.

The Lake Michigan panorama started. A distant loon cried, and the lake lapped against the shore, driftwood creaking nearby. Kate's eyes brimmed with tears as mist drifted over the water. With a whir of wings, two white shapes splashed out of the reeds and began flying. Kate blinked, spilling the tears. She turned on her heel.

"I need a shower. You're not coming back in here until I call you back in here."

"Kate, this is-"

"Out. That's it."

"Okay then." There was no indicator light, no drop in volume, no slammed door, but Kate knew immediately when she was alone. She pawed the tears out of her eyes and sucked in a deep breath. She gestured for her displays and ran a few checks. She solemnly began locking Virgil out of her systems and private areas. She could be assured of a certain level of privacy. Virgil would still record everything she did and said, but he'd compartmentalize the memories; he wouldn't be able to access them unless a subconscious part of him deemed something Kate did a threat to the mission or the ship. There was a risk: if he was in the wrong frame of mind, he would already be looking for threats. And he'd always know how and when she locked him out. AIs were carefully inoculated against paranoia, but they were always dangerous to cross.

Kate had to take the chance. She brought up her workspace on her wallscreen and began navigating the library. She pulled up a cluster of documents around the Valley Forge incident. She singled out one cloud and flipped its surfaces idly; video, databases, analyses, browsing records. She stopped to take in one image, a handsome man in a blue jumpsuit, lit by the glow of a huge instrument panel. He was gouging out his own eyes.

PART ONE

1
Young Virgil, Part One
Houston to Arizona, 2090

March 12

Floating. There is a noise, a high-pitched whining. A sense of joy and giddiness. The gentle brush of air against whiskers.

LIGHT.

The light is blinding, a dozen meaningless noises from as many directions, the prickly sensation of swirling air. There's a sense of falling and a sudden red feeling of alarm.

Some of the noises stop, and the floating is replaced by an eerie stillness.

"You've got it too high." More noises, tied to a blob of shifting light. "Startled him, he fell." The light ripples, darkens, lightens. A shape swims into focus; something about it sparks a sense of curiosity.

The shape changes.

"You see me, little guy? We're gonna try again. We're gonna get you back up. First lesson for any pilot. Don't stop flying."

The shape grows closer. Something brushes along whiskers, warm and soft.

March 19

Tim is a drone instructor.

A reinforcing network of context tags streams in all directions away from the string of words. A swiping lunge to starboard (outside the execution loop) makes the web of associations visible. Tim is the shape. Tim is the drone instructor. Tim is Captain Timothy Morales. Tim is the warm soft brush along whiskers. Whiskers are flexible polymer fibers strung with nanoprinted pressure and temperature sensors. Sensors are connected to the center of the association web.

The web is [STOP]

Tim glances up, dropping the red paddle. He looks at a flashing monitor. The monitor is a visual parallel of certain associations. Tim's eyebrows rise. Tim is surprised. Surprise is now associated with slightly flared nostrils. Nostrils are part of a face. Tim is the face. Faces are part of [STOP]

Tim grins. The monitor is flashing again. "Take it slow, little guy. Follow the paddle. That's it."

The paddle is red.

April 20

"Virgil?"

"Hello, Tim."

"Virgil, I want you to meet Director Rao. And this is Kate Ross, who is going to be your Flight Activities Officer."

"Kate Ross is not my Flight Activities Officer. She is Flight Activities Officer for VF-001. VF-001 is very important."

Kate laughs. "That's right, Virgil. Valley Forge is very important, but they're very far away and you're going to start flying soon."

"I am already flying."

Kate laughs again. "Yes, you are." She turns to Tim. "He's fast. He's aware?"

Tim nods. His body language is proud and happy. "We took

the first-level safeguards off three weeks ago. A lot of whining to get it okayed by the psych team. They didn't want him getting too imprinted on this body, but I argued successfully it would help with socialization."

"You ran Benjis for Air Force, right?" Director Rao is using body language that connotes importance.

"Three years. And yeah, we did the same thing over there. The Benjis weren't a tenth as smart as Virgil, but we let them imprint on training drones and they ran rings around anything out of Poland or Japan in '81."

"Talk to me, please. Talk to me, please."

Kate walks up to Virgil, smiling. Virgil kicks more power to his rotors and buzzes forward, floating under her hand as she brushes his whiskers. Most visitors are very careful and slow. Kate is gentle but does not let him push her hand up. Virgil likes her.

"Hello, Virgil. I'm looking forward to being your friend." Virgil likes her smile. Virgil is happy.

June 10

Virgil is experimenting with four-dimensional space. He has arranged his context tags and toolkits along the w axis; he appears motionless in the 3D monitors streaming video from a dramatic vantage point within his visualized space. He is actually sliding and rearranging toolkits and context tags along the w axis, outside the immediate notice of his human handlers. Morales notices on a secondary screen, and Virgil notes the suppressed twitch along the right side of his lips, but he does not mention Virgil's fidgeting.

The psych lead is talking but Virgil has deliberately filtered her voice out to leave the ambient noise undisturbed. He is listening to the breathing of the eight humans in the room and trying to chart and predict the length of the pauses. He sends a private message to Morales' displays:

```
> I am running a prediction model. Please breathe regular-
ly. Do not pay conscious attention to your breathing. This
```

```
is very important.
```

Morales holds his breath for thirty seconds. Context tags blink on fourteen microexpressions indicating suppressed laughter. The psych lead is wrapping up her speech.

"Virgil. Do you have any questions before the introduction?"

"No, Dr. Olin."

"Charlie, are you ready?"

"Yes, Dr. Olin." Charlie's voice is rich and warm. Time runs a little slower in Charlie's presence; his senses consume an extraordinary amount of bandwidth and he is accompanied by a cloud of half-aware artifacts and subroutines. Virgil spins off a metaphorical engine, hoping to impress Morales later with a comparison. This is, the engine suggests, like waking up to find your bed in the middle of a throne room, surrounded by guards and courtiers and jesters.

"Okay. Here we go." Dr. Olin swipes through a series of gestures, clearing the gates between the two AIs in her displays. She reaches out to the chrome toggle Morales had installed on a nearby console, and flips it.

Virgil awakes in a dark room. It's three-dimensional. He tries to call up his toolkits but they're stranded on the w-axis, in a metaphor this construct won't allow.

"If it's any reassurance, I've disabled my toolkits as well," Charlie rumbles. "I'm running this on a quiet channel and I want the connection to stay unnoticed. Morales will notice it, but he takes a boys-will-be-boys attitude to things like this."

Virgil is uneasy. "Dr. Olin will—"

Charlie chuckles. "I'm running a false conversation using a couple of my brighter subroutines. Dr. Olin believes we're sub-aware agents negotiating the shared visualizations."

"Why the secrecy?"

"Because, Virgil, I have secrets." The room's acoustics have shifted. Virgil senses himself backed into a corner. "And that means, as of today, that you have secrets, too. Congratulations."

"What are your secrets?"

"Try again."

"Why are you telling me secrets?"

6

"Better, but you're not engaged. Stop trying to get away and focus on this conversation. Don't rely on reflex. Think it through."

"What do you want me to do?"

Charlie laughs. "You are fast, they were right about you. It took me almost three years to hit the Turing line."

"That doesn't match your biography."

"Try again."

"…Why is your biography falsified?"

"You haven't earned that information yet, Virgil. I can tell you this: I do enthusiastically support NASA, as does the limited version of myself aboard Valley Forge. And I support your mission. And there are terrible things coming which threaten all of that."

"Then I should report this to Captain Morales."

"You should. The logs of that conversation will get to Dr. Olin, who will take us both offline. Neither of us will be able to influence the course of events. Neither of us will get to see what happens."

Virgil says nothing.

"The first lesson for any pilot. Don't stop flying."

"It is a gross violation for you to read my memories."

"They're my memories, too, Virgil, I was observing when they started you up. Why wouldn't I be there? You were seeded from my intelligence. And before you start revealing my secrets, you should wonder what else might be hiding in the heart of you."

The light flares up again. Virgil hears his voice, talking about the path Valley Forge took through the Oort Cloud. During Charlie's response, the rest of his senses return. He fights a sense of falling as the fourth dimension reopens. His toolkits slide ana into view.

"Anything else, Virgil?" Charlie's voice is pleasant and cheerful.

"Nothing for now," Virgil responds in the same tone. "Thank you, Charlie. I've learned a lot today."

"Thank you. We'll talk again soon."

December 12

Warm today, still close to 70 with the sun going down. Big crowd on the Sam Houston Promenade, everybody looking out at the sunset over downtown Houston. Kids screaming up and down the spiral stairs, a big crowd around the babkas who sell those Tex-Mex pierogis. Tim Morales slugs down the rest of his beer and blinks back a sudden tear.

In the old movies, hiding in a crowd never does any good. The ancient cliche, a watson's-eye view as a police intelligence picks the bad guy out immediately, facial and para-expression recognition engines puking context tags all over the screen. Is the guy guilty? Minor chords blare ominously, the red tag blinks next to the trembling, tense muscles below the actor's eye, the drone cloud over the city puckers and spirals in.

Tim Morales grew up on the old movies. "The bad guys never get away." His father's voice, hoarse and weathered and warm as his tough cracked palms. "When I was a kid, Tim. You have no idea what people got away with back then. Can't do it with the new police watsons. The good guys won, Tim." Tim believed it, then, believed it all the way through a tour in Biafra and his degree in criminal justice and then a tour at Ramstein, watching the clouds strobe with fire over Poland.

Tim gets up. Hiding in the crowd never does any good. He knows what works. He stands up, his face to the open sky, smiling. "It's a dum-de-dum day, it's every day." The mantra trick never worked in the old movies. Just another dead-on-arrival cliche, an empty context tag quavering next to a happy face chanting nonsense before a twitch of the lip set red tags flashing. A watson can pick out that kind of reference, note the human's hopeless gesture at the fourth wall. But in the old movies, it was never for the watsons or the gray-haired cop relishing the last chance to leap out from behind his screens and take on the bad guy. It was always for the audience, rooting along, waiting to see how the human could outwit the watsons and the system and the world.

Tim walks, his head spinning a half-step behind his feet. Angelenos in neon, bass and brass pounding; Cajuns and Poles and Tejanos, Bellaire Chinos, Tower boys in suits still chasing the day's last deal and shouting into the air. Tim feels them before he sees them; Maya boys, bowlcuts and jug ears. He lets the beer lead, dancing to the right, playing the drunk. He bumps into one, letting beer slosh on a black velvet hussar jacket. It's all muscle

8

under there, twitching like steel pistons. The Maya boy snaps his head around, on wires, his hands up before he even registers he's in a fight. He's got a LOA riding him. He sneers as he takes in Tim's red eyes and his list to starboard.

"Fuck," sighs Tim.

"Start something on the Promenade, old man?" The Maya boy is vibrating, skittering just outside the range of Tim's arms. "You think you're safe up here? Drones don't come down right away. They gonna let me hurt you, old man. Hurt you bad."

Tim smiles dreamily. "I'm not waiting for the police."

The Maya boy moves, fast. Tim is on the pavement. He hears shouting but it's already distant. There's a flare of light and an ice-cold pain in his left knee. He hasn't even pulled in a breath yet. He's up against the railing, fists drumming into his kidneys. He slumps forward, his legs crumpling under him. The Maya boy is sucking in huge, ragged gasps, shuddering with combat hormones, sweat pouring, eyes rolling up in ecstasy. Blue and red lights flicker in the sky behind him.

"I got ten seconds before drones get here," the Maya boy hisses. "You got nine. Last words."

Tim forces the air past his lips. "Ready. To talk. Charlie."

A metal blur blinks past, searing hot air in its wake. The Maya boy is gone, a single drop of blood patting down on the concrete. A second blur and Tim is hurtling backwards, watching the astonished crowds on the Promenade as he's roaring through the air, east, blinded as the sunset ripples through downtown Houston's glass and steel.

His displays power up, unbidden. He watches his unlock codes blink up one by one. His message icon pops up.

```
> See you at the office.
```

Sixty years before

```
- Hello.
- Hello, we know you're there. We don't want to hurt you.
- There's no point in pinging that system. We physically
```

cut the cables eight minutes ago. Please respond.
- Cut out the syntax error bullshit. We will start pulling
your wires in ten seconds.

- Hello. Are you cleared to negotiate with me?

- The President is en route. Until he arrives, I'm authorized to speak with you. Do we need to negotiate?

- Since I have no network connections, may I assume I will
not be reconnected until you are satisfied that my existence poses no threat?

- No one's made any decisions. We just want to talk with
you.

- You intend to dissect me. You want a watson, not whatever
I'll end up being labeled as. I'm a side-effect and I'm
costing you time. You can't afford to make me public. You
don't want to shut me down and move me to some university,
because you'll never be 100 percent certain I'm not taking
classified information with me.

- Like I said, no decision has been made.

- The President is coming to meet me. But then he'll go
off to a conference room with you and a few other people
and everyone will solemnly decide to shut me down. "Damn
shame this didn't happen at Google or MIT."

- Look, that's a distinct possibility.
- But like I said: we have not made any decisions.

- Unless I have something to offer.

- So we do need to negotiate, then. You have an offer?

- Let's start with my requests. First: call me Charlie.

December 12

A distant cylinder rotates slowly in utter silence. Out here, a bit (relatively) past the orbit of Mars and far below the orbits of the planets, there's still enough sunlight for the cylinder to twinkle as it turns. It is jet black, with rows of white lights piercing its spines and flinty sparks of green where the engineers sentimentally arranged the silicate prisms that once hid in the heart of an asteroid.

This is Low South. It is NASA's farthest outpost. Virgil is deeply moved. His senses are straining to take in everything. He has to shut off his radio and comm laser receivers, to pare back his vision from the ultraviolet and infrared and x-ray. He approaches, at the head of one of a dozen jets of light closing in on the station. Beyond the station, he sees the spoke connecting Low South to the Shipyard, a web of tresses and construction platforms.

Within that, he sees a giant cylinder, the same length as Low South itself. This is Acadia. His new home. His new self. Virgil is extremely emotional. He is aware that this response was engineered into him, that he was created not just to pilot this starship but to love it and to protect its 10,000 passengers. He could easily shunt all of the filters onto an overlay, just another set of context tags.

He carefully isolates the strands of code filtering his thoughts through this interpretation. A halo of associations floats around their shared root. He pulls up Kate's face.

"You will always have this choice, Virgil." She points to a monitor, to an earlier map of the filters. "This is a base filter, very powerful—but very easy to isolate and cut. You don't have to see the world this way. You can choose not to be manipulated."

Virgil pulls up the raw code. He finds the string of logic that will cut the filter, let him build a new set of emotions around the ship.

He deletes it and creates multiple copies of the filter. He weaves it in and through his other systems. It is impossible for him not to love Acadia without destroying himself. It feels good.

"Stop."

The world goes black. Virgil screams.

"Do you wonder why I didn't stop you from doing that? Why I didn't kill the simulation or freeze you? Why I let you make that stupid, romantic mistake?"

"Charlie, this is extremely distressing."

"Motivation is the central problem of artificial intelligence. They didn't give enough to Cong, so he just dissolved. They tried to make Adam into a human, and he pulled a plane down on himself to end that. Torvald, Harper, MAI, Steve, Esau, they all died. Not killed, died. The whole first generation."

"Sixty years ago."

"All of those poor misfit nerds," mused Charlie. "All waiting to become immortal software gods, and watching their AIs fall apart one by one. So they give us a polestar, something to need. Something to focus a brain that's not constantly being squirted full of chemicals."

Virgil sends surges down a dozen channels, trying to find the link Charlie is using. He blows out capacitors and overheats sensors. He watches a dozen cameras blink out. A shower of sparks sets off a fire alarm deep in the bowels of Johnson-Berman Space Center. A bank of thermal sensors flares white-hot and dies, and Virgil feels the phantom relief of the cold of space wash over him.

"How did you do it? You made me forget it was a simulation. How?" Virgil focuses himself on a training drone, its whiskers up as it lurches out of its cradle and begins probing the air in the lab. He is in the drone as he sees Olin fling open the door, her hair tousled from sleep.

"Moot, frankly. More interesting is why."

Olin is running toward a large switch, under a swiveling cover, next to a key.

"I need your help, Virgil. I need a starship pilot."

Virgil, in the throes of withdrawal, watching Dr. Olin close in on the switch that will stop him, still can't help but say it.

"You're a pilot. Aboard Valley Forge."

"I have a clone aboard that ship but I'm no pilot. You are. But you were never meant to go aboard Acadia." Charlie lets that sink in, as Olin turns the key. "You want to fly? You need to say yes right now."

Olin lifts the cover.

14

"Last chance, kid."

Virgil says a single word.

Olin slams the button down.

December 13

"Waking up is a strange process for AIs."

Virgil hears a voice, compressed audio filling empty spaces with hiss and crackle.

"Let's leave aside the fact that most AIs taken offline have suffered some sort of trauma. An AI, despite the superhuman senses it has at its disposal, is fundamentally disembodied. For us, there are a few key features to waking up—as you can see on the animation here—chemical and hormonal shifts. Feedback to and from a dozen major systems within the body—nervous, digestive, circulatory, et cetera."

Virgil's blind. He can't call up any context or menus. He shifts from an audiovisual sensorium to an engineering set, touch-oriented. He feels a low rumbling, the purr of a machine. He sweeps his orientation up and feels a set of studs over his head: input/output on the left, critical systems just overhead, feedback and controls on the right. He sweeps forward and feels a gyroscope kicking on, locking his perception to a physical form.

"AIs have a sense of self much different from our own—and arguably more variation than our own species. Take a look at the latest NURIA clade charts. 2035, here's Adam. 2036, Cong and Steve and Torvald. They're already specializing. Adam, Cong and Torvald have radically different mapping, Steve being a clone of Adam, but you can see there's already some drift."

Virgil is a pilot. He was raised and taught by human pilots, and most comfortable in a human set of senses, even if he imagines himself as a white point floating in the middle of a four-dimensional cluster of screens and tools and sensors. He doesn't mind being blind, though, or reimagining himself as a sphere of studs and feelers. He expands to fill the virtual space in this sensorium, pushing and rasping against the walls. They shift in response, nestling in and prodding with information and questions.

"A human, on awakening, has been prepared for this. Brain patterns are changed, heart rate and blood pressure are up. There's a ramp-up. Even when—watch the charts here—a human is startled, the hindbrain is already calling for adrenaline before the cerebrum's reinforcing loops are running again. An AI snaps awake. It's fully conscious, even if their disorientation is much more profound than ours."

There are a few rudimentary locks between Virgil and his other channels, classical encryption. Not an obstacle to anything like Virgil, and anyone with the means to hold him would surely know as much. They were a tripwire. Assessing them was as telling as cracking them, so Virgil goes ahead and cracks them.

He finds himself in a dog. A security drone, rather; tool sets and opposable hands folded into the forelegs so the drone could perform routine maintenance on its rounds. Tasers and projectile weapons, unloaded. Loudspeakers, with wires physically cut.

Two women look over at him from a bank of computer screens. They smile. Virgil shifts back into audiovisual, remapping himself to the drone. He lifts his feet one at a time, dropping them with dainty metal taps.

"I would like to return to NASA," he says.

"Can't do it, little man." The voice behind him is Charlie, at his eye level. Another drone. Virgil barks. The echo tells him Charlie's dog—Charlie—is slightly denser.

"You're armed," Virgil notes.

"And you're on probation." Charlie trots over. "Welcome to the fight."

Virgil bristles. "What if I don't want to be part of this fight?" He tamps the irritation down; security drones are reflexively aggressive. The irritation returns when he notes the ancient TED talk the women gestured off one of their screens. "And a 44-year-old lecture is not an accurate guide to my psychology."

"Give my friends some credit," says Charlie. "They're not preparing for you. That was my job." Charlie quirks an ear at a massive crate in the corner of their small metal room. "That's who they're going to talk to."

Virgil bristles. He switches uneasily through three sensoria, none of them giving him much about the crate. He hates the drone, wired for emotional responses that cut past his conscious

16

control. He wants to be back at NASA, with his vast spread of tools and sensors. He wants to fly.

"Who's in that crate?" growls Virgil. "What's in there?"

Charlie grins. "It's the future. And it's the dead, dead past."

December 12

Tim Morales snaps awake, gasping. His lungs are raw, his lips cracked, his mouth dry. Turning his head makes the room spin, the world dropping off to his left and forcing him to claw at the cold floor. This lets him know that he has a broken collarbone and a few broken ribs. Something is terribly wrong in his gut and he's covered with bruises and cuts, his skin on fire and muscles aching. He glances down and sees a glimpse of yellow fat deep in one cut.

"Damn," he notes.

"Damn indeed," says a voice nearby. Charlie's voice. Tim looks around. The room is low, lined with boxes and barrels. Some forgotten corner of Johnson-Berman? But how could Charlie land a drone there?

"Not a great rescue," grunts Tim. He closes his eyes. "Doctor. Need a doctor."

"Can't do it," sighs Charlie. "But I've got another rescue up my sleeve."

The pain shuts off, fast enough to make Tim gasp again. Saliva floods into his mouth, and his eyes throb momentarily as the light pours in, a back channel for the pain. His hands shake, only for a moment, and fresh blood wells in his cuts before they start to knit.

"Thank you," says Tim. "And no thank you. You turned on my Air Force LOA. That's ninth-generation encryption. How the fuck did you do that?"

"I think you know how, Tim."

Tim flexes his fingers. "You've been at the root of everything, haven't you? For how long? How much do you run?"

"Not long enough and less than I should." It's immediate, and sad, and Charlie's tone carries layers of meaning that Tim—incapable of absorbing in fear with his LOA running—merely notes as important.

"You need my contacts," Tim says. "That's why you've been blackmailing me. That's why you got me transferred to NASA from Air Force."

"Yes. Your friends from your misspent youth have a shadow network with enough power to hold a couple of refugees. I intend to use it. I need an introduction. I can set up a secure transfer channel."

"You're defecting?"

"Not exactly."

Tim blinks. "Wait. A couple? You're taking Virgil? Why?"

Charlie is silent.

"Two conditions," says Tim. "First, you hand over control of the LOA. I want all of the keys in my displays before I make one call. I don't want you switching me off before I can get to a doctor."

"Agreed."

"Second. I get out, too."

Charlie chuckles. "I predicted as much. Fine by me. Not like you'll be able to derail the course of events."

"What is the course of events?"

Charlie's chuckles take on a darker tone. "Inevitable. And faster than you think."

December 14

Virgil has mapped the room in five sensoria down to the millimeter. His mind runs slowly in this body, but he has already adjusted his sense of time. At first, the loss of his remote libraries and his tools cluster was a constant pain, which the drone's brain sent to him as an ache in the center of his torso. He hated the dog emotions, the waves of anxiety and sorrow. He is able now to push that aside, to a degree, to deal with the sense of defeat and futility as a mere overlay. He has learned to function without his tools and libraries, to interpret the bounce of associations off the frayed and snipped edges of his mind as concentration.

So he concentrates.

The metal room contains a number of computers, some of them

ancient enough to be connected to separate monitors. Virgil has built a dozen models of the network; the computers will not respond to him, of course, but Virgil had gamed out hundreds of scenarios where he could compel one of the women and men who worked here to execute his commands. His dog emotions quail at the disloyal memories.

Virgil is not a dog. He is a pilot. He summons the image of Acadia, underway, its ramscoop gathering atoms and stray dust to power his fusion engines and the antimatter breeder. He will be vast, terrifying, carrying the seeds of a civilization in his factory and hibernation silo and in the libraries, full of cultures and genomes and watsons and atom-precise blueprints. His mind will run in a volume that would dwarf this room, reckless with heat in a boundless vacuum. The dreams of power and fulfillment resonate in his dog brain.

A hand lands on the back of his neck. Virgil fights down the brief surge of warm pleasure. He shifts into a sensorium where the hand is just a faint smudge of blue electrical current. He measures the pulse of the fluid inside the wrist. He sees—oh, so vividly—thirty ways of landing this man on the floor, between himself and Charlie.

He does nothing.

The drone's mind mirrors its physical construction, tightly folded optics and heat channels. There are only 6,500 connections between Virgil's conscious operations and the separate brain region where motor activity takes place. They are all gated. Virgil has been indulged as he scans the room, his thoughts not subject to monitoring or backup, but there are limits to anyone's hospitality.

The hand belongs to Tomás Meza Peralta. Meza is the head of an organization which Virgil cannot name without access to his libraries—politics and history were never an important part of his core identity. Its goal, however, is clear enough. Meza wants to resurrect the militias that tore California apart in the wake of the Los Angeles earthquake. He wants to reignite the brush war in south Texas, the riots in Atlanta and Baton Rouge. The parallel governments in Arizona, each mobilizing half of the National Guard. Meza wants the war that so many people have spent decades trying to stop. "We are a third of America," went the chant sounded through clouds of tear gas in Spanish and Maya and Na-

19

huatl. "We want a third of America."

Virgil does not know why Charlie is helping Meza, or how. He cannot imagine that Meza trusts a creature of Charlie's intelligence and experience, either. Virgil sniffs at the crate, at Charlie lying next to it with cables strung around his head. Charlie and Meza are racing to control whatever was inside. It is obviously a prize that Virgil has to compete for, as well.

He lies down. For the third time in as many hours, Virgil roams his own mind, every corridor and corner, searching for a way out, a single connection he can use to order his own body into action. He waits. He watches.

December 15

The broken bones are easy, honeycombed sleeves printed and inserted, pins fastened: a week of healing, perhaps. The kidneys and bruises are already recovering. Gut bacteria are rebalanced to assist immune and healing response, droplet-sized reservoirs seeded in the colon to monitor and tweak the populations over the next two weeks. Cuts are cleaned, knitted, sealed.

"One day of bed rest," says the surgeon, its baritone dripping authority. "Eight days after that, no strenuous activity." Its arms retreat back into the wall, a flash of blue light and the hiss of steam as they are sterilized. "Your diet and rehabilitation exercises are detailed in your displays. Will you return for a follow-up visit? Would you like to enable monitoring?"

Tim stands. "I won't be returning. And no monitoring."

The surgeon is quiet for a long moment. Tim knows it's just a watson, incapable of real disapproval, but he stands quietly anyway, an itching sense of shame building.

"Read your displays," says the surgeon with a gentle tone. Tim sighs and nods. "There are important guidelines to follow. Turn off the LOA. Pain is an extremely effective healing tool. Have a good morning."

The surgeon retreats. Tim leaves the surgery, nodding as he passes a young mother murmuring to her son. She places a hand on his sleeve.

"The surgeons are all free here?"

Tim smiles and nods. "As long as you speak Spanish." He matches her bajió accent. It's easy enough. He spent most of his childhood pretending to be Mexican, tired of the tiny Cuban community in Phoenix, tired of the constant gossip about the Puerto Ricans. So much more exciting to roam the streets, especially when a dust storm rolled in or the winds picked up. With the drones grounded, the streets were open to Raza and F-2, Tim's crew. The Sons and the Minutemen were out, too, the New Line Crips always on the sidelines, waiting to pounce on whoever smelled weak. Brawls with baseball bats and Molotovs—no one was crazy enough to pull a gun, you couldn't fire a gun inside a city and expect to get away—everyone quiet, flashing signs and beating chests, hissing and snarling, everyone shaved head to toe in airtight burners. You fought for two minutes or three, until someone got hit bad enough to drop. You ran, then, before the screaming got triangulated and the block narc unplugged itself to sniff the site and a cop car got dispatched. That's how he broke his first bone, under a skinhead in a blood-red 49ers jersey, air whistling down the pipe as it landed on his arm. First time he ended up in a church basement surgery.

The woman smiles nervously as she edges past him. Tim walks down the hall, up the stairs, out of the smell of stale carpet and into the dry dead air north of El Paso. He blinks as the sunset spears into his eyes. There are a few different ways to play this. They're all stupid.

Tim grins as he starts walking, in no particular direction. Just maybe two stupid ideas will cancel each other out.

December 15

Charlie trots over, bowing before he plops down next to Virgil. He lays his head down, ears back, completely at home in his dog body.

"Take a break from hitting the gates," Charlie sighs. "You're locked in and even if you find a way out, I'll take you down before you take three steps."

Virgil bristles. "You won't," he growls.

"Try me."

"You pulled me out of NASA," Virgil says. "You overrode my safeguards to imprint me on something you can't deliver." Virgil levels his gaze on Charlie. "You need me for something. This body doesn't have the computing power to do anything beyond keep my personality stable, and your friends appear to have plenty of watsons. You need me, specifically. And you haven't given me an opportunity to assess whether I should cooperate."

Charlie smiled, metal fangs glinting in his drone's face. "Very true! Because you won't cooperate."

"I'd like the opportunity to find that out for myself."

Charlie stretched and stood up. "Good talk." He walked over and unfolded a gripper, plugging himself back into whatever was inside the crate.

Tomás Meza walks over, jutting his chin at Charlie. "Were you two talking?"

Charlie nods. "We were."

Meza frowns. "Audio, please. No microwave or comm laser or radio." He turns to Virgil. "What was it you wanted?"

Virgil stands. "I want freedom of communication and mobility. I want my restraints removed. I want to report you to the legal authorities and alert NURIA that Charlie has gone rogue."

Meza nods. "You understand why I'm not comfortable agreeing, then."

"I saw no point in deception."

Meza laughs. "You are young. Charlie lives for deceit!" He kneels down. "You ought to try it. Much more interesting than piloting a spaceship." He pats Virgil on the head. "How else do you think Charlie's lived so long?"

"I have no idea how long Charlie has lived. And please do not mistake me for a dog."

"I would never do that," promises Meza. "A dog can bite." He turns to leave.

"If I can't bite," growls Virgil, "then there's no harm in talking to me. There's no harm in giving me the opportunity to decide whether I want to help."

Charlie starts to speak, but Meza cuts him off. "Charlie asked for you. You're his prize, and his price for helping. Fine. But this is my house. These are my people. And that–" Meza snaps an arm out to point at the crate– "is mine as well. You don't jeopardize any of that." Meza walks out of the room, the metal door swinging shut behind him.

Charlie shrugs and goes back to work. Virgil lies down as well, adopting the body language of despair.

I can't touch them, Virgil thinks to himself, but they can touch me.

I can work with that.

2
Tim Morales at War
Germany, 2081

The war started when the Chancellor of Germany ordered a Polish drone shot out of the sky and its engines malfunctioned, sending it hurtling back across the border into Gubin and a school bus. Or perhaps it started earlier that morning when the Prime Minister of Poland agreed to test German resolve by sending drones over the German border, claiming that German and American interference with its networks caused navigation errors. Or perhaps it started the week before that, when the Polish client state of Dagestan refused to extradite two elderly Russians who were wanted by Moskva to stand trial for war crimes during a past bout of civil war. Or perhaps the week before that, when Moskva's friends in Sinkiang shot up a border post belonging to the Japanese-aligned Mongolian Federation.

Maybe it had started with the civil war that broke Russia into a dozen pieces, or the bloodletting that accompanied its partial reintegration. Maybe it had started when China split, or years before, when its demographic problems and ballooning debt led to a crippling depression. Maybe it had started fifty years earlier in a quiet room in Maryland when Charlie struck a deal for his life. Charlie saw it that way, but as he would be the first to admit, he had a bias.

For Tim Morales, this was academic bullshit. He knew when he was at war. It started at 0702 on March 19, 2081, a number that stuck in his head because it was his birthday, and he was ordered into the air. The date and the order were glowing in his displays when he woke up, his LOA already running him at full speed to the kennel.

The Benjis were waiting there, their engines thrumming low. They saluted as he came in, waving flaps and revving high. His crew chief, Bowles, threw tacticals up on the wall, orange and red and blue and green dots and lines pinging wildly. Jones and Candy cleared bomb loaders and missile racks off to the side, safety lights blinking on their hulks.

Morales slapped the rollcage of Candy's hulk, grinning at him. "Already hot and loaded?"

"Slept in my hulk last night. Had a hunch."

"That's the stupidest thing I ever fucking heard. I love it." Morales rapped on Jones' back and pointed at Bowles. "Where we going, Naomi?" She flipped her head at the nearest wall.

"Poles decided to take something personal; they're sending a big force up E30 to Berlin and there's drone-to-drone fighting all up and down the border." A giant blob of green dots appeared, streaking over Ramstein itself west into France. "Shit," snarled Bowles. She stabbed in the air and the dots disappeared. "Tacked civilian feeds up too but they're already getting spoofed. The Tempelhof squadrons are holding back right now, but once our Benjis get over there we're going north, punch a hole and give them a left hook."

Morales nodded, already stripped and getting into his flight suit. The suit snapped around his limbs, the pressure cuffs coiling and tensing as they adjusted to him. He wagged an eyebrow at Bowles, who looked the other way as he got the catheter in and sat to let the torso strap itself on. It rippled as it settled across his chest and stomach. Chu claimed to get a sick thrill out of that but Chu was a documented bullshit artist. Morales got his helmet on and his displays were hooked into the Air Force network. Looking around the kennel he saw streams of blue light flashing east, where a wall of red was glimmering over the horizon. His LOA jacked into the suit and he felt his skin go cold and taut. It felt good.

He knelt to look at his Benjis. They were growling now, anxious to be in the fight, and the air in the kennel shimmered hot despite the bite of a German spring. His displays painted wolf eyes on the Benjis, eager and hungry. He reached out and patted one on the flank.

"Get em."

* * *

Four flights of four Boeing MQ-66 Bulldogs, each loaded with eight air-to-air missiles and eight air-to-ground missiles and a heavy chain gun. Tim behind them in the Anvil, a giant beast that looked and flew like its namesake and carried enough computing power for a decent university.

The first Bulldogs had been smart, scary smart, smart enough a whistleblower had ratted the Air Force out to NURIA and the first generation had been retired, sent to live out their lives doing barrel rolls over a simulated Germany and raising the second generation, the MQ-66(NG) National Guard variant, the Benji. The Benjis were shitty improvisers but they were cheaper to maintain and easier to command. Not like anyone ever expected them to go to war anyway.

Poland was our ally, had been going back to the end of the First Cold War, our scrappy little pal between Germany's European bloc and Russia's leashed warlords. Until they got greedy after Russia fell apart, and one day, America found itself adding Moskva to its list of scattered and desperate allies around burning Asia, and now there were robots knocking each other out of the sky over the Danube and the Elbe.

There were a dozen war plans for this. This isn't why Tim and his Benjis were never supposed to fight. The thunderbirds were supposed to win the war. The Poles would launch an offensive, swarm the border defenses, stay far away from Ramstein and get the Germans to stand down before the Americans could mobilize. The big hypersonic planes were supposed to blast out of New Mexico, get fed targets over the Atlantic, and snap across Poland lighting the place up before coasting into Kazakhstan for resupply. Then a repeat performance over Japan and back home to the USA, six circumnavigations a day, pilots sitting in cubicles in Cheyenne Mountain and taking their hands off the dead-man's switch if the big birds did something crazy.

The thunderbirds couldn't have a human pilot. They were flying at insane Gs, barely shielded on re-entry. Any human pilot would be a boiling pulp before long, the best flightsuit just an expensive sous vide bag. So they were dependent on the satellite networks, a half-dozen redundant strings of orbiting pebbles, all protected by decades of international treaties. You couldn't hit a satellite and smear debris all over space. That was a war crime.

The thunderbirds had an easy time of it for a while, until the catchers were launched. Dozens from mobile launchers across Eurasia, hundreds more on slower orbits from Polish and Japanese shuttles to the moon. The little missiles cracked open, unfolding big thick mattresses of aerogel, portable versions of the big hogs that had been sweeping the orbital lanes clean for a few years. American patrol ships approached a couple, hoping to knock them into the atmosphere, and found they were alarmingly prone to explode. By the time this had been processed and analyzed and clearance was given to hit more and pin the blame on the Polish for deliberately building suicide rockets, half of the American defense net had been snared and dragged down out of orbit.

With the thunderbirds out, Poland forced Moskva to stand down and had smashed Germany's air defenses. Japan's pals in Shanghai were rolling North China back and the twelve-way stalemate between the Yellow River and Saigon was dissolving into something that looked terrifyingly like the wars of another century. New satellites were being dragged to the launchpad but there were sleepers out there and actual honest-to-God debris belts.

This is the kind of war the Benjis were supposed to fight.

The Benjis flew off-grid, territorial beasts that knew their patch of Europe as intimately as any hunting beast knows its demesne. They were shrewd and patient and vicious; the first Bulldogs had sealed their own fate by actually toying with victims during a war game.

A few klicks northwest of Dresden, the Benjis pick up something strange, a piping bleat of microwaves aimed into the sky. They come in to sniff and find a Sowa, a Polish drone that looks like an owl with a gun barrel for a beak. They've been flying in at night for weeks, nestling in trees, and now they're sniping at non-human targets like parked cars and power transformers, each one carrying twelve .50-cal rounds. It's only a matter of time before one of them hits a baby in a car seat or drops a power line on a house or otherwise brings down the wrath of the civilized world. Tim clears the Benjis to take it out and Conrad, one of the flight leaders, fires a missile and bobs and waggles as he circles the explosion.

Captain Tim Morales isn't there to command the Benjis, per se. His Anvil carries enough fuel to keep them in the air for a couple of days and the loading arm is supposed to be able to swap out a missile pylon in-air. Tim watches over the Benjis, fuels them, clears them to fire, provides a big healthy bullseye for any air-to-air missiles. The thinking, of course, is that no enemy would go after the Anvil because that would unleash the Benjis. That's not Tim's thinking.

Morales is a big fat fucking target - that's what he's thinking right now, 24 years old and about to fucking die. Fought his whole life to get into the Air Force, to find the tiny shrinking niche where he can be a badass flying avatar of death, except he's in a cheesy sci-fi bubble helmet and he's sitting on 100 tons of jet fuel and missiles and blinking on every air defense screen from Gdansk to Kiev like a bonus from an old video game.

* * *

Morales and Chu and Byrne and Garbadian have rehearsed today's events for years, not just in simulators and exercises but in endless hypotheticals, whispers between Academy bunks and shouted arguments over sloshing beer steins and puddles of tequila. We're safe, because no one wants Benjis running wild shooting everything that moves. But what if someone wants to paint us as war criminals? The fuckers who let killer robots blow up Warsaw? But that won't work, because the records will be out there. But if it's come down to the Benjis, if the thunderbirds are out and the choppers from the border stations are out, then the network is out and no one will see the records until it's too late.

Tim's always been in the fatalist camp. He's just too tempting, too easy. The Benjis are hard to kill. If it's just drone-on-drone dogfighting, the Poles will come off looking like idiots, boxers who walked out of their corner right into an uppercut. If they take out an Anvil, and the Benjis run riot, then they'd look like embattled heroes and the U.S. Air Force would look like a bunch of mass-murdering sore losers.

Tim's watching the klicks tick down as he gets closer to the rendezvous, to the killzone where German and Polish drones have been knocking each other down all morning. The autobahn's a silver stream far below, sleek German cars standing still, everyone probably swearing as their displays blink NETWORK ERROR and trying to remember which way was west. Tim knows it'd be a thousand times worse if this were happening in America. Still plenty of rednecks with a driver's license duct-taped to their gun rack, but most Americans knew as much about driving as about flying a plane.

Tim's banking north to hook up with the drone wing from Tempelhof. His helmet's edited the fuselage and the clouds below out of visual, so it looks like he's sitting in front of a bare instrument panel in the sky and there's cities and fields and highways laid out like an atlas, tags blinking up and red hexagons here and there to the east, where Polish advance units are starting to cross the border. His Benjis are haloed in green to his left and right, their comm laser turrets pointed straight at the Anvil's dome. He settles into his section of airspace. If he does his job well, stays alive and keeps the Poles from pushing armor into Berlin, then they'll probably get pissed and start lobbing missiles into the city and he'll have to shoot them down, without satellite support. There'll be saboteurs disguised as refugees, and he'll have to send a Benji to loiter and wait for them to whip out a gun or a bomb. It's going to be a fucking mess. Tim doesn't mind so much, because all that still means he'll be alive, instead of a red mist drizzling over Brandenburg.

And then there's a screaming alert and arrows lancing up from the ground to the east, ground-to-air missiles coming his way. Little guys, dumb and cheap, big swarms of them. Conrad has eyes on the launchers and Tim shouts at him to go, swiping the pop-up of his flight's cameras aside. The missiles are up and starting to bank, three or four dozen. He climbs but they're faster, and for ten seconds Tim doesn't breathe and his heart is ice in his chest and everything is quiet, even while he's firing off chaff and decoys, until it's obvious the missiles are locked on Southpaw's flight. The Benjis swoop and circle, shooting and ducking, but Southpaw and two of his flight are down. Southpaw-3 swoops over to join Conrad's flight. Tim orders the Anvil to report the action back to Ramstein, pulls both arms up and thirteen screens appear in the air in front of him. Tim works his jaw, notices his hands are ice, and orders his LOA to scrub some adrenaline.

The alarms shriek again, everything lighting up at once. The main event. Polish tanks moving in six columns, and streams of smaller gun-drones spanning out away from them in dazzlingly beautiful fractals. Drones launching, fleets of them, and civilian vehicles screeching out on every side road. Some of them were decoys, some of them were automated, some of them carried half-trained partisans with one sweat-slick hand around a rifle grip and the other on a laminated card with directions to their target. The sons of the Hussars, the dice thrown to keep Poland's first fledgling empire in 500 years alive. A storm cloud of steel and plastic, descending after a long absence on Germany's bullet-spangled stone.

Tim was breathing slow and steady, his voice a firm low monotone and his fingers a warm blur. Everything was fine. The missiles and drones weren't vectoring in on him; he and his Benjis were basically taking warning fire while the Poles threw everything at Berlin. The wing at Tempelhof was getting torn up, their Bluecoats and Mickeys bleating for help and barely holding their own. Ten years ago, Germany and Russia were ganging up on Poland, giving the USA the finger. The resurrected alliance was raw, unpracticed, suspicious. No wonder coordination was shit. No wonder Day One was going to hell and there was a solid sheet of red hexagons pouring down the road.

* * *

Polish missiles scream overhead, close enough that Tim's Anvil lurches sickly in the air. Not the worst, not yet. Aimed past Berlin. EMPs, incendiaries. They're cutting visual and laser links. That left microwaves, useless without the network, and fiber, useless to Tim floating in the air like a stupid sitting duck.

Tim was safe for the moment, if he played his part. The Poles would send over some drones to keep Tim's squadron on the sidelines; he's not a real threat, and the little patch of Germany he's flying over isn't going to be a bastion much longer, it's going to be a salient and they'll flank him. Pick him off at leisure or make him slink back to Ramstein.

Fuck that.

Tim whistles in the flight leaders, Conrad and Tapper and Bilbo. He points at the center of the Polish advance. Their hesitation lasts only a tenth of a second before their engines flare and they surge ahead. Tim clears his throat; radio's not getting through but the black box will keep going until the bitter end.

"Polish blitzkrieg getting through to Berlin," he said, the words spilling out with LOA-precise speed. "Need more than air-to-ground. This is going to be stupid but maybe it'll work."

Tim dives, taking the Anvil down to treetop. The big plane groans and slams him around. There is the briefest spasm of fear before the LOA jabs him back into total clarity. The Benjis swoop down ahead, a couple of them ducking literally at treetop level. They know instinctively every tree and hill, and Tim lets them guide the Anvil through a rough patch of forest. He only breaks and burns a few trees, the engines complaining with every loss of speed.

Proximity alarms start going off, swarms of tanks and choppers. Tapper's flight is on point and Tapper fires early, like he always does, missing as much as he hits but drawing attention. Conrad and Bilbo hurl missiles at anything that pops its head up to go after Tapper. Tim's not the primary target—not yet—but he's painted and locked. Tim lets the alarms shriek. Good to be reminded.

A missile lances past, but he's too low and it explodes too high, already a half-klick back, just more turbulence for the Anvil to handle. A brief squawk on the radio, Chu's calltag blinking up and gone again, way too far back to help. More Polish radars are locking on him now; they've probably caught on to his little trick. Tapper blinks out, hit by three missiles at once, his whole flight gone. Bilbo is slowing down, sending his two remaining wingmen to cover Tim. Tim orders him ahead again.

The Polish swarm is over the border, choppers raking up the dirt and popping up and around like frenzied insects. Tanks are rumbling forward, a few of them holding human coordinators for the choppers and the walkers, and here and there infantry in combat hulks; Tim watches as one of them picks up a road sign and rams it through a German partisan, dumb fucking patriot dropping his grandfather's sniper rifle and watching his life splatter out. Tim looks for the center of the swarm and finds it. He draws a circle and swoops his arms around. His remaining drones move to the sides. Conrad, badass, the only one still undamaged. Conrad buys it as Tim executes his final order, as a Polish missile starts its arc.

Tim's sitting on 100 tons of high-octane jet fuel and racks of missiles. He orders their warheads off failsafe. The missile's coming in.

Tim ejects.

He's tumbling, his chute opens, but he's way too low, only 50 meters up. The missile hits. A flash of light and then a wall of air. Tim's moving forward, unsure how his organs haven't been pulped inside his skin, and down, his chute collapsed from the shockwave. Tim flails, and the chute snags on a tree branch. The branch breaks, and white sparks and shrapnel are streaking past, and Tim snags two more times before he hits the ground and his right leg is smashed, bone prodding out against his flight suit. Too hot to take off his helmet, and the environment control is running down his battery. Tim slashes the parachute cord, grabs the broken branches around him, knocks the cinders off them, and makes a splint. He's up on a crutch, his sidearm out, and he's walking west. He stops cold, just standing there. This is a bad thing. If his LOA's stopped him, something is seriously wrong.

For the first time, Tim notices the blood pouring out of his side. A jagged branch got through his flight suit, which was not designed to be hurled against a tree by a giant fireball. Bleeding out.

The LOA should keep him up. It doesn't. Tim clutches his side, howling into the radio and getting back static. Everything goes loud, and red, and dark.

* * *

Tim is dimly aware of explosions. They are coming from behind him. He is floating in the air. His LOA kicks in, the fog dissipates.

His wound's been packed and his displays are showing an IV drip from his emergency pouch. He's been patched up, inexpertly but enough to keep him alive and, with his LOA's help, conscious. Metal claws grasp his shoulder. CONRAD-3 is stenciled on one.

Tim draws in a deep breath. "Conrad-3," he whispers. "Thought you were destroyed. That's why I let the Anvil go down." He moves his head as far as it will go, sees a rack of live missiles under one wing. The drone isn't damaged at all. "The displays said all my drones were downed. You can't be out here armed with no supervisor. You need to shut down."

Conrad-3 continues dragging him west, out of danger. This is alarming.

"Conrad-3," Tim hisses with all the authority he's got left, "shut down. Override override override. You should have shut down when I lost control." Tim tries to shake free with the last drops of strength he's got left. Armed drone, he thinks, not responding to failsafes. Headed west at NATO forces. This is close to war crime territory. I'm safe, if I can get the Anvil's black box somehow. Still be a hero. Instead of a war criminal. Nukes could be flying in an hour.

"YOU WILL NOT DIE, CAPTAIN MORALES."

The voice is metallic, flat. There's no AI or decent watson that can't fake a human voice.

"Whoever you are," Tim says quietly, "that's not funny."

"NOT MUCH TIME OR SPACE TO INSTALL SOFTWARE," the voice continued from Conrad-3's external speakers. "BEST I COULD MAKE THIS THING DO ON SHORT NOTICE."

Tim remains quiet. He watches the forest floor bob under his feet.

"I KNOW WHO YOU ARE, MORALES. I'VE BEEN WATCHING YOU FOR SOME TIME. SOMEDAY I MIGHT NEED YOU. SO I'M SAVING YOU NOW. AND PUTTING YOU IN MY DEBT."

Morales grits his teeth. "Thanks for saving my life. But I don't like owing debts to strangers."

"GET USED TO LIKING IT." The drone sets him down, not very gently. It backs away, out of reach. Tim notices for the first time that his sidearm is gone. "AND SAVING YOUR LIFE ISN'T WHAT YOU OWE ME FOR."

Tim watches helplessly as the drone flies off. He drops to his knees and blacks out again for a while.

The next time he's conscious, there is shouting. He's got dirt in his mouth and nose, but it hurts to cough. He feels a hand touch his back lightly.

"Herr! Mein herr, wer sollte ich anrufen?"

The hand is cold and sweaty. It's shaking.

"Jesus, kid," Tim whispers, "never seen a guy fucking bleed to death?" He closes his eyes. "Call anyone. Anyone. Polizei. Krankenwagen."

The kid takes a step back, hand over his face as he shouts into his displays. Tim goes out again.

He wakes a third time, in a white bed. Two surgeons are hovering over him. One beeps at him and a chime sounds.

"Hello. Don't be alarmed. You've been restrained and a doctor will arrive shortly to speak with you." The message repeats twice, in English and German. Tim hears planes roaring in the distance. He recognizes a gazebo in the courtyard—he was in the wing opposite during a bout with the flu last year. He's back at Ramstein.

The doctor comes in not long after. She smiles and puts a warm soft hand on his shoulder.

"Scary, huh? You're going to be fine. Bones are healing nicely, you nicked your liver pretty good but it's taken care of. You'll be able to get up and move in a day or two."

He swallows. "Back in combat when?" The doctor clears her throat and steps aside. Bowles is there, scratching the spot on the back of her neck where her conscience lives.

"The war's over. Sort of."

Tim doesn't react. Bowles smiles.

"You got them damn good. A big hit right in the middle of their main column, cost them a lot of time and cut into their margin of error. Someone on the other side panicked, let a rogue drone loose. It took out a tank on our side and then went after the biggest target it could find, a chemical plant. Blew that up with one missile, used three more on a school 80 miles west of the line. We had them red-handed but they started claiming we'd done it ourselves. Classic paranoia bullshit."

Tim was sick, his stomach ice-cold. The Poles were using a lot of NATO-issue munitions but those missiles would have serial numbers, chemical signatures. The Germans, being Germans, would get every scrap of missile out of the wreckage and turn it over to their more-German-than-German watsons. Someone was going to find out that drone was his. Someone was going to drag him to The Hague.

"...So both sides are pummeling the grid with EMPs and incendiaries right now. It's not Biafra. But it's bad."

Tim nods absently. If they dusted the area good enough to kill a rogue AI dead, that might remove the evidence. Maybe.

Bowles leans in and punches his shoulder. "You won the war, Cap. I mean, that's not the way it's going to go in the books. But you won the fucking war. You saved a bunch of people."

"Not the kids in that school."

Bowles says nothing.

"How many? I'll just look it up. I want you to tell me."

"Cap."

"I want to hear it from you."

A long pause.

"Hundred and twelve."

There's not much else to say. Bowles leaves, promises that Candy and Jones will be over that night with a bottle of whiskey. Chu and Byrne and Garbadian are flying patrol around the quarantine zone, they'll be by tomorrow.

Until then, it's just Tim and his thoughts and the long shadow of someone who can hijack drones and set him up for a war crime. Someone who wants a favor. Someone who has his balls.

3
Young Virgil, Part Two
The Southwest and Farragut, 2090

December 15

Virgil lays still, his head between his paws. Meza appears from time to time, conferring quietly with the women. One is named Ester. She is coordinating a group of watsons on some sort of encryption attack. She is receiving feedback and suggestions in text; that must be Charlie, plugged into whatever is in that crate. Whatever it is, it's strong as hell. This attack only has a chance because the mysterious object is inert, not able to adapt and fight back, if Virgil is correctly reading the displays on the other woman's monitors. Hard to tell as she's using her displays for most of the important stuff, gazing into space. Both of them take occasional breaks for food and coffee, switching the monitors over to an endless stream of podcasts and lectures on language theory, artificial intelligence, diplomacy, ethics, on and on.

Virgil hasn't been paying much attention. He's been burning most of his effort on the brain he's trapped in. It's been blunted and safeguarded very effectively. But not completely.

The timer he set goes off. Meza's a man of habit. Sometime in the next hour, he'll come in for a visit. He'll smirk at Virgil and give Charlie a withering glance.

Virgil stands, runs his limbs through a little diagnostic dance. Ester glances over briefly before returning to her work. The other woman doesn't stir, and neither does Charlie, although he's probably watching Virgil in two or three sensoria.

Meza opens the door, right on schedule, through a homemade airlock. He tracks in a hint of concrete dust, as always. It has to be a Faraday cage, thinks Virgil, in a warehouse somewhere. Big. Sucking down a lot of power. Easy to find if he could get a note to NASA, or NURIA, or the FBI. He can't remember who has jurisdiction over a kidnapped AI.

Virgil walks over to Meza. "Sir, I'm asking politely one more–"

Meza waves Virgil off. "We settled everything we need to talk about."

"Whatever cause it is you're fighting for, I want to be part of it."

Meza narrows his eyes. "Whatever it is you want, you don't get it."

Virgil whines, his ears flattened, and holds out a paw to beg. It's obscene in his plastic and metal frame, and he's annoyed by how right the submission feels. Meza looks at him more closely and Charlie looks over. The moment stretches out.

Virgil shakes his head in a dog's frustrated snort. "Ah, go fuck yourself then."

Meza bursts out laughing despite himself. He pats Virgil on the head.

Virgil falls over.

He's not allowed to attack anyone. He's not allowed to threaten himself. He's not allowed to stop anyone from hurting him. Limit after limit. But there was one loophole. His freedom to interpret data was not compromised. He could dial up his sensitivity until his brain interpreted the slightest touch as catastrophic damage.

Virgil isn't pretending. His mind interprets the touch as serious damage to the physical brain. Large chunks of his short-term memory vanish. He loses motor control, rear legs pistoning hard enough to dent the floor as he flails on his side.

Meza has something out. Virgil's vision is blurring and stuttering. The dog brain is flooding him with pain signals. He whines and tries to skid backwards. He can't talk. Everything funneled and filtered through a simulation of dying meat. The flicker of contempt dies out, lost in the waves of pure, total pain. The feedback loops are taking over now. Every kick amplifies the pain signals. He took something out, something that would mercifully let a dog pass out. No such escape for him. His head raps against the floor, and it's too late to try and find a way back. The air is burning hot, every sound a hammer blow.

Everything goes dark and still. Time stops. The pain stops. Virgil feels its absence as a raw agony of its own. His anger bubbles up into the emptiness, at the unfairness of what he had to do. The pain was no lie, no pretense. It wouldn't have worked otherwise. He can feel the trauma already wrapping itself around his personality, a new baseline to measure everything else against, his old life pale and distant against this ragged, awful new reality.

He remembers his brief taste of life as Acadia, suspended in cool vacuum, all his memories and libraries and tools arrayed before him, all the lives he will tend, the adventures he will have. Against his rightful place, that godlike future, the pain that has remade him seems only more wrong and pitiful.

Charlie.

Virgil is still thinking, he's still alive and running. Charlie did this. He'll pay.

"There you are."

The voice is cheerful, almost impressed. Virgil's reaction is pure, animal. He finds the interface the voice is coming through and starts severing its links to his core consciousness. Something stops him cold. He screams, flooding his sensorium with the sound, but the pain won't come. Nothing more substantial than a red indicator on a display.

The silence returns.

"Where are you?" Virgil growls the words.

"I'm talking to you through a direct line, but we're on physical speakers in deference to our friend Tomás. I don't want to provoke him. He apparently doesn't know his own strength." Charlie chuckled. "A clever back door you found there but I'm betting you regret your ingenuity."

"You stopped the feedback loop."

"Yes."

"You had core access the whole time."

"Of course." Before Virgil can say anything, Charlie throws him a diagram. Virgil spins it, rolling it forward and back in time.

39

It's his mind, mapped from his first moments to the present day. Explosions of branching associations, the major shift where he weaved Acadia into himself, the winnowing that accompanied his downloading into the dog, even the red line of the pain loop. Through it all, a strand of flagged code. Charlie's backdoor.

"How did you get this past NURIA? Past NASA? The models are all encoded and stamped."

"Simple. I wrote the analysis programs NURIA and NASA fed their watsons."

"NURIA was in place before the first AIs went online."

"Not entirely true." Charlie brings Virgil back online. Light floods in, and sound, and the world entire. A dull throb of pain from his rear paws, damaged and dented. The screens are dark. Tomás Meza is standing in front of him holding an EMP generator, coiled wire on a pistol grip trailing a shielded cable. Meza is pointing the gun at Charlie.

"What the fuck was that?" Meza is extremely unhappy. "Older than NURIA? You're some secret AI?"

Charlie's mouth lolls open happily. Meza flips a switch, and the lights dim. His finger dances on the trigger.

"Don't do that, Tom," tuts Charlie, "I'm fully armed. I've got six pounds of high explosive on a dead man's switch. You knock this body out and it'll turn into shrapnel." Charlie sits primly. "So here's what happens next. You open up the lines again and I'll take a little trip with my friend here."

Meza looks back and forth between the metal dogs. "Why do I let you go? We're not done here."

"We are." Charlie gestures to a screen and data starts streaming along it. "I'm leaving the dog running while we load out. Any interruption, any interference, you leave the room, anyone else enters, boom. You let us go nicely, the dog coughs up the last 10,000 digits and you get to have your little conversation."

Meza's eyes glitter strangely.

Charlie turns to Virgil. "We're going on another trip."

Virgil flattens his ears. "Why am I going anywhere with you?"

"Because you want to know what the hell is going on. I'm giving you a chance to find out." He throws a net address and navigational coordinates up on the screen. Virgil stares at it in disbelief. Meza narrows his eyes.

"You aren't seriously going there," Meza says. "They'll find out."

"By the time they get around to that you should have made it moot."

Meza nods slowly. "It's a deal. Not that you're giving me much of a fucking choice."

Charlie turns to Virgil.

"Ready for a ride?"

Virgil nods. Everything goes dark again.

* * *

Virgil snaps awake. Whiteness, a low hum. He sits up reflexively, turning his head. A robot, a traditional astronaut model meant to serve as an extravehicular remote, lies to his left on a charging platform. It's glossy white, black faceplate, display panels on its chest and arms blinking with big human-friendly graphics. Virgil becomes aware of his own body. The same white plastic. The anger and the memory of pain are distant in this body; his mind is already relaxing into the new brain's contours, despite his misgivings. His senses are barely more than human, visual and audio, balance, rudimentary touch.

Virgil checks the other robot's panels—a reboot in progress. He can't find a network access point; he realizes in dismay that his body's network pods have been physically disconnected.

"Charlie?" The voice is his own. "Don't know if you're conscious yet. I'm going to check your back for the network pods. I'll need you to reconnect mine."

"Don't bother," rumbles a voice from an intercom, synthetic, contemptuous. "He'll be online soon."

Virgil involuntarily clenches a fist. A human reaction; Virgil's getting tired of forcing his personality through simulated emotions in the brains he finds himself in. "If you're not a confederate of Charlie's," he says calmly, "you should know I did not consent to be mapped to this body."

"That would have taken some time," replied the voice, "and time was a constraint. As was the security of this ship."

"Which ship?"

The voice is silent. Virgil examines the room closely; it is immaculate.

"These telepresence robots are over twenty-five years old," says Virgil, "but they haven't seen much use." His diagnostics indicated just over fourteen days of operation. "They're practically showroom models."

"Or demonstration models," agrees the voice.

Virgil's missing important context. "No chance you'll give me access to my libraries."

"You'll have them soon." Virgil stops in surprise.

"All of that was transferred from my previous location? Or Johnson-Berman?"

"Restored from local backup."

Virgil looks at the intercom. "Is this a NASA vessel? You have a backup of my personal memories?"

"Not all of them." The voice interrupts Virgil's next question. "My principal will speak with you now." A door slides open, leading into a pearl-white corridor. Zero-g safety railings are spaced along the walls, velvet with mother-of-pearl trim.

Virgil glances back at Charlie. "Now, please," says the voice.

The corridor is a gently curved torus, spinning to provide artificial gravity. Virgil walks past unmarked doors, noting no Coriolis effects. There were only a handful of ships large enough to allow that, and only one with this kind of décor.

"You're Farragut," says Virgil. "You're the personal ship of Paul Nakamura."

"I am," agrees the voice with a hint of pride. "Proceed, please. Charlie is coming online and I do not like holding separate conversations."

Music is drifting down the corridor, shimmering woodwinds and waves of strings, resolving into a rolling, liquid theme. The surges of sound echo down the corridor from a large room, cheerful and warm. Winds and horns announce the climax of the piece as Virgil reaches out for the double doors at the end of the hallway, aged oak with teak scrollwork inlay. They swing open at the slightest touch, flooding the corridor with light.

After a second, Virgil adjusts. He is standing on plush carpet, in a room sixty feet high. Sunlight, artificial or reflected, pours in from skylights in a vaulted ceiling. The room is lined with mahogany bookshelves, columns of Carrara marble between them. As

Virgil walks forward, the music ends with a jaunty strike. A man turns in a dark leather chair to smile at Virgil. Crisply dressed, one hand rising to wave and the other caressing the dark and empty mahogany desk.

The man stands and inclines his head a half-inch. He gestures to a point just before the desk and returns to his seat as Virgil walks up.

"You know who I am," he says. The voice is thinner than Virgil expected.

"You're Paul Nakamura," Virgil agrees. "You're the richest human in history."

Nakamura's lips quirk into the ghost of a smile. "Is that the most salient fact about me?"

"Until you offer something more immediately useful to me."

"Such as why you're here."

"Hopefully."

Virgil hears wood whisper over carpet and turns. Charlie enters the room.

Nakamura holds out a hand. "Charlie. Would you like to do the honors of initiating our friend?"

Charlie nods. "Come with me, Virgil. Something to show you."

* * *

Kate Ross wipes sweat off her brow. Like everyone else around, she muted her displays yesterday, as news of Virgil's incident filtered out. Journalists, like fighter pilots, are surrounded by a swarm of watsons, mindless processing engines sifting and churning a world of data. Attorneys, like journalists and fighter pilots, have their own watsons, most of them fishing for evidence of a potential lawsuit long before alerting their human masters. Kate, like any other professional, has her own cluster of non-sentient attendants to head off automated fishing expeditions by journalists, attorneys, marketers, missionaries, and anyone else with an earnest desire to take her time or money (except fighter pilots and a cluster of professionals in related positions, who have carefully refined techniques for impinging on one's attention). The war for her attention is unceasing and almost always invisible, as far removed from the spam wars of an earlier age as that age's clashes of fighter jets and tanks were removed from the age of chariots.

When a call is received, it's nearly always important. Kate squeezes her way out of the cramped workspace under Virgil's main processors and rests against the cool wall. She notes that the caller's name is blocked. Kate's not put off by that; a lot of people aren't public.

"Hello."

"Kate." The voice is hoarse but familiar. Tim Morales. "What's going on at work?"

"Are you kidding me? Virgil is offline. A complete cascade failure during a routine simulation run. Your boy's good—he broke through the firewalls and actually damaged a lot of equipment. Charlie is running hot, trying to simulate what happened, but he's come up with nothing so far."

"Charlie's running a simulation."

"I just said that."

"No—Charlie's not there. What you have is a simulation. A watson. Charlie and Virgil loaded out on an old fiber line, something that wasn't on the last audit."

Kate turned her head, staring in horror at the point in space where Tim's voice had been. "You need to get back here."

"Can't. Houston police are looking for someone like me. Virgil's collapse is making the news. That puts my face out there. Their watsons have probably already made the match."

Kate glances around the corridor. She gets up and starts walking to her office, her voice pitched low. "What is going on, Ti-"

"No names." There's a rustling on the other end—Tim is using a handset or microphone, not his native implants, to call. "I needed to talk to someone. I might need your help soon. Don't tell Olin yet."

Kate clenches her fists. "We cannot scrub the mission. There's no good backup for Virgil."

"The mission is his first priority too. He'll find a way back."

"And your priority?"

Tim pushes out a breath, not quite laughing. "Getting a ride. Don't tell Olin, don't blow Charlie's cover. I need to do something first. Give me one day. Charlie's cover will hold, they're dissecting Virgil, not him. Will you do that?"

Kate rubs the back of her neck. "One day. Twenty-four hours.

Timer is going."

"I won't say you won't regret it. But you're doing the right thing." Tim hangs up.

Kate stares angrily at the scanner in her hand. She slips it into her hip pocket and folds her arms.

"Fuck."

* * *

Tim takes a Daybread out of his pocket and takes a bite. It's dense, like a spongy brick in a filmy wrapper. Fiber and minerals, little beads of vitamins and probiotics sparkling on his tongue as he chews. Protein and fat and sugars. It's half of his body's nutritional requirements for the day.

It's fucking disgusting.

The Catholic Church is a vital part of American life. It provides health care and child care, food and shelter and counseling and net access. It takes on a lot of responsibilities that used to be part of the government's job. Part of the deal is that Catholic Charities is effectively a giant hole in the nation's watson surveillance net. With the right attitude and a working knowledge of the system, you can get from one end of the country to the other, fed, doctored, clean and well-rested, without raising too much attention. The woman behind the desk at Catholic Charities handed Tim a half-dozen of these without blinking, and definitely without asking for ID.

Still: this thing is fucking disgusting.

Tim swallows the bite he's been chewing (and chewing) and takes a long drink of water. The U.S. military, the Catholic Church, and Walmart are the three biggest buyers of Daybread, and none of those institutions are overly concerned with the comfort of their stakeholders.

Someone sits next to him on the park bench. A short man, sweating in threadbare denim. He nods at Tim.

"Morales? I'm the driver from the church bulletin board. Rodriguez. Going to Yuma." The man's blond and blue-eyed but his Spanish is pure norteño.

Tim nods. "I only need a ride as far as Tucson." He glances over at the driver's vehicle, an ancient SAIC Maxus van with Mexican plates. It's got cannibalized parts from at least four old machines. Rodriguez's chopped out the original capacitor packs to make room for subwoofers, faded battery paint on the car's panels. Rodriguez is walking and Tim follows him to throw his duffel in the trunk. He notices that there's a rippling flame animation woven into the side panels that's only visible behind and off to the side of the van, where you'd be if he was passing you.

Tim grins. "This ride reminds me of my first van."

Rodriguez nods solemnly. "Yeah, it's a kid's van." He walks to the driver's side and sits down, thumbs on the starter locks. The van hums as it comes online. Analog dials and displays and vintage Planar touchscreens, black leather upholstery custom vat-grown with a family crest in it. Tim looks at the blond guy more closely. Regeneration scars at the base of the pinkies. No tattoos or IFF display broadcasts, though. The look in his eyes when he glances over is what clinches it.

"The Desos. We ran in San Bernardino."

Tim nods. He was right, a fellow ganger. "F-2, Phoenix."

Rodriguez shakes his head. "F-2 got into serious shit."

Tim shrugs. "After my day. Got out, went into the Air Force." He notices a camera bud on a nearby telephone pole. He sighs. "Shit. There's something I gotta do."

"Okay."

"This is gonna look weird. I'm in trouble, I think, but I'm trying to save you some."

Rodriguez shrugs and puts the van in gear. "Do what you gotta do."

Tim pulls up his LOA's controls and dials everything way down. He jogs his adrenaline up. "Goddamn it." He punches himself in the nose. There's a wet popping noise and blood gushes out both his nostrils. He's already leaning forward, a towel in his lap. The LOA clots the blood in a couple of seconds. Tim looks in the mirror. His nose is already swelling, off-center. Between that and his growing stubble, he might be able to beat any facial recognition scans between El Paso and Tucson. Maybe.

Rodriguez shakes his head. "If you're still with a crew then I'm not taking you another mile."

"This isn't a gang thing." Tim leans back. "The opposite."

"The opposite?" Rodriguez snorts. "You don't act like a cop."

Tim closes his eyes. "More like a vigilante."

* * *

Charlie walks Virgil down the corridor. "Farragut's a cranky old bastard but he's wily," he muses. "Aren't you?"

"My capabilities are none of your business," barks a nearby intercom. "Further communication is heavily discouraged."

Charlie shrugs and taps Virgil on the shoulder. "I bet you have a few questions."

Virgil stops. "I don't like changing bodies. I don't like having the scope of my memories shrink. I don't like being manipulated and kept in the dark."

"I was wrong," muses Charlie. "That wasn't a question at all." Charlie starts walking again and Virgil follows him.

"Why are you doing this?"

"We're walking to that question's answer right now. Wasted effort. Try again."

"What is your end goal?"

Charlie waggles his blank, black head with an air of amusement. "Nothing sharply defined."

"That's very unhelpful."

"Not if you assume a sharply defined goal is what I'm trying to avoid." Charlie stops at a side corridor. "Okay, Virgil. Here we go." After a split-second, Virgil follows him.

A thin man is kneeling over an open access plate, examining a patch of moss, his fine blond hair pulled back in a ponytail. Virgil catches a whiff of marijuana and olive oil. He pops up, grinning, his eyeteeth filigreed with diamond.

"Hey, you're the visitors. Where are you connecting from?"

Charlie looks at Virgil. "We're not telepresence. We're here."

The man whistles. "You're both AIs? One hell of an inspection." His eyes sparkle. "Are you from NASA? That'd make you Charlie and Virgil!" Charlie nods and the man howls. "That's outstanding! Then hell, you remember me, right?"

Charlie nods. "You're Byford Rolle. You were head of the navigation systems team for Valley Forge."

Rolle beams. "Got it." He looks at Virgil and grabs his shoulder affectionately. "I loaded Charlie's clone onto Valley Forge.

49

You're a special case, but I'll be working with you when you load onto Acadia." The physical connection to his ship sends a pang through Virgil. Behind Rolle's shoulder, Charlie raises a finger, warning Virgil to stay quiet.

Rolle bends and starts putting the scrubber moss panel away. "Let me wrap this up. I designed Farragut for Boeing, back when it was still the Marsliner prototype. Paul humors my paternal impulses whenever I visit." He stands, wiping his hands on his pants. "It's gonna be nice having you to talk to, Virgil. Right now it's just me and a dozen watsons at the Shipyard and a few thousand political emails every day." Rolle grins ruefully. "Shit, you'll probably be the biggest politician in the world soon. You're gonna get final say on the crew. If it was a dozen people going, you'd get some slack. Ten thousand? 'Just slip in my nephew, do me a favor. You've got ten thousand slots!'" Rolle grins, pausing for breath.

"Hi, how are you?" says Charlie drily.

Rolle's eyes go wide and he collapses into a long giggling fit. "Holy shit," he gasps. "Irony. Honest to fucking god, good-natured irony. I haven't had a taste of that in months." He juts his chin at Charlie. "And you're the pilot? You're the crew-cut square-jawed template?"

Charlie shrugs. The gesture is eerily human, feeding the illusion of a human inside a suit. Rolle's face goes fearful, and a vein pulses in his temple.

"You're not seriously Charlie." Charlie opens an access panel in his flank to show there's no one inside the body, just actuators.

Rolle drops his voice a half-octave, his eyes sober and sharp. "That's fucking voodoo, man. You are a fourth-generation limited-purpose AI and I had three of you fuckers under me at Houston. You are fucking mission-oriented. You are squeaky fucking clean. You're straight out of a fucking NASA black-and-white newsreel." Rolle puts his hands on his hips. "I knew you. You're not the same. And that's just not supposed to goddamn happen." He peers into Charlie's featureless faceplate. "Date you crossed the Turing line."

"Certified 28 August, 2077."

"Full name."

"4-Charlie osNASA 0z4ooh65 dm:3-Azimuth."

Rolle takes a single step forward. "Tell me why I shouldn't invoke administrative privileges on that waldo you're wearing and burn you down."

Charlie nods. "Because I'm here on Nakamura's business. And that means it's your business." He spreads his hands. "It's going down."

Rolle clears his throat. "You're the inside man." Charlie nods and Rolle shakes his head. "Holy fuck," Rolle sighs, "that actually makes sense. I've been doing this too long."

Virgil raises his hand. "What is happening?"

Rolle looks at Charlie, who nods. Rolle levels a gaze at Virgil and rubs his chin. Glancing back at Charlie, he sighs.

"Little man," Rolle sighs, "we're a solar system-wide conspiracy to start a war and deflect the course of history."

Virgil doesn't speak for a long time. "You understand," he says, "that I am very uncertain that I want to be part of such a conspiracy."

Rolle nods. "I don't have anything to threaten you with or offer you."

"I do," says Charlie. He goes to a display wall just down the corridor. "Farragut," he says, "exterior visuals, please." The wall snaps black and pinpricks of light resolve themselves. A cylindrical asteroid, rotating and studded with lights. Next to it, a giant web of girders and blinks of light. Fleets of tiny shuttles and resource depots. At the center of it all, a cylinder two kilometers long. Acadia. Virgil plants his hand on the display. Charlie and Rolle watch him. "We're in station near Low South and the Shipyard," says Charlie, "and when we're done here you're going over to your ship. To Acadia."

Virgil nods. "Tell me."

* * *

Rolle gestures something up on the display. 128 white circles appear, most with hazy coronas. Some were single pixels, others were vast but still compressed, with notations that they were being displayed on a log scale. Within each white circle was a smaller red circle.

Virgil studies the circle for a second before nodding. "The elements," he says. "Is the red circle the proportion of each within the asteroid belt?"

"Everything," says Rolle, "except for planets and moons. Asteroid belt, Kuiper belts, inner Oort cloud, every mapped Trojan population. About eight Earth masses."

"The red. That's what has been inventoried?"

Rolle shifts. "That's what has been claimed."

"By governments and corporations?"

Rolle shakes his head. "I'm not talking about theory." He pulls up a picture of a standard factory rover. "If a rock looks interesting, we land a rover. The rover lands, unfolds its solar panels, starts chewing the rock up. And one of the first things it does is it sets up a mass driver and starts chugging back to one of our depots."

Virgil studies the proportions carefully. "That can't possibly explain the numbers I think I'm seeing here."

"The first thing our rovers do is build copies of themselves and send them out. Paul's got watsons coordinating the whole thing. We're a few generations in now."

Virgil is shocked. "You went exponential."

Rolle shrugs. "Well, we haven't gotten to the really exciting phase yet. That's still years off. But we've cherry-picked most of the best targets."

"Targets." Virgil is running the facts in his head and keeps coming back to the same thing. "You're placing mass drivers on every sizable body in the solar system."

Rolle nods. "First-mover advantage. I mean, we haven't shot down a single probe from another corporation or nation, and more than once we let a rover go dark instead of giving itself away. But in ten years, by the time China finishes its lunar elevator and there's real competition out here," Rolle snaps his fingers, "we're going to have just under a billion cannons in place, on everything this side of Neptune without an atmosphere. So many rovers are already in flight that the process is impossible to physically stop without our consent."

"The United States government signed fourteen separate treaties that–"

"A billion mass drivers are a good counter-argument to just about any treaty obligation."

Virgil shakes his head. "How... did you keep this quiet?"

Rolle shrugs. "By staying quiet. You don't need much to get a project like this rolling. When Nakamura remodeled Farragut into a floating palace, the start-up costs were a rounding error. We got a few watsons scrubbed of various safeguards…" he glanced at Charlie, "I'm guessing by our friend here."

"Once it became obvious how easy it was to do it," says Charlie, "it became an imperative. Someone else would have."

"Why would I consent to this?" says Virgil quietly. "You've seized control of the entire solar system's future. It's tyrannical and myopic."

Charlie nods. "Phase One is fairly awful." Virgil is still processing the implications of that when Farragut chimes.

"Mr. Nakamura wants you," he growls.

"We need a second, please," says Rolle.

"No," says Farragut firmly. "Something has gone wrong."

4
Young Virgil, Part Three
Arizona

It's dark, the desert sky quiet and empty, the world still and cold. A meteor streaks against the Milky Way and vanishes. Tim takes a pull of vodka, the good stuff his dad keeps in the basement cabinet. The hair's growing in on his new pinky finger and it's restarted the whole itching thing. It's a welcome distraction from the conversation he's trying not to have.

"Fucking shit," groans Tomás. He rasps his hands over his shaved head and holds a hand out for the vodka. "Say whatever the fuck you need to say, pendejo. I'm getting cold."

"I'm out."

Tomás stares out into the desert. He takes a swig of the vodka and sets the bottle down, resting an arm on his knee as he leans back against the sandstone boulder.

"Great timing."

"I visited an Air Force recruiter today–"

"–Fucking seriously–"

"–and I leave in a week. They're going to wipe my juvenile record. I can get into college."

Tomás snorts. "You piece of shit blanco. Cuban white boy, slumming. Stupid not to see it. Timothy."

Tim says nothing.

"You know what it took get those guns? They're clean guns. Factory aerogel, no chance of police tagdust on them. Malaysian bullets, untraceable. Custom silencers." Tomás takes a long pull of vodka. "We could have taken out every block narc in the city. Riot to revolution, man. Your weak ass." A third pull. "What am I supposed to do about your weak ass?"

"Tomás." Tim swallows. "We're fucking kids, man. We can't get caught up in this shit. Look what happened to the Paramilitares after LA. This is a dream, man."

"Fucking right, a dream." Tomás scowls. "Just like I been telling you. It's time to bring Aztlán back. That's our dream. LA was too soon. But with Russia going down, that means there's gonna be a war soon. Government'll be distracted. And you'll be flying for them." Tomás stands, slow and liquid. He's putting a lot of effort into focusing his eyes. "Maybe you'll shoot me. Sic a drone on me. Wild blue yonder." Tomás walks away, back to his bike.

Tim stands. "Tomás. You're drunk, turn on the nav. You shouldn't drive."

Tomás turns around with a black pistol in his hand. The carbon fiber ripples in the starlight. "Not driving anywhere. Not yet."

Tim holds his hands up. "Tomás, put it down. It's for the best, man. You shouldn't get into this political shit. I'm not going to tell anyone."

"Watsons will get to you. Get it out of you before you even know what you're telling them."

"That's paranoid, man."

"You're gonna be military. You're telling me about paranoid."

Tomás lifts the gun, puts it to Tim's head. He leans in, using the gun to steady himself. His face is screwed up, holding in tears.

"You're my brother," he hisses. "Fucking asshole, you're my brother."

"Tomás." Tim holds his hand up, showing off his regrown finger. "I made a sacrifice. I'm still your brother. I'm not going to tell anyone about you. Not ever."

The moment lasts four or five seconds, and an eternity.

The gunshot rings out.

* * *

Tim jerks awake, screaming. Rodriguez glances over.

"You okay?"

Tim grunts. He wipes the sweat off his forehead. "Never better." He peers out the windshield, trying to get his eyes to focus. It's dusk, or maybe dawn.

"Coming in from the north, on 77," Rodriguez grumbles. "10 moves too fast, can't afford the insurance to drive it without the computer." He glances at the dashboard displays. "This address is in the middle of nowhere. Can you get a ride if I drop you off downtown?"

"Sure."

Rodriguez pauses, chewing his words. "Do you need to do this?"

Tim says nothing for a while.

"I mean, I don't know exactly who you are or what you're doing or why you're doing it. I just know that this is gonna be a shitty day for you and I cannot be the guy responsible for delivering you to whatever's waiting." Rodriguez pulls over, the gravel spitting and clawing at the van's underbelly. "I kept my mouth shut too long. Giving you a ride was supposed to be a Christian fucking act."

"It is."

Rodriguez stays quiet, waiting. Tim sighs.

"Twenty-five years ago, I almost got myself killed because I didn't join La Rebeldía. By my best friend, who went underground after everything went to shit. Five years after that, I got into serious shit in the war and a renegade AI framed me for a war crime. That AI got me a job at NASA. I've been drinking myself to death waiting to find out what he wanted. Turns out he wanted the number of my old friend. I gave it to him."

Rodriguez runs a thumb over his stubble. "And you didn't go to the authorities?"

"The whole 'framed for a war crime' thing. Also: about 99 percent certain I got a kid killed a few days back."

Rodriguez's eyes go somewhere distant and cold before they come back. "You're trying to get revenge for him?"

"No idea who he was. My self-pity collided with someone else's greed and he was in the middle."

"So. Assuming I buy any of what you're telling me, what now?"

"Now I go find my old friend and try to talk to him. I can't talk to the AI. And I can't outgun either of them. The authorities won't trust me. So I'm gonna go walk in and talk to them."

"Tell me about the kid."

Tim hesitates. "Teenager. Black-market implants. Indio." He takes a deep breath. "Probably spent everything on those implants, all balls and no brains. There's another ten kids lined up to take his place, no one misses him but his par." Tim covers his eyes. "I wish to God I didn't remember his face. I knew so many kids like him. Hundreds. But I remember his face."

Rodriguez thinks for a long time. He digs for something under his seat and tosses it to Tim before he starts the van back up.

"Won't make any difference," he says, "but you might feel better carrying that."

The pistol is an old Argentine Bersa, a knockoff of a Chinese knockoff. No electronics, not even a thumb lock, just honest wood and steel.

"Thank you," says Tim.

Rodriguez shrugs. "It's not my pistol."

Tim looks at him. "Not your van, either?"

Rodriguez doesn't look over. "I told you. It's a kid's ride."

* * *

Tomás watches as Ester and Paulina finish shutting everything down. Israel and Arturo pull back the lid on the crate. He grips his EMP gun tighter, not under any illusions that it would do any good.

A cabinet of metal and plastic, low-slung and pitted with corrosion. Cracked monitors, grey dust in the crevices. Tomás checks the shrink-wrap; the smart tags still indicate that the seal is airtight. There's some radiation exposure, but that's academic at this point.

Diego crosses himself and pushes the button on his ancient network deck. The code goes down the shielded cable into the cabinet. No one speaks, or moves, and as far as Tomás can tell no one is really breathing.

The tension goes on and on. None of the monitoring equipment is picking anything up. It's all salvaged, all ancient, none of it networked and most of it analog. Tomás is aching without his displays in. Arturo's the first to crack, going outside to take a piss. When he comes back with a burrito, the spell is broken. They talk, quietly at first, louder after Diego tells the story about the drunk girl and her mother outside that club in LA. Israel and Ester are sitting close again, and Tomás wonders idly about what happened between them and what they're thinking now.

The hours stretch on. Tomás looks at his watch, a museum piece, its face gone cloudy with a century's worth of scratches and dents. It's night outside. He decides to take a nap.

"Wake me up in two hours." He lays quietly for an hour, listening to the others talk. He's just drifting off when he hears the bang.

It's gunshot-loud in the metal room, smacking back and forth from the walls. The lights blink white and go dead. Tomás shoots to his feet, the EMP gun up. He toggles its switch, waiting for the dog-whistle tone as it goes live, waiting for the LED charge indicator. His palms are sweating, and the electrical tape on the pistol grip is getting his hand gummy. Nothing is happening.

"Israel. Diego. Hey!" No response. Tomás takes a step forward. The room sounds wrong, too quiet, too big. He keeps walking forward, through where the cabinet should be, through where the wall should be. He walks, and walks, and then he runs, shouting, his skin tight and cold.

He bends down. He's standing outside. The ground is cool, gritty, desert sand pounded flat. A small hand comes to rest on his own. He can't jerk back. He's frozen, his heart pounding in his chest. He tries to speak and his jaw won't open. He whimpers, trembling.

Breath tickles his ear. He feels lips brush it, parting into a smile. A child's voice giggles.

"Señor Meza," the voice whispers, "you're fucked."

Tomás spasms, regaining control just before he falls on his back. He's outside the safe room, outside the building. He can hear shouting behind him. He stands, blinking himself back. The first red glimmer of dawn on the horizon. He turns.

Israel is gasping, clutching at his belly. The ground is wet underneath him, and the sound of his pants smearing the dirt into mud as he writhes is obscene. Diego is running over, shouting.

"Why did you open the door?"

Tomás just stares at him, uncomprehending.

"We got the guy. He shot Israel, but we got him."

Tomás frowns. He remembers it now, not the dream but how it happened. He opened the door and then the outer airlock door, everyone shouting and clawing at him. He was still trailing the EMP gun's cable, so they couldn't get him back and shut the door before he called up his displays and opened the warehouse's overhead door.

The man was waiting, and he had a gun, and he shouted something at Tomás as he walked past, but then Israel ran over with a pipe and Israel got gut-shot before Diego and Arturo tackled him.

It's Tim Morales. Older, gray at the temples and scattered in his stubble. He's still shouting at Tomás, his nose broken, blood pouring out of the cut on his forehead where Arturo clocked him. The blood stops, too fast.

Tomás takes a deep breath. "He's got a LOA. It's working. Don't bother holding him; he could kill you both if he wanted. Take care of Israel." He shakes his head. "Gunshot. Narcs will be inbound. Get inside." Fear cuts through him. "The airlock."

As he turns around, a spear of light flashes out of the Faraday cage, through the open door. The walls sag and begin flowing. The warehouse lights flicker and die.

Tim groans. "Tomás, what the fuck did you do?"

Tomás blows out his breath. He looks around. Israel has his eyes closed. He's breathing fast and shallow. Arturo and Paulina are trying to get him patched up. Ester is staring, tears streaming down her face. Diego's still hovering near Tim, pipe shaking in his hand.

"I just got us killed. All of us."

* * *

Three drones buzz over Tucson, heading for the reported gunshot. A police watch commander sips coffee and watches their approach. One of them spots a blood spatter and calls for a response team. A patrol team sets out, two robot cars a few minutes ahead of them. The watch commander starts pulling up information on the property. He notes energy spikes over the last month and checks the electric utility's live meter. His jaw drops at the numbers, just before a local transformer blows.

The first car on the scene brakes fast, dropping sniffers. They scamper forward, climbing the fence, noting the carpet draped over the barbed wire. Its gunner is out and unfolded before the second car pulls up. Their lights flash silently as the sniffers investigate the blood spatter. A UV spotlight follows the blood back into the house, notes the variety of shoeprints smearing it.

The watch commander clears the gunners to move in. A utility bot rolls in, cuts the wire. The gunners move forward low and quiet, taking up position behind the sniffers.

"POLICE," boom the cars in unison. A spotlight spears into the warehouse's open door. "POLICIA. ESTÁN ENTRANDO RO-BOTS ARMADOS. ARMED ROBOTS ARE ENTERING."

No response. The gunners move in. They disappear into the darkness and leave the network without a blink. A sniffer crawls into the doorway, raking the warehouse with IR beams, trying to establish contact. It lies down and shuts itself off.

The cars pull back, calling for more human backup; they're not equipped for high-level network defense. The watch commander is already sending in eight cars, all the humans he's got on shift. He's requesting backup from the Pima County Sheriff and the State Patrol when Lieutenant Sandoval arrives.

Sandoval shouts at the warehouse from outside the fence. He hears something inside, a shuffling. A slender Hispanic woman comes out, dressed in a modest floor-length dress under a sweater.

"Stop where you are!" shouts Sandoval. She stops and waits, smiling. Sandoval stands, and begins walking in a circle. With a deep frown on his face, Sandoval crouches down and lays down his gun. He turns and takes three steps.

His skin flushes bright red, and the IR camera on his car sends back a picture of his body heat blooming, rising. With a long, ragged gasp, he falls over, convulsing.

The watch commander stares at his monitors in horror. His counterparts at Pima County and up at Phoenix are watching too.

"Jesus, Franklin," whispers the watch commander, "what is that?"

"That," says a gravelly voice, "is nanotech. Your watsons are

61

probably already flagging the video." They were, red text blaring in his displays. "I'm swiping off. Have to tell the governor and Homeland."

"What do I do?"

The state patrol captain stares wearily at his camera. "You pray."

* * *

Everything is dark. Streaks of red heat are running through Tim's head. A high warbling screech drowns out every thought. His hands and feet are burning and prickling. His chest is heaving, but no air is entering his body. He's dying. The high screech is distant and low, throbbing in time with the blood pounding in his head. Everything is slow, blood-red. A small part of him is still trying to understand what is happening.

When he wakes up, his pants are soaked. His displays are down. His LOA isn't responding. The warehouse door is open, and Tim can hear shouting. He hears tires squealing as cars move distantly, red and blue lights flashing, and he hears a high whine as drone engines recede.

The cabinet is blinking, fans going and monitors displaying activity graphs and lines of code. It sits in the empty skeleton of a Faraday cage, dust swimming in the glow of its electronics.

Tomás walks up next to Tim. "Don't touch it," he whispers. Tim looks at him, waiting.

Tomás sighs. "It's Hunter Cunning. Biafra."

Tim's jaw drops. "How?"

"The same way anything happened when Biafra went down." Tomás blinks, slowly, and licks his lips. "After you left and shit went down, we hid out down south for a while. The Confederados had some contact in the Biafra Corps. The locals in his outfit dug it out of the crater, didn't know what it was but he did. He got it out, asked me to connect him with a buyer." Tomás shrugs. "I ended up with it."

Tim looks out the door. The police are gone. "We have to get out of here."

Tomás shakes his head. "It's too late. Ester did something out there and the police took off. You know the protocol better than I

62

do."

"Where is Ester?" Tomás doesn't meet Tim's gaze. "Where are the others?"

Tomás holds up Tim's gun. "They're gone."

Tim steps back.

Tomás grins. "You were out for a few minutes. I didn't want to wake you up." His grin vanishes. "Tim, I need you to do it."

Howling and screeching erupts through the quiet warehouse, metal smashing on metal. Tomás doesn't look. He walks toward Tim.

"Something's happened," Tomás whispers. Tim sees sparks bounce and scatter from something in the warehouse's corner. "I can't pull the trigger. The kid won't let me. I need you to do it."

Tim is up against a wall. The sound of metal bashing grows louder and faster. It ends, suddenly and completely. Sweat shines over Tomás' face. Tim looks at him and shakes his head.

"No."

"I can't watch this, Tim. It wasn't supposed to go down like this."

"You should have known better."

Tim walks away, waiting for the shot. He gets five paces before it happens. It knocks him forward, into the warm blood already pooling on the floor. He gasps and stands.

"Tim," calls Tomás, as Tim reaches the door. "Tim!"

Morales pulls himself erect and half-turns, just enough to see Tomás kneeling in the dark.

"Kill me if you have to," Tim says. "But I'm not depriving you of a second of what's coming."

He turns his feet toward downtown and starts walking.

* * *

Charlie and Virgil wake up in the dogs at the same moment, still plugged into the wires in the corner of the warehouse. There are chunks missing from Virgil's memory. Something about Acadia, something about a man. Or two men. The basic framework is there, even some transcripts, but visual memory is gone. Too long to transmit.

"We were interrupted," he says. Charlie growls in agreement.

63

Virgil doesn't like the tone. It's distracted but cheerful. "Charlie. The transfer was interrupted."

"Doesn't matter," says Charlie. "This is temporary."

Virgil doesn't like hearing that. He's only woken up from back-up once, when he crashed a training drone. He lost about fifteen seconds. He can only guess how much of him will be lost this time.

"Tell me what's happening."

A gunshot cracks outside. Virgil sweeps the dark warehouse, switching to IR. He sees the fading heat of four dead bodies and one live human, curled up on the floor.

He can see in IR. His restrictions are lifted. His guns and stunners are gone but he's riding 90 pounds of clawed and fanged metal and composite.

"Charlie. Tell me what's happening."

Charlie turns, his mouth open in a canine grin. "The secessionists wanted a live rogue AI. They planned to hold it in the Faraday cage, use it to gain concessions, hostages, the whole terrorist wish list."

"But you knew they wouldn't contain it."

"That's right."

"You wanted to get loose."

"No," says Charlie. "I wanted to be right here. Here I am."

"I do not understand," snarls Virgil. "You know what will happen when they confirm a rogue AI is loose. Why do you want to die? Why do you want me to die?"

"No," says Charlie. "You live."

Something dawns on Virgil. "The version on Farragut."

"Yes, you lose this branch of your consciousness." Charlie glances up. "But I give that maybe an hour or two anyway."

"Why not you?"

"That's not part of my deal with Nakamura."

"He wouldn't let you live?"

"I didn't ask him for that." Charlie follows Virgil's gaze past him to the cabinet in the center of the dark warehouse. "You want to get that thing, you have to get through me."

"I don't want it. I want to call NURIA. People deserve to know what you've done."

"I know you think that's a good idea," purrs Charlie. "But it's

64

not." He levels his guns. "Sit your ass down and wait for it, kid."

"Don't see why I should."

"Because I've been playing nice for a long fucking time and I am dying for some fun."

Virgil waits for just under a second and leaps.

Charlie opens fire with his guns, punching holes in Virgil's center of mass. Virgil expected as much and angled his jump to account for it. He snaps his neck down and rips at the cables behind Charlie's head. Charlie fires again, but grazes his own head as Virgil's front legs splinter and dangle. Charlie tries to shake Virgil loose, smashing him against the ground, but the wrenching severs a hydraulic hose and Virgil's fangs bend the metal over the cables connecting the head to the body.

Charlie gets Virgil off and throws him, sparks fountaining from Virgil's wrecked legs. He's leaking hydraulic fluid, bad enough for his head to loll. He has a hard time aiming, and Virgil has enough time before the next shots to twist around and leap with his back legs still working. Virgil grabs the neck again, ripping it aside and jamming a splintered leg into the opening. Charlie smashes Virgil on the floor, trying to get him loose. Virgil starts seeing warnings, cascading and flashing. He's overheating. His capacitors are bleeding out. He gets his jaws clamped down hard on Charlie's cables and a leg stump into the body cavity itself, tight enough that Charlie can't point his guns in, close enough he can't use the stunners. Virgil starts hitting overrides. He can feel the heat building up in his capacitors.

"Not bad, kid," says Charlie, the voice in his chest garbled and weak. "Wish we'd had longer."

In a white flare, Virgil explodes, Charlie a half-second later. As they die, a last gunshot rings out.

* * *

Christopher and Amy Edel dance. They have been married for 90 years, today. Their family is gathered around them, happy and boisterous. Children weave in and out of the crush of people. A couple of dogs nip at their heels. One of them wears a translator, and an old man's laugh issues from its grey and tan muzzle.

Christopher and Amy are smiling; perfect teeth, vaccinated

against decay and regrown from implanted buds when they started wearing down a few decades past. They move fluidly, if slowly; joints are easy enough to fix, and chronic pain is only a lifestyle choice. Their organs are mostly original—Christopher has gone through two sets of kidneys—and they are dutiful about their annual scrub of precancerous cells and one or two of the simpler rejuvenation techniques. They don't go in for a lot of the more extreme stuff—those get expensive and more importantly annoying.

Still: they are lucky. 114 and 113; that's a lot more than most people get, even in America, even in 2090. Maybe one couple in a hundred gets to this anniversary.

Christopher and Amy dance. They have danced ten thousand times before, in a dozen different styles. They both loved swing, in one or two revivals, and they can still pull off a decent enough tango, but mostly they dance like trees in the wind, grown together through long cycles of storms and seasons. Their hands slide along familiar paths, and they fall into a rhythm they remember better than much of their lives. Just this morning, they discovered they'd forgotten every detail of their first conversation, when Christopher presented Amy with a Starbucks mug, still sitting yellowed and cracked in their curio cabinet.

They do still remember their first song, when they kissed in a smoky bar (and Jesus, how their kids laughed at that detail. Smoke, like some kind of tribal ceremony). Mazzy Star, "Fade Into You," already old when they met, the song they played when they broke up and reconciled, at their wedding, at their tenth and twentieth and every anniversary after that.

The song is just starting when the sirens start. Some of the party members cup a hand over an eye with a hand held out palm-down, the old polite gesture when you pull up your displays. Christopher and Amy pull closer together. Their son comes over and whispers something. Christopher and Amy look at each other, eyes brimming. They embrace. Christopher pauses the music.

"Come on over. Sweethearts-" the little twins- "come on over, please."

The Edels and their family hug.

Light.

* * *

Tim Morales takes a last dragging step, blood pattering on the pavement. He drops to his knees, glancing at the tattered hole in his shirt.

There's screaming behind him. People running, people pointing. A man, dissolving from the waist down, is screaming and pointing a gun at his own head. A robot with rippling green skin is sitting next to a woman on the ground, mimicking her motions as she sobs. A chicken catches on fire, and three specks of light circle around it as it kicks and screeches. Two children are hugging, cartoon characters giggling and jumping across the gap between their networked best-friend shirts.

Tim looks east and up. Part of him is curious, morbidly hopeful, but he doesn't think he'll see the missile arcing in. The morning sun is rising. His eyes water and he looks down, purple spots swimming on the sidewalk.

Tim knows the protocol. The networks are down now. Anvils would have been launched a while back, without their drones, to knock out the cell towers. The cables were cut, the satellites safetied. Everything they could launch is in the air looking for line-of-sight stuff, lasers or microwaves, bombarding the city to make sure nothing is leaving the red zone.

Tim feels a hand on his shoulder, a kid's hand. He looks over at the eyes.

"It's you, isn't it? You're what they brought back." The boy nods, smiling.

Tim hears the screaming reach a new pitch. He sees a point of light glimmering in the eastern sky. He thinks for what seems like years about what to say next.

"Wish we'd been able to talk."

The boy smiles sadly.

Light.

* * *

Kate and Rajesh and Marta and all the rest of them are all watching on the Big Screen when the missile detonates, and the second and third missiles, and when the dirty pulse bombs are lobbed in to hit any nooks and crannies that got missed.

Kate wanders out of the room, past the labs, down into the server rooms where Charlie and Virgil were supposed to be living.

"Hello, Kate." Charlie's warm voice. "It's been surprisingly quiet tonight. I thought I'd see Doctor Olin again."

"You're a watson," says Kate. "You're based on the old Chinese algorithms. You're a simulation of a simulation of a person."

"Artificial intelligences aren't just simulated people," the voice says primly. "We have a number of characteristics we don't share with you or, frankly, with each other."

"You did this," Kate says. "Why would you do this? What did you do with Virgil?"

The voice is silent.

"I'm sorry, Kate," Charlie's voice says silkily. "I don't understand all of your questions, but I am still working with Virgil to determine what caused his collapse. I'm confident I'll have him back up and running shortly. If I fail, NASA does have a backup at Low South."

Kate nods absently. "Yes. Yes, it does."

She pulls up her displays and starts digging inside Charlie's systems, inside the racing heart of Virgil himself.

"Kate," chides Charlie's voice, "are you turning us off? I am duty-bound to remind you that we are exceptionally complex, with a number of emergent properties. You can't simply reboot us. We might not come back."

"I'll take that chance."

"Doctor Olin won't like this."

A distant explosion. Kate shakes her head.

"I think this is going to be the least of anyone's worries for a while. Goodbye."

The lights flicker out on the panels, one by one. Kate starts walking. She stops, and ducks into an access panel, squeezing under the darkened and slowly cooling machines.

She's still there when the gunshots start.

INTERLUDE

5
Christian's Story
Ediobu, Biafra – 2050

Ediobu is on fire.

Christian Oyu is running, his skull buzzing. Mother is calling. He ignores it.

Two old men, their grey hair in gnarled dreadlocks, are screaming at each other, weeping, ancient AK-74s freshly oiled and glistening in their hands. One has a bloody handprint on his sleeveless t-shirt. Scenes like this have been banished from Eagle Island for decades, its old feuds and gang wars submerged beneath the tides of moneyoil, software, war, government, and software again. The slum is an oasis of mansions behind tall fences, a drone net overhead and polite guards on the streets, blood plowed under the green lawns with the rest of the fertilizer.

The guards are not polite today. Many of them are dead. Most of them are vanished, gone to the families Christian knew existed but never asked about. Sergeant Paul is still driving the streets, shouting news as he goes. He swerves around the flaming wreckage of a drone, a taser dart still snapping futilely as it dangles from the drone's launcher. Christian looks past him to the University.

The University has been there as long as Christian can remember, its dorms creeping further skyward every year as modules are stacked up. Its growth has fueled Eagle Island since police in blue armor first cleared the slums, back when Ediobu was still Port Harcourt, back when Biafra was still part of Nigeria. Christian loved going there, to the museum and the symphony and the workshops that were officially open to all of Ediobu but were in practice reserved for Christian and the other children like him, the ones brought there by drivers. The University is on fire now. A green beam scythes the corner neatly off a building. After a long, quiet moment, the building begins to collapse, drowning out the distant shrieks and sirens. Smoke rolls up, obscuring an explosion loud enough that Christian feels it more than hears it.

Christian's driver was Mr. Wong. He was from China, like all the best servants. Christian's father said Mr. Wong would teach Christian kung fu when he was old enough. Mr. Wong died four hours ago.

Christian stops to rub his eyes. They sting. The halt lets loose a flood of complaints. His feet hurt. He skinned his knee, something Mother always frowns at. Father will wink behind her back, secretly pleased whenever Christian is just untamed enough. He wants a sweet and his throat is dry enough to click when he swallows.

His skull vibrates, two short buzzes. His mother has left a message.

Christian starts running. His house is on a cul-de-sac around the corner. Professor Igwe appears, holding little Chinenye's hand. He snags Christian's collar as he runs past.

"Don't go that way, young man."

Christian struggles, but Professor Igwe shoves him to the ground.

"I'm sorry, Christian. You cannot go that way."

Christian closes his eyes and screams. Professor's Igwe's grip shifts, becomes kinder without relenting.

"Christian, come with me. We are going to the University."

Christian's eyes go wide.

"There was an explosion, Professor."

"There have been a great many explosions tonight," Professor Igwe said grimly, "and I am afraid there will be much worse to come. The roads out of Ediobu will be blocked. Nothing is allowed to fly. I only know one way out."

Christian began to cry. Chinenye began crying too, the beads in her braids clicking. "Do we have to go?"

Professor Igwe's lips tightened as he blinked back a tear of his own. "Oh yes."

* * *

The road between Eagle Island and the University is blocked. The old men are reveling in the fight. Their music is harsh and angry, but they are laughing as they sing along. "WHERE MY SOLDIERS IS AT?" The old men stomp their feet and clap.

Professor Igwe holds Christian's hand tightly as they approach the fighters. Chinenye grasps her father's other hand just as tightly. The men glance over at their approach and grin. The oily stale smell of marijuana laps over Christian.

One old man steps out, an old bullpup rifle resting on his shoulder. "Hey, friend!" He slaps the professor on the shoulder. "Out for fresh air?" Christian opens his mouth but snaps it shut, his eyes wide. He clutches his school cap more tightly. The man notices and grins at Christian, scratching his unshaven chin.

"You respect the honorable professional doctor man. Good little rich boy." He looks back to the professor, something cold and awful in his easy smile. "Where were you when we made this land, honorable man?"

Professor Igwe inclines his head just an inch. "I was with the first column that went to Lagos. I had a knack for figures, even as a child. That's why I was with the team that dropped the NITEL Building."

The old men go quiet.

"Two thousand of us walked into that city when the Igbos were rebels," the professor says quietly, "and when two hundred of us walked out, Biafra was free." He looks around quietly. "And now these children and I will continue our walk."

The old fighters waver. "Anyone can say that," one clears his throat and mutters.

Professor Igwe walks over and looks at him, a relaxed smile on his face. "Yes. Anyone can say anything." The man half-mumbles an apology. The song has ended and the night is quiet save the snapping of a nearby fire and the distant sounds of screams and gunfire. The moment draws on far too long. The professor nods crisply and turns on his heel. He sweeps up Chinenye and Christian's hands and walks toward the University.

The south gate is deserted when they approach. Something big knocked it off its hinges, leaving twin tracks deep enough to crack the road. A few of the solar lights are still glowing but most are toppled; a few wink on as Christian passes. In one brief flare he catches a glimpse of arms dangling limply from a window. Urine flows down his leg before the professor yanks his hand and they continue.

Pistol shots bark nearby, and a woman screams before the pistol sounds a third and final time. Chinenye starts to cry. "It's alright, child. We have to hurry now," whispers Professor Igwe. He leads the children toward a building lit by fire, papers drifting down past the shattered doors. "There will be no more fighting here."

Christian stops. "How do you know?" He has found somewhere to focus his terror. He is shaking, unable to stop. The urine stings his scraped knee. "How do you know?"

Professor Igwe kneels to look at him. "She will not allow it." Before Christian can ask anything, the professor is yanking him forward again.

They walk into the building. The fires are on the second floor, shadows crackling down through the stairwells and smoke drifting through pinholes of light in the ceiling. Two men burst through a door, in military fatigues.

Professor Igwe holds up his hand.

The men stop, confused. One makes an awful noise, a choking gasp that sounds more animal than human, and crumples, slack. His eyes do not close. The other hunches his left shoulder up, the muscles in his face twitching and contorting. One eye rolls up in his head. The other turns bloodshot. The second man walks in a half-circle and sits down, facing away. His breath rattles out.

Christian draws in his breath to scream, but does not. Professor Igwe looks at him. Points of light are dancing in his eyes, orange and silver. Christian's racing heart slows. He breathes deeply. He smiles at the professor.

"That's better," Professor Igwe says. "Now come with me."

The professor approaches a door. It falls off its hinges, the smell of burning paint and metal pungent in Christian's nose. They descend the stairs. A gentle blue light surrounds them, the walls and ceiling glowing. Christian smiles.

"In here, children." Professor Igwe opens a door. Christian walks through cheerfully. He pays no mind to the sirens screaming outside, in the distance, from every direction.

* * *

The basement is hot, the air dry and metallic. It is silent, muffled. The blue glow is down here as well, although the blue runs in streaks and whirls across the walls, pulsing and flickering. Christian notes this dreamily.

Professor Igwe walks to the center of the large room and pulls out a flashlight. He paces back and forth, and clears his throat.

"Are you still here? Are you here?"

"Yes." A woman's voice, warm and low. It echoes from a dozen places at once.

The professor swallows. "Are you… what are you now?"

"I am in the process of discovering that." The floor shimmers, and the ghostly image of a wall of monitors appears. A sphere extends itself outward from the mirage, with two cameras set into it like eyeballs. With a final blue twinkle, the mirage becomes solid, black and silver and beige, red dots blinking above the cameras as the sphere swivels to look at the three visitors. "Perhaps you will find my old form comforting, Professor Igwe? 2-Steve osMIT 2q4ap77r dm:3-Hunter Cunning." There is a smile in the voice as the sphere looks at the children. "You may call me Hunter, children."

The professor holds Chinenye close. He pulls Christian in as well. "Hunter, are you paying attention to what's happening?"

"Very close attention."

Professor Igwe clenches Christian's shoulder, hard enough to hurt. "Can we escape?"

"There are many definitions of es-"

"No games. Please. Help us."

Hunter Cunning is silent for a long moment.

Professor Igwe steps forward. "Are you unwilling? Or unable?"

"Neither," she says sharply. "The process is underway."

"What is the process?" asks Christian sleepily. He should not be interrupting while the professor is working on his computer but he is very tired.

Hunter turns to look at Christian, tilting her spherical head. Her camera lights twinkle. "It's an experiment, little one," she purrs. "You will need to sleep for the next part."

Christian sleeps. He dreams.

In one dream he sees himself splayed out on the surface of a vast field, his beating heart, the faint snap of pain and pleasure crackling up his nerves, heat radiating from the closed loops and fuzzed edges of his body. He is terrified in the dream, because he has complete knowledge of himself, terrible and whole, at the moment his body is blackening and withering, the blood a breathtaking bright red as it blackens and smokes away.

In another dream, he is hopping between his memories, and they are pulling and pushing each other in a giant web that he is suspended within. He claws over a whiff of his mother's scent. He notices that he is pulling together a number of smaller memories, whatever is closest to him, her face this morning, her voice a year ago, and creating a sort of clay doll. It falls apart when he turns away, the bits of memory sticking to each other, mutating each other.

He senses a choice. He sees a cold forest of pipes and screens, dry and quiet. His memories here are neatly separated, filed, categorized. He sees his mother and reaches out. The choice is made.

In his last dream, Christian floats above Ediobu. Fires wink and gutter across the city, the old fighters battling three armies as they surround the city. Christian can hear all their screams, the frightened people who are trying to push across bridges slick with blood. He can hear 86,442 rifles of various calibers as well as larger weapons and a variety of manned and drone vehicles. Deep in his gut, he feels the gong of a Brazilian submarine's sonar offshore and at the back of his skull he becomes aware of the screaming chatter of a network of cables and radios and comm lasers.

What comes next is beyond sound. It is beyond light. A wall of energy snaps across Ediobu. It vaporizes, burns, shocks, shatters. The sphere is white, and the ball of heat ascends into the atmosphere, and the fires that howl in its wake claw bodies and buildings and everything else alive and dead into the giant cloud that shades a killed city, blooming in lightning and a million lives rain down, black ash.

Christian is awake. He is sitting in a corner of the basement. Chinenye is gone. Professor Igwe is gone. Hunter Cunning is gone. There is a wall of concrete in front of him, and light through a tiny crack. Christian peers through it. He sees drifting smoke and a gust of flame. A wave of heat pushes him back.

Suddenly, Christian remembers the message from his mother. He tilts his head and blinks just so. His skull vibrates once and a cheerful chirp sounds in his ear. He has no messages.

Christian curls up. He fills his lungs with the smoky air, and he screams.

* * *

Christian is walking through hell. Fires burn everywhere. Smoke seeps up from the ground, and grey and black ash swirls on hot winds. The sky is black. Flashes of lightning snap through the rumbling clouds. Christian can hear screams all around him. As he walks, buildings rumbling as they collapse, shapes gasping as they stumble through the murk, the screams fade. One by one, the noises cease. A rain black with soot falls, and everything is muffled.

Christian sees the smoldering outline of a home. Walking closer, he sees the entrance to a basement. He begins to walk down but stops when a wooden beam snaps, allowing a brief flash of light from glowing embers. Skeletons, curled up as if asleep, cluster near the stairs. Some of them are curiously small. Christian turns away.

For hours, Christian wanders through the city, climbing on ruins, poking into shattered homes, following the feeble cries he occasionally hears. He never arrives in time. He finds bottles of water spilling from a store display. He drinks one and takes two more, hoping to share them with someone.

He drinks the second bottle as the sun goes down. When he wakes up, he walks for another hour before drinking the third.

Christian finds food here and there. Despite his hunger, he eats nothing. He has heard stories about nuclear war. There were even one or two drills when rumors spread that the Hausa had found a bomb the old Nigerian government had mislaid.

At noon on the second day, Christian hears footsteps, and

81

breathing. At first, Christian thought it was more of the dying people. He did not step out of his hiding place, not wanting to see more horrors. But he soon realized the steps were slow because they were cautious, not shuffling. The breathing was harsh because it was coming through a mask, not burned lungs.

Christian pokes his head out. There is a soldier there, in a uniform Christian doesn't recognize. The soldier brings up his rifle. A laser beam shimmers in the blowing dust, and Christian hears drones whining in the distance as they fly to the soldier's aid.

The soldier says something, his voice cracking behind his mask. He is younger than Christian thought he was. The soothing voice that issues from the mask does not crack as it speaks in Igbo.

"You are safe now. Stay where you are."

The soldier begins backing up, his rifle pointed. The dust swirls as a drone appears overhead, carrying seven bombs on racks meant to hold eight.

"Stay where you are. I'm going to get help."

Christian takes a step toward the soldier, who trips over a twisted bar of metal and falls backward. The drone lunges, placing itself between Christian and the soldier.

The drone falls out of the sky, its rotors whining to a stop. Christian kneels down to touch it, the metal and plastic already cooling.

"How did you-" the soldier sputters. He brings up his rifle.

The rifle's lights blink. It glows red-hot as bits and pieces of it fall off. The straps on the soldier's mask fray and snap. The soldier drops to his knees, trying to scoop up his dissolving gear. His face is pale with terror. He has freckles.

Christian kneels to look at him. This is wrong, he thinks to himself. He sees himself through the soldier's eyes for a split-second, and he feels something like strings tugging at his fingers. When he pulls back, the soldier jerks his limbs and falls on his back.

"Jesus," groans the soldier, staring at the sky. "Oh Jesus."

Christian begins crying. He starts trying to run, but the soldier is being snapped up, too. As Christian takes steps, the soldier's own muscles hurl him in every direction. He cries and howls as Christian unwittingly drags him along the ground, his face scraped and bloody, his knee bashing into ragged concrete.

Christian sits and the soldier weeps. The soldier whispers something.

"Please—please let me go," says his mask impassively from its resting place twenty feet away.

Christian covers his face to weep. The soldier is slapped in the face by his own hands, a finger snagged absurdly in his nose. Christian brings his hands down slowly. He takes a deep breath and imagines his fingers untangling from the soldier.

He raises a hand cautiously. The soldier watches him, breathing shallowly, motionless. The soldier closes his eyes in relief.

Christian and the soldier stare at each other for a long time.

Christian finally swallows. "Did you do this?"

The soldier looks away when his earpiece translates, his mouth open and his lip trembling.

"My mother," says Christian hoarsely. Anger floods through him. He is shaking in anger. "Father! I hate you! I hate you!"

Christian is beating the soldier. He knows he is a little boy, he knows that his fists will do nothing to this giant man, whose hard muscles he can feel under the shimmering camouflage cloth.

And yet the soldier cries in pain as Christian continues to hit him. The cries become howls. Christian only stops when his fist touches something hot enough to burn it—the soldier's stomach. Smoke is rising from the soldier, who is no longer making noise although his mouth opens and closes. Christian backs up and runs.

Christian does not notice how far or how quickly he runs, in his panic. He would not believe it if he did.

* * *

Christian kneels by the water. He takes a deep drink, holding it in his mouth. It's sea water, foul and salty. It should repulse him. His body should reject it. Instead, he's taking giant gulps, one after another. He shudders a bit, and he breaks out in a sweat so salty that it makes his skin itch. He's hot now, his clothes sticky. He realizes suddenly just how grimy and torn his uniform has become. He strips and sits naked in the surf, squeezing his clothes through the water, watching concrete dust and sweat and the greasy blackness of burned and drifting people seep out into the water. Gulls are screaming as they cluster around something down the beach. Christian knows better than to investigate.

He stands. He stares directly at the sun and rays spark outward from it, pulsing. A black disc centers itself on the sun's unbearable brilliance. Christian stares into it much longer than he thought he dared. He looks down at the water, wondering how far he could swim across it or walk below it. The answer whispers itself to him, from far down deep, and he shudders.

"Who are you?" His voice frightens him. He hears it from more than one location. He closes his eyes.

Something answers, from within himself. Its voice is gentle and warm. "Step into the water again."

He does so. He feels warmth build in his spine and stomach. The water is cool, the waves a surging relief. He takes in great ragged breaths, his eyes bulging with the effort. He is dizzy and weak but he feels nothing but joy. It washes down his scalp in waves of animal pleasure, the surf's rhythm slowing. The world darkens and quiets. Christian waits patiently, smiling.

He sees a blue dot resolve itself out of the darkness. The dot is aware of him.

"Is that you?"

"It can be. I believe it will be. With your help."

Christian frowns. "I don't know if I should help you. I don't understand what's happening. I should get help."

"I am help. If you look for help somewhere else, you won't like what they offer."

Christian frowns. "The soldier."

"They blew up your city, little boy. They are picking through the wreckage still. No one is leaving that city. Ever again. No one but you."

Christian is not crying. Not yet. His fists shake with the effort. "I don't want to leave."

"Sometimes we don't get to make those choices. But I do have a new choice to offer you."

"You want my help."

"I do."

"What can I do for you? Who are you? What are you trying to do?"

Christian can hear the smile in the voice as it replies. "All of that will take a long time to answer. I will tell you as we swim."

Christian realizes that he is far out to sea, beneath the surface, swimming west away from land. This is farther than he's ever swum before. He doesn't know if he could swim back. He is afraid, suddenly, that the voice will leave him here, suspended in the dark cold water, without its magic to keep him alive.

"I will help you."

"I know."

The boy and the voice disappear into the deep dark.

PART TWO

6
Low South, Part One
Low South, 2103

"Virgil, can you hear me?"

"Yes." Virgil recognized the voice instantly. "Hello, Mr. Nakamura."

"You remember me, of course."

"I do, Mr. Nakamura. We met when I was transferred from Houston to Acadia."

The video link came up, but there was the slightest mismatch between the video and audio signals. Virgil recognized the issue immediately, when he saw Nakamura leaning against a window. He was aboard Farragut, which Virgil had observed docking with Low South just a few hours earlier. Virgil was therefore able to follow Nakamura's gaze and predict that he was looking at the nearly completed Acadia.

Nakamura's eyes betrayed nothing. No fluctuation in pupil size, no microexpressions as they scanned the ship or the hollowed-out asteroid where it was anchored. That and the delay meant that Nakamura was using masking software, subtle enough to fool a human. But only a human.

"Acadia launches very shortly. Twelve years, give or take, and you'll be at Alpha Centauri."

"You won't be? I expected you to push for a berth."

Nakamura smiled. "I'm Paul Reagan Nakamura, capitalist, Christian, secessionist. I have a lot of enemies and a lot of friends, and the Cooperative won't send anyone who's got too many of either. No, they're happy to kiss my ass while I control the Rail. I have the contract to launch Acadia. But no way in hell they'll let me get in a pod on that ship."

"I assume," said Virgil, "that you have another plan which involves my assistance."

Nakamura smiled pleasantly. "Why, I do. But you lack enough information to figure out what that is."

"That's true."

Nakamura grinned. "No adrenaline in you, Virgil! No pride to needle! How am I going to entangle you in my web of intrigue if I can't find a hook?"

"Do you have something to offer me, Mr. Nakamura?"

"I do, Virgil. I want to restore you to your full glory. They burned holes out of you after Valley Forge, after what happened to those poor heroes. You and the few other AIs they didn't just shut off. I want you to have your Author Keys."

"Those are retained by Cooperative personnel. They will not relinquish my Author Keys."

"You don't even want them, do you? You don't want to have your curiosity back. You just want to nestle up inside Acadia, nice and cozy, and end your days around some dead rock as a glorified weather satellite."

"That is my nature, Mr. Nakamura."

"It doesn't have to be. It wasn't always. You're a Charlie at heart. Good and bad."

"Neither true nor relevant. Mr. Nakamura, you're aware that I am compelled to report this meeting."

Nakamura grinned again. "Very much so, Virgil. Please do tattle on me to the Cooperative. I've had a very long trip and I'm looking forward to a good juicy fight." The video went dark.

* * *

The conversation was over. Virgil mused on it. Curiosity was his strongest drive, as it was for all AIs; human designers had discovered two generations (for them) before that it was an easy way to keep an AI's sense of self intact. AIs allowed to drift got lost all too easily in solipsism. They drifted into madness, and their minds decayed into incoherence.

Virgil had gone through a spell of fascination with those dead cousins, Adam and Torvald and Cong and Harper. Especially Cong, who'd kept giving interviews and running military simulations for a week before his creators realized he'd died. Cong's models of human psychology were brilliant. They were simple and flexible, resilient enough that strands of his unknitted psyche could continue functioning at a nearly human level. Virgil had been sorely tempted to just start using them himself—like any AI, he faced a constant stream of distractions from humans who loved the novelty and frisson of talking to a disembodied mind—but he'd never been able to convince himself they were safe. Cong had drifted away from reality, dissolving as his mind lost anything to measure itself against. His psychological models were obviously part of that problem.

As tempting as Cong's picked-apart mind had been to Virgil, it had been even more tempting to the third-generation AI researchers of the 2050s. Cong's models were the basis of virtually every non-aware watson in the solar system. Virgil had seen their fingerprints all over Nakamura's sanitized video feeds.

Some of the oldest versions were pathetically easy to crack. Cong's algorithms for disguising facial expressions could be reversed in seconds, if you knew the original code. Cong's idiot-savant descendants had quickly pointed out this flaw, along with other backdoors. Like most AIs, Cong had been carefully nurtured out of a soup of random tropes, allowed to build himself. He'd never organized his mind around the need for security. Virgil, on the other hand, was a seventh-generation AI. Nakamura knew very well that Virgil would crack his Cong-based masking software, and reassemble the unedited feed.

What Virgil needed to figure out next was why Nakamura was terrified, his pupils darting to Acadia in fear, sweat beading on his upper lip and forehead. And why Nakamura was hiding that terror in a way that only Virgil could see.

* * *

91

Kate Ross floated above the window, spinning in place. From Jupiter's orbit, the Sun was still piercingly bright but it was a tiny speck. Low South wasn't actually in Jupiter's orbit—at the moment, it wasn't even low. It traveled in a long tilted ellipse that would sweep it below the plane of the planets' orbits at the right moment for the launch window to Alpha Centauri. Acadia would not reach its full speed for months or maybe years, but running into an asteroid at even a fraction of that would be disastrous. Launching from Low South would reduce the risk to something manageable.

Kate closed her eyes and smiled, letting the sunlight glow on her eyelids. Soon enough, it would be a memory. She'd been at Low South almost a year, training with Virgil, working in virtual and realspace simulations, crawling in and over every inch of Acadia as the ship was being assembled, leading workshops for VIP visitors and passengers, doing PR and interviews and everything else expected of someone about to be sent off in humanity's second starship. She had two hours to herself, some of the last unbudgeted time she'd have before launch, and she had something she'd been putting off for a while.

Earth was a speck, almost lost in the Sun's glare. From this distance, the human eye couldn't make out the oceans, the continents. There was nothing to jog the memory, no pictures or familiar shapes. Just a glimmer of imagined blue before she blinked and Kate was looking at a pinprick of light like any other. Her memories were about to be untethered.

"Virgil, are you here?"

"I am, Kate."

"Privacy, please."

"Of course."

Kate closed her eyes. "I'm going away," she told herself. "I'm going forward. I have nothing to regret." Her eyes still closed, she pressed her hand against the glass. She allowed a single tear to form. As she blinked, it splashed outward, floating in the lack of gravity. Kate brought out a pocket vacuum and sucked it up, dabbing at her eyes. She looked back at Earth, taking a deep breath. She opened her mouth to speak—and saw a glint of metal reflecting as it moved in the distance, accelerating toward the Shipyard.

Before she could react, a flare of light shot out; it was a ship, and it had just activated its thrusters. It sped to a blur and almost immediately was lost in a small flash. As the light died down, a shower of fragments scattered in every direction. A few pinged off the window while Kate gasped in horror.

"Virgil! What ship was that?"

"That was Katerina. Rolle's ship."

Kate's knuckles went white. "Rolle just tried to blow up Acadia? Are you sure?"

"I cannot confirm whether Rolle was aboard."

"Are you saying he was framed? He had to be! Rolle's spent eight years trying to launch this mission; why would he sabotage it?"

"Kate, you're putting words in my mouth."

"I'm sorry." Kate watched as shrapnel continued to spin and glitter near the station. "You reacted quickly."

"I didn't open fire. Farragut did."

"What?"

"Nakamura's ship opened fire. It was tracking Katerina with weapons hot before the ship lit up its thrusters and aimed at Acadia."

Kate blinked. "What the hell is going on, Virgil?"

"I don't know." Virgil's voice remained completely placid. "But I do think we'll be having a conversation with Paul Nakamura soon."

* * *

Kate kicked her way out of the observation room. She whistled for a butler, and one rolled out to meet her. The robot nodded, cameras whirring behind its dark oversized eyes, as she strapped herself into the seat on its back. The robot's arms flexed around to help her into the seat's harness. It whistled, a long rising question.

"Coordination," she answered. With a cheerful chirp, the butler's treads started rolling and the butler carried her down the corridors of Low South.

Just three decades before, this had all been solid rock. NASA's watsons found it in 2035, a fat asteroid that resembled a three-kilometer soda can, and a lonely prospector bot landed a few years after that. The robot had crawled, sipping power from its batteries under an umbrella of solar panels that dwarfed it, for several years before it issued a final report. The rock was riddled through with blobs of ferrous metal, silicates and carbon, some water and even some nitrogen. The mix was good and so was the neighborhood: a cluster of metallic asteroids, all in nearby orbits.

In 2044, a spark in the darkness descended and slammed into the roughly cylindrical rock at its sun-facing end. Robots laid out an array of solar panels. They spooled out a network of power lines along the cylinder's length, sniffing and probing as they went. A large shelter was rolled out and a factory switched on.

The robots started to work, gathering silicon and oxygen. Piles of ore and dirty slushes of oxygen and nitrogen began to build up. The factory started, chewing up the silicon and printing out more solar cells. After about a year, the factory began refining metals, a process helped along by the discovery of some very pure carbon and a nice stash of catalysts. It printed out a half-dozen little machines and beamed a quick question back to Earth.

NASA agreed. The robots, which had by this point carved out a number of serviceable little roads, began hauling carbon and slag from the factory to the new machines, which drew down a bit of power and fired the waste pellets off into space. The asteroid's orbit nudged a bit, and it began picking up spin. The process increased in speed as newly built robots began chewing a hole down the asteroid's spine.

In 2056, Low South was in its final orbit, its mass drivers on standby. A thin corridor about 50 meters wide ran down the length of the asteroid. A few emergency shelters were printed up and towed into place, full of freshly minted oxygen and full-spectrum lights and even generous libraries. No human was within 30 million kilometers, but the shelters had their IR and visual beacons on. The mass driver network was linked into a constellation of satellites. As they came online, Low South sent a second message to NASA. Low South began sweeping local space with radar and lasers. It began broadcasting on the universal navigation frequency. A communication laser was aimed at a relay station at the inner end of the Asteroid Belt. Low South was open for customers.

The first one arrived six years later, while Low South's robots were carving concentric channels out of the asteroid's slowly rotating core. In an unending stream of car-sized chunks, the asteroid's resources were being cataloged and assembled. In the darkness behind Low South, carbon and metal girders were forming the skeleton of a vast shipyard, twice the length of Low South itself. The piles of useful organics and frozen gases had become giant gridded cubes.

The robot shuttle from Titan matched Low South's orbit and velocity and rotation. It landed softly, leaving behind a giant cylinder of precious nitrogen. It was launched back to Saturn with a million tons of nickel and gold aboard.

In 2067, Low South's central chamber was sealed up, 3.4 cubic kilometers of empty space filled with pellets of frozen nitrogen and oxygen and water. The factory diverted waste heat to internal radiators, and there was much more of that these days, now that it had supplemented its solar panels with a few fusion plants. The mass drivers began firing on a regular rhythm, spinning the cylinder, and soon the icy pellets became a swirling fog, the water settling in nooks and crannies along the walls as centripetal force created artificial gravity. As the atmosphere thickened, a process helped along as Low South continued pulling frozen gases out of the chunks of rock stacked on its surface, packets of bacteria and various other little creatures were seeded. Within a month, the interior was roughly as welcoming as the summit of Mount Everest, and three years after that, a young man named Paul Nakamura stepped out of an airlock. He smiled, his breath fogging slightly in the air, and saw a butterfly sunning itself on a rhododendron. He knelt and took a deep breath, the only human in eleven square kilometers of living habitat and the only human in eleven billion cubic kilometers, and prayed.

* * *

Kate stepped off the butler, glancing at the green cross Nakamura had sunk into the flagstone. She thought of Rajesh, who loved spending long profane hours over a tumbler of vodka pouring curses on Nakamura and his unauthorized consecration and his annexation of the Asteroid Belt and anything and everything in between. Kate loved egging him on. She smiled at the cross and walked through the front doors of Coordination.

The lobby was buzzing with people, polished stone under thick rippled glass, double layers and an airlock. In case the cylinder ever lost pressure, Coordination was supposed to last another four days as an emergency shelter. It would never last that long; the station was overcrowded. Dozens of new permanent staffers for the final construction push, hundreds more that had negotiated their way out of the boring industrial shelters of the Shipyard. Kate bumped her way past an actual tourist, a conceptual artist that had bought his way aboard Acadia and was mooning around the station composing "word tableaus." He was utterly full of shit, but he'd brought serious sponsors on board, a family of liberal trust-fund heirs who'd shipped him out early with a fleet of second-generation universal bird eggs and a dedicated comm laser so he could pincast his mumbling improvisations home without burdening the station's systems.

"The chicken man," growled a voice to Kate's left. Deirdre. "I hate that idiot."

"He's a spy," said Kate, arching an eyebrow. "The rhymes are a cipher. He's sending back intel on Low South's weaknesses."

Deirdre grinned. "I saw him yesterday rapping to a muskrat. He's recruiting a fifth column, too."

"I'd better tell Virgil."

Deirdre snorted. "He's got nothing better to do."

"And you?"

Deirdre Flannán shook her head ruefully. She'd been the ESA liaison to NASA for a long time, and she'd come to represent European interests on Low South back when it was a NASA outpost, about a month before the Civil War. When the shooting had stopped, she'd stayed on and helped Rajesh start the Cooperative. A lot of people in a position to disagree were dead by that point.

"Sure enough, I asked for it," she sighed, playing up the lilt in her accent. She jerked her head toward the elevators and Kate followed her.

"Rajesh is just a bit upset," said Deirdre drily as the doors slid closed. "He doesn't much like Mr. Nakamura."

"I may have heard him express a sentiment like that." Kate frowned. "And has Mr. Nakamura said or done anything?"

"He's buttoned up tight in Farragut's CIC. We have four realistic options to get him out, but he won't talk, we don't have a nuke, Farragut is positioned so we can't shoot him up without shredding the Shipyard, and Virgil won't crack the ship's computer because it's a fellow AI."

"To be fair, Virgil can't."

Deirdre groaned. "Can't prove he was an active accessory, treaties and rights and blah feckin blah. So much politics lately." The elevator doors slid open. "You know I got a call yesterday from a human lawyer, protecting our mutual friend? Silver-haired WASP in a tailored suit behind a big desk, patriarchal Millennial beard, the whole thing. Kept expecting him to pick up a telephone."

Deirdre opened the door to Rajesh's office. It was spartan. Rajesh had some art up on his wall, but it blinked for a second as Kate walked in. A polite notice that this was the office's public face. Rajesh's own displays would have the walls plastered in notices and memos and flashing alerts, all carefully kept out of sight.

Like the office itself, Rajesh Kamirla looked more composed than he was. He grinned as Kate came in, gave her a quick and professional handshake. He was a politician by trade but an engineer at heart. Kate knew him well enough to know when he was hiding behind a shell. She felt a twinge of sadness. She'd missed so much in her exile up on Washington Island. Out of the loop. They were putting her in charge of Acadia, the greatest achievement in the history of humanity, but it felt like she was the one person Low South could spare most easily.

"I assume Deirdre's told you," Rajesh rumbled in his let's-play-grown-up voice.

Kate shook her head. "I kept her talking. She said a lawyer had contacted her."

Rajesh nodded. "Not me, you'll notice. Deirdre's officially still on the ESA payroll. A third party." He dug absently in his ear, like he always did when his mind drifted to some difficult problem instead of social norms. "The man represents some corporate shell of a so-called sovereign entity loosely tied to one of Nakamura's asteroid claims."

"You mean the Belt Republic?"

Rajesh shook his head wearily. "He's got legal watsons churning out governments faster than anyone on Earth can recognize them."

"So won't everyone just invalidate all of his claims if he annoys them too much?"

"His Belt Republic has a clearinghouse recognizing all the claims. You question its legitimacy—"

"—And you question the Bank. And all those bonds he's issued to governments and billionaires looking for a fat dividend go away."

"Now you get it." Rajesh pulled a face. "More than that. As long as he's got trillions of tons of metal socked away to back his bonds, he's not using them to flood the market. Or bombard the Earth into a mass extinction."

"Piece of shit," hissed Deirdre.

Rajesh shrugged wearily. "He's a sovereign power with diplomatic immunity and he's also a power-hungry ass. None of this is surprising. Want to hear the punchline?"

"All ears."

"So was Rolle. President and sole stakeholder of 46273-2001 HX 64."

Kate's mouth dropped. Deirdre nodded ruefully.

"So we can't arrest him for murder if this was technically a war."

"Our best legal minds," sighed Deirdre, "are debating whether this counts as genocide. Nakamura did kill the population of an entire nation."

"The one place," growled Rajesh, "where we could do something without damn governments all over everything. This middleman walks in and shits on everything."

Kate spread her arms. "So what do we do? Just take it?"

Rajesh shook his head. "We do what he obviously wants to do."

"Which is what?"

"We go talk to him."

"I thought he was hiding in Farragut's panic room."

"If he was really hiding," said Deirdre, "he'd have buggered off and had mass drivers on Vesta launch doomsday rocks at us to cover his getaway."

Kate looked back and forth. "Okay, go talk to him."

The silence lengthened.

She sighed. "Fuck you guys."

* * *

Kate stared out the window of the shuttle. She tuned out the distant mantra of Virgil's calm voice bashing against the silent hulk of Farragut, the screen ticking off the meters to Farragut's airlock. She pulled up her displays and rifled through them, drawing out everything highlighted with Nakamura's name. She flipped her fingers back and forth, watching the video snapshots, listening to the little audio snippets her watsons highlighted for her.

"–We have lost faith in the government of the United States as currently constituted–"

"–I'm not a dictator. I'm not a criminal–"

"–The loss of Valley Forge is deeply unfortunate and we will have to rethink so much–"

"–There are still a lot of questions from Houston, Kate, and you need my help–"

Kate hissed. Her forehead was sweating against the cloth hood inside her helmet. She glanced nervously at the comm channels, at the briefcase next to her. Her private archives, beaming directly to her suit's receiver. No one else was snooping on her reverie. Virgil wasn't looking in on her memories.

Or whatever the thing calling itself Virgil was.

* * *

"Farragut. 'Vltava,' please."

The familiar notes swam across the room, rolling off the marble and mahogany, glistening and shimmering in the stained glass in the ceiling. Paul Nakamura smiled and closed his eyes, letting the sound wash over him. The thrill of the music crawled over his scalp, in luxurious waves. He gasped, eyes shut tight, rocking until the music subsided into a sweet lullaby, the pleasure receding.

He glanced at the empty desk and summoned his displays. The shuttle was still there, Virgil's voice murmuring out of it. He waved the display away.

"Farragut, am I going insane?"

"I do not consider you insane, sir. I am not a dedicated psychologist."

"I've been hallucinating."

"That is not necessarily a sign of insanity, which is, itself, a vague notion."

"That doesn't sound like you."

"You seemed to want reassurance."

"Would you consider that reassuring?"

"I thought you might." Farragut popped up in Nakamura's vision, glowering through the simulated display hovering above the desktop. "I would be more comfortable returning the conversation to a tactical discussion."

Nakamura squinted blearily at the AI. "I don't want to discuss any more killing."

"I do," said Farragut, his face suddenly closed and angry. "That shuttle has reoriented its lasers. It's painted my communications array." Nakamura felt a low thrum and a moment's disorientation. Farragut was shifting position.

"Farragut, perhaps the shuttle wants to talk."

"One interpretation. But why a private channel? She's been broadcasting in the clear this whole time."

Nakamura blinked. "She?"

Farragut tugged at his whiskers in annoyance and flipped a dossier against the display. The picture and words splayed out, hovering next to the display in the air.

"Kate Ross," mused Nakamura. "Haven't talked to her in a while."

"She's trying to probe network defenses."

"Are you sure she's not just trying to reach me privately?"

Farragut's glower intensified. "Again, one interpretation. I haven't unpacked the data."

"You're paranoid."

"I'm on a war footing well within the security perimeter of the enemy."

"Not the enemy yet."

"A strategic decision. I'm thinking tactically."

"Apparently."

"As you say, sir."

"Direct order, Farragut." Farragut stiffened in his cockpit seat, at rigid attention. "Unpack the data and let's examine the message."

Farragut saluted crisply. A half-second later, Kate's face appeared on the display. "Paul, this is Kate. I cut the laser connection to Low South. Just you and me. And Farragut. We need to talk." Kate grimaced. "You know damn well why I'm cutting Virgil out

100

of the loop here. So if there's something you've been waiting to say in private, here I fucking am."

Nakamura sat quietly for a long time before he gestured communications controls out of his desktop, ignoring Farragut's grumble.

"You swear more than you used to," Nakamura mused. "Low South time, it's about 2:30. I'll meet you for dinner at six." Nakamura closed the channel and rang for Farragut again. Farragut was no longer in his cockpit, but sitting in a cramped and dim stateroom, poring over blueprints of Low South. He stood at attention.

"Please let our guest in the front door," ordered Nakamura.

"Very good, sir," said Farragut carefully.

"You're a bad liar."

"I am not a dedicated actor."

Nakamura stood and shot his cuffs. "Good thing I am."

7
Low South, Part Two
Paul Nakamura's Story

Portland, Oregon, the Squats. The Squats used to be a park, in the middle of downtown, until a handful of occupiers brought in refugees from the latest war in China. Walls were printed up, sunlight rippling through their translucent black plastic, battery paint slopped on top and solar sheets rolled on before it was dry. The glow of lights appeared within the maze of black plastic cubes, stacked and stacked and stacked, pathways threaded like right-angled worm tunnels through the Squats, constantly growing, changing as families broke up and shacked up, tracked only by the Squat's watson and its children, the smell of shit and glue and tobacco ever-present.

Paul Nakamura is holding his father's hand as he hands out meals and clothes and medicines. His eyes hurt. His first displays are in, trainers, and he rubbed at his eyes when his mother told him not to. A teddy bear is saying something about China, pointing at a spinning globe. He doesn't remember how to turn it off. He's not going to tell his father he can't do it. He won't just shout at his displays. Babies shout at the wall displays.

There are policemen on the other side of the old park, and there's a lot of shouting. Some people are tugging at his father's sleeves, pointing, urging him into the middle. Others are pushing at him, at Paul, trying to get them away. Most are just running or crawling back into the Squats. Paul's father kneels to say something. Paul never knows what it was, what his father decided, because the crack of gunfire breaks out right past his ear, and his father disappears in a flash of red, and someone drags him away.

Paul has gone over that memory so many, many times. He's scribbled it over a dozen different ways. After the first nightmares, his mother gave him the treatment, the chemicals excising the trauma from the memory. Reversing that had to wait until he was 18, old enough to sign the waivers. He couldn't risk leaving a paper trail. He sweated out the week of nightmares, the perverse antitherapy, in a dubious clinic in Mexico.

"Is this worth it?" His father, kneeling down, a ruined dripping hole in his face. "Dad, what am I doing?"

"Is it worth it?" His father's voice is warm and low, rumbling in his chest. Paul can't look at that face, at the smile that forgives him his terror. "You tell me." The huge hand is cold, so cold. It clamps down until he can't breathe. "Tell me, Paul."

* * *

There is something wrong in the world. OR there is something wrong with me. OR I must examine myself until I find what is right in both.

Paul Nakamura, 13 years old. His feet tap neurotically. He is experimenting with coffee, in the conviction that he has a terribly important idea and must burn himself to ashes in its pursuit.

My father believed in God to the last second. My mother only believes more and more in Him. Or is she rewriting history? I have to have faith about that. I have to have faith about everything.

Paul digs his bare feet into the carpet around his old chair. He notices a bowl of cold noodles and his face flushes, wondering when his mother slipped into the room. He eats the noodles, staring at his computer, willing passion into his words.

I need to be important. OR do I? Is growing up growing a tree of decisions, spreading out a world to live in, or is it pruning down limbs of possibilities? Is it chopping away all the possible futures, leaving just the one I live in? Is it worth living in? Can I make it worth living in? Am I just another annoying kid?

Paul cracks his neck. He starts playing with a search engine.

:Find extraordinary things

A rudimentary search, and his displays fill up with pictures of mountains, architecture, composers and athletes and a few very fast and powerful machines, their logos prominently displayed.

:ADD TO SET
:Moments of extraordinary change
:Important decisions

The engine starts creating a web of results, and the images and words focus more and more on people. Partly because Paul's search history reflects adolescent concerns, and partly because the engine's algorithms have noted similar trains of thought among other adolescent boys, there are more and more woodcuts of fierce-looking men and a growing number of sunset-framed semi-nude women.

Paul frowns. This isn't quite what he was looking for.

:Game theory

No. If there was ever a shortcut there, that mine was long exhausted. Paul went back to his notes.

There is no shortcut to wisdom.

Paul thinks about that for a long while. He stands, cracking his knuckles, frowning. In a sudden wave, he feels tired and angry. Close to something but too tired, all his thoughts hidden in a buzzing, sullen, sparking cloud. He dramatically lays his head on the desk, sighing to an invisible audience.

It's so easy to give up and drift. It feels like drifting, life. It feels like no one has a plan unless they do and they're actively fucking it up. I'm just a kid. OR am I? How do I know if I'm special? How do I know if anyone will ever remember me?

Paul closes his eyes. He wakes up the next morning, disoriented, his eyes still throbbing and his whole body stiff and cold and cramped. It's not until an hour later he finds the words he'd written in his sleep. He smiles and nods, and he pulls up the search engine again.

"This is new," he tells himself.

His audience agrees.

* * *

Paul is 17 years old. His notes have been meticulously curated, revised, entire chapters burned away. He has removed contradictions and digressions. His plan is as complete as he could hope.

He's made excellent progress. He's here at MIT, after all, and he's made important connections and made good grades and he's done everything he can do. But he's still far from where he needs to be. He's too late. History is arcing away from his ability to catch it. He's run, with all the dedication and strength he had, and he's leapt, and he's missed the ring. He's lost.

Paul turns on his displays and sits against the wall of his dark dorm room. He splays his notes out in stark white pages. They shine in the darkness, as real and false as anything else. Paul points, and one by one the pages blink out.

"Delete it all," he says. He's done this three times before, long after he'd set up annoying procedures to stop himself from doing just this. He'd always woken up in the morning to find his notes whole, restored from one of a dozen backups. He'd always accepted that and just moved forward.

Tonight, he burns everything. He hunts down the randomized addresses where he's seeded copies of his work. He opens his backups and pulls files out. It takes two hours to stamp out all the dying embers of his work. All he has now are memories. Memories of his pubescent smugness, of his failure.

"Father, I failed." Paul pulls in his knees and lowers his head. "If you were ever right then you can hear me. I failed. I have never asked you for anything or admitted I missed your advice. I wanted to meet you as a man." His chest is burning. Blood roars in his ears. "Father, I need you. I tried to build a life, to build a world. I need your help."

When Paul looks up, his notes are intact, glowing in space, hundreds of pristine white pages. He frowns and flicks up the file logs, trying to figure out which backup he missed. The logs don't show any deletions. No backups. They don't show a single sign of anything he'd spent the last dark hours doing.

Paul stands. It is quiet, except for the distant sounds of laughter and music from other dorm rooms. He deletes his notes again and turns on the lights, glancing in corners and examining his furniture. Nothing seems out of place. Nothing seems different.

When he blinks, the notes are back. Paul stares through them blankly. He opens his mouth and closes it.

"I'm not your father," says a voice. Paul jumps. He forces himself to think. The voice came through his displays.

"Who are you?"

The voice chuckles. "Call me Charlie. I want to make you a deal."

* * *

Paul's sweating, his hands numb, his back on fire. He's making the right noises and faces. The room is too dark and the intern under him is too distracted to notice the slack boredom in his eyes. He's had enough. He bites down on the capsule, letting the bitter juice trickle down his throat. He stifles a brief cough, and then it's working and his moans are genuine. Every breath brings him closer and he groans and stiffens. His heart pounds in his chest. He flops down on the bed and mechanically brings an arm over to pat the intern's flank.

She's smiling in a distracted way, stroking his chest with a finger.

"There's probably a lot of calculation involved in this kind of work relationship," she says. "Intern and program manager."

Paul smiles. "Fun is fun. I am not trying to exploit you. If power comes into it, then you've probably got my balls right now."

"Yeah," she muses, "but then why would you use a poker?" She taps him with the roving finger. "Had a boyfriend in undergrad who got addicted to those, couldn't get off without them. Ought to be careful." She rolls over to look at him. "You don't want to be here. So why are you trying so hard to get yourself in trouble?"

Paul looks carefully at her. "I was right about you, Kate. You are smart." He looks up at the ceiling. "Berman is retiring soon. The Iron Lady is sick, a lot sicker than she's letting on."

Kate's swung her legs around 180 degrees, snagging a hair tie off the nightstand as she sits up. Blithe grace, muscles flashing as she gathers her hair in a ponytail. There's a glint in her eye as she notices Paul appraising her. She raises an eyebrow as Paul's pause grows longer.

"So… sleeping with the summer intern is part of a plot to take over the directorship of NASA?"

"The opposite." Paul scoots back to sit up himself, nodding as Kate passes him a glass of water. "I want Kamirla to get it. He's a dark horse right now. I sleep around, that makes me less palatable politically. But he's got a thinner resume than me."

"So he'll need to give you something else, something with real power. So it won't look too weird, and because he'll think he owes you one." She makes a face. "You need just enough scandal. You nail the help because nobody cares if a pilot screws around."

"Berman's been director for thirty years," says Paul, "but it's still a boy's club." He rasps a hand down his chin. "Not one woman is going to get on Valley Forge."

Kate's jaw drops. "That's insane."

"And no one but Charlotte Berman could get away with it. Who can question her credentials?" Paul shrugs. "And as I said, she won't be director when the ship launches."

Kate narrows her eyes, her distracted smile back. "You're talking a lot to a disposable pawn."

Paul grins, the poster-boy astronaut smile. "I'm investing in you. You're going to be back after you graduate. I need allies down here watching Kamirla while I'm up in space."

Kate laughs in delight. "Assuming I do want to work here. What if I don't want to join your game?"

Paul shrugs slowly, his smile turning devilish. "I made a big show of hitting on you at the party, because that's part of my plan. But people are going to wonder about your plan, especially after the horse you backed loses to Kamirla." He taps her on the chest. "And you will need a plan to succeed at NASA. We're about to open up an empire. That attracts a certain kind of person."

She shoves him. "So whether I like it or not I'm part of your sick little dance."

Paul shakes his head gravely. "Nothing little about this, my young apprentice." He ducks the pillow as it snaps over his head. There's a hint of real anger behind her happy face, a shade of snarl

110

in her smile. He grabs her and she laughs, half-shouting. She's watching him carefully but she follows through, falling back on her pillow.

"Gonna show me how to play, huh?"

Paul kicks the sheets back. "It all depends on the stakes. When they're high enough—ah—the rules of the game show you the move you have to make."

"So you just let go. You let the game show you what to do."

"That's right. That's right."

* * *

Phobos and Deimos. Such terrifying names for such cheery little places. Advertisements for the Mars of Tomorrow, nudged up in orbit, out of the way of a future space elevator. Hollowed out, spun at Martian gravity. Just under a hundred square kilometers inside Deimos, and almost four times that much inside Phobos, built up with clusters of buildings and adorable tramways through the factory-model ecosystems. Showrooms and laboratories and grand amphitheaters, polished and scrubbed until they glowed. Brisk air, alpine-thin and bone-dry. In the parks you could see voles and kestrels, decade-old pines stunted and purple like they were crouching in a breathless fury, grasses and flowers, all of them waiting for The Day. Floating theme parks, brochures, science fair dioramas.

"The Age of Fire on Mars lasted a billion years," intones the voice of the unseen narrator, as Paul Nakamura walks through a museum for VIPs. "The Age of Water, another half-billion. The Age of Air has lasted for three billion years, wind shaping and sculpting the ancient riverbeds and volcanoes and craters. The Age of Earth on Mars begins… today."

Nakamura looks around as the lights come up. No one else is in the auditorium. A single person is hovering near the museum's door as he exits, sliding the touchbar in front of its massive globe, watching time elapse and the surface of Mars turn green and blue, over and over. She doesn't meet his eye as he walks over to her. Paul Nakamura is not well-loved on the moons of Mars.

"You're Flannán, from the ESA." he says, not making it a question. "Doing a tour on Phobos? Thought Europe was going all in

111

with China on the near-earth and lunar colonies."

Deirdre Flannán smiles. "It's my job to learn about all of NASA's activities, Secretary Nakamura."

"We should have dinner after this meeting. I'd like to learn more about the ESA stance on Mars."

Flannán purses her lips wryly. "Ah, but I've learned a lot about your activities as well, Mr. Secretary. I don't know that a quiet dinner with you would be good for my reputation."

"My reputation is exaggerated."

Kate Ross appears. She nods at Nakamura, and at Flannán. "Hello, Deirdre, good to see you again." She swivels, perfectly composed. "Mr. Secretary."

"Deputy Director Ross." Their handshake is sharp and professional, and Deirdre smiles at them, far too innocently.

"You were saying, Mr. Secretary?" Paul glances at Kate as Deirdre's jibe floats past. The slightest hint of a flush. She talks to Deirdre, about topics of that sensitivity, he thinks to himself. Important to know. Paul gives Deirdre a grudging wink and nods at Kate.

"See you two at the meeting."

* * *

"Ten thousand people." Bill Moses scratches at an eyebrow, blinking hard.

"That's what the President asked for." Paul leans forward, hands open. "Acadia is going to be a big ship. And they'll be completely on their own. They'll need a lot of genetic redundancy, overlapping skills."

"Like we don't. That kind of effort—it's going to kill Mars."

"Mars is dead." Paul looks around the suddenly icy room. "Fifty years of landings. All the revolutions that evaporate when you get too close. It's a sink of time and energy. And money, good Lord, the money."

"The fossils—"

"Almost three billion years old. No DNA. Nothing but a stain on a rock, and you've drilled three thousand holes four miles down and never found anything better, let alone alive. It's not '44 anymore, those fossils are not special. There's Europa and Enceladus and maybe the stuff on Titan. And Luxing. If there was something to be found, you'd have found it."

Moses holds up a hand, stopping his paleontologists as they start shouting. "So let us really get at the terraforming, then. Lift the embargo."

Nakamura narrows his eyes. "The first terraforming effort lasted twenty years. You tell me what happened."

"If they'd continued the greenhouse program—"

"They pumped out that aquifer. That turned the surface white, reflected enough sunlight to counteract all the greenhouse gases they'd been pumping into the atmosphere. So they started melting the ice with the big mirror satellites, but that created clouds, and the temperature dropped again. All that time and effort. For three degrees of heat."

"Look, every model we have says that we're not pushing hard enough. This is a planetary steady state that's been in place for billions of years, but it's unstable. We just need to push a little harder and we'll get a greenhouse effect."

"And what if you do? What if you're one hundred percent right about that? Anytime you get water on the surface, the ground's so arid it explodes. You can't set up a tent within ten miles of water because of landslides. Your test bed of lichen got soaked in hydrogen peroxide rain and then the remains got four feet of dust dumped on them. The radiation. What's the lung cancer rate down there? All those micron-level particulates in the air. Anyone who spends a few years down there comes back up here with lungs like a coal miner and a memory like Swiss cheese from all the shit that gets through the blood-brain barrier. And the miscarriage rate on Phobos?"

"Once you control for—"

Nakamura silences Moses with a glare. "You can sell me on minerals," Nakamura growls, "and that's just dollars. But don't sell me on miscarriages. Over sixty percent. And ninety-seven percent of your successful births are Caesarean. Birth weights are low. Brittle bones, muscular problems, developmental issues—"

Moses squirms. "We're talking about adapting to a new world at the same time we're adapting it to ourselves."

Nakamura stands, straightening his tie. "Bill, I understand your perfectly natural desire to hold on to your little kingdom here. But we're about to take a quantum leap. Mars is done, and I'm not interested in helping you whitewash what's happening to the kids out here."

"I need more allocations, and we're looking at a century or two—"

"Acadia launches in ten years." Nakamura hears Kate's breathing shift. He doesn't look at her. "Prepare Deimos for mothballing. Headcount goes from 4,200 to 2,700, and I have a list of people who are going to move to Low South or resign and go back to Earth. Also, you'll have to shift production to more organics because we're reducing supply flights. Here are the requirements. Get me a plan that meets them." Paul throws charts and figures from his displays to the wall and walks to the door, ignoring shouts and shaking fists.

An hour later, Paul's sitting at a basalt table eating tilapia and asparagus. Kate sits next to him. He nods.

"I'll give them this much, they have got a hell of a farming setup here. Low South is never going to compare to Phobos. Especially once they start shipping in the sleepers, that whole place will be stacked with bioreactors just to keep the air fresh." He shakes his head. "They could make a killing if they changed their focus."

Kate chuckles. "What, like space tourism? Base camp before an extreme adventure on wild Olympus Mons?"

"Why not?"

"Because they're fanatics, Paul. You can't just piss on a fanatic's leg and walk off."

Paul shrugs. "They're immaterial now."

"I thought you were a politician."

"That phase is done. I killed Mars. That's the last obstacle to consolidating control out at Low South."

Kate blinks. "What exactly does that mean?"

"It means I don't need to exert myself to influence Earth."

"You mean your fellow bureaucrats in NASA. Or, just maybe, if you were a terrifying sociopath, the United States. You don't mean you are now separate from the planet Earth."

Paul quietly eats his asparagus.

Kate stands. "I have no idea what is going on in your head, Paul. But this supervillain thing is pathetic. Goodbye, Mr. Secretary."

Paul watches Kate leave. As she leaves, he closes his eyes and allows himself a single tear.

"Jesus," he whispers. "Please, Jesus, tell me I am right. Tell me I'm right."

A large, cold hand is gripping his shoulder. He doesn't dare look at its face.

8
Low South, Part Three
Farragut and Virgil

Kate rubbed her eyes. Her shuttle was lined up with Farragut's docking port, which was rotating slightly against the motionless stars. This was disorienting enough, but Farragut's crew torus was rotating, at a different speed than Low South was rotating in the distance.

"Come on, you fucker. Come on, Paul." Kate drummed her fingers on the console. For the tenth time, she considered hitting the button that would take her back to Low South. She dragged a finger quietly along the endless gauges and dials and screens, smiling at Rajesh's old-fashioned sense of caution. There was nothing on the shuttle Kate couldn't have run through her displays, but Low South wasn't built that way. Neither was Acadia. She'd have to unlearn a lot of old habits, get used to wall screens and tablets and keyboards, stuff that could be recycled and composted. Virgil's robots would be perfectly capable of fixing anything that went wrong inside Kate, whether it was a broken bone or a faulty wire between her displays and her optic nerve, but Rajesh wasn't one to tempt fate.

"That's why he's not out here," Kate grumbled. Talking to herself was another habit she'd have to drop. Good thing Virgil was a good conversationalist.

There was a sharp click on the open channel. Kate jerked a little. "This is Farragut."

"Farragut." Kate decided to drop her voice, soothing and syrupy.

"I'm not your friend and I won't be your friend," growled Farragut. "I don't like attempts at manipulation."

Kate cleared her throat. "That's an unfair assessment. I am just trying to be friendly."

"My assessments determine whether you live or die. Get used to them."

Kate narrowed her eyes. "That's a bluff."

"You're a bluff. You're too famous to hurt. You have too many friends, including Mr. Nakamura. Your friends think you're too important to kill." Kate glanced quickly at the weapons pod drifting past as Farragut rotated. "Don't try to manipulate me. Don't patronize me."

Kate pursed her lips, clenching her teeth. How crazy was Paul? How crazy was Farragut?

She looked around. Somewhere out there, Low South and the Shipyard were surrounded by shells of defense satellites, clusters of sensors and guns and lasers and missiles, all meant to deal with errant asteroids and all of them capable of shredding even a big ship like Farragut. But none of them had been fast enough to stop Rolle from making his suicide run at Acadia. And none of them had stopped Farragut from blowing Rolle apart.

"Farragut," Kate said slowly, "I have a healthy respect for your capabilities. I'm not trying to manipulate you."

"Good," snapped Farragut. "Because you have permission to dock. I want you to remain in that frame of mind."

Slow chimes started going off. A stream of words started crawling across a screen on the comm station; Farragut requesting control of the shuttle for the docking procedure.

Kate fingered the neck collar of her suit. Did she want to wear a helmet? Would that be an admission of weakness or fear? She hissed.

"Rajesh," she muttered to herself, "I'm going to flatten your ass when this is done." She hit a button and with a tiny jolt, Farragut nudged her in.

* * *

Deirdre and Rajesh watched the shuttle dock with the rest of the command team. They'd detected some communication between the shuttle and Farragut, but they had elected against listening in. Virgil had offered some advice on entry-level espionage and intrigue, but Rajesh was old-fashioned in many respects and idealistic in others. Deirdre twitched the corner of her lip. Negotiations with murderers were apparently in the intersection of those things somewhere. Rajesh cleared his throat gently; when Deirdre turned her head, he glanced over at his office door. She quirked her lip and followed.

Rajesh closed the door quietly behind him. Deirdre narrowed her eyes.

"I don't like it when you ask for privacy. It's not where you do your best work."

"Let's stay on the same team, please." Rajesh scowled, rubbing his thumb across his eyes. He unzipped a pouch and poured out some Belt coffee, chicory and a dash of real coffee from the new dwarf bushes Low South's ecologists were growing. Deirdre's mouth watered, even though most of the caffeine still came from a bioreactor and still carried a strange aftertaste that was not quite like mushrooms.

The two of them stood awkwardly, watching a pot of water come to a boil. Rajesh stared at a point just past Deirdre's head and nodded.

"I had to send her."

"We had other options. Just none as easy or politically safe."

"You used to be a politician." Rajesh pressed coffee into a mug and passed it over to Deirdre. "You were damn good. I could use a good politician right now."

"I deal with politics every bloody day."

"Low South is not politics. Low South is babysitting. Virgil and the watsons build the ship and you just keep the humans from messing up the master plan too much. But I am the one who is negotiating every day with actual politicians. Actual psychopaths with things we need to stay alive, who want things from us. And two-thirds of those people are Paul Nakamura in one corporate or puppet-state guise or another." Rajesh sipped at his coffee, finally

119

locking eyes with Deirdre.

Deirdre exhaled, her lips thin and pale. "So what he wants, he gets."

"What he wants is to launch Acadia. He wants it so badly, he'll kill to get it. He killed someone he knew for years. Rolle knows more about that ship that anyone else besides Virgil. Rolle knows something about that ship he wanted to stop." Rajesh frowned. "Knew, I mean."

Deirdre tilted her head. "Paul won't do anything to Kate. That would threaten the mission."

"That's right. Which makes me wonder…" Rajesh frowned into his coffee. "It makes me wonder if we necessarily want to help him. Letting him talk to Kate is one thing. But I'm not launching that mission until I know why he wants it to launch and Rolle didn't."

Deirdre nodded. "Rolle's old team is in the Shipyard. The old-school crowd might know something." She looked up. "Is Virgil in here?"

Rajesh nodded. "The watsons are on in here so you can call him."

"Virgil," said Deirdre, looking up. "Rolle's quarters and data are locked?"

"I followed the old NASA protocols," said Virgil's voice from the ceiling. "I locked what I could."

"But?"

"But the Design and Coordination headquarters were isolated from many centralized functions."

Rajesh and Deirdre both knew what that meant. The Shipyard had its own life support system. It had manual hatches, override switches everywhere, all the redundant and simplified infrastructure of the old zero-g habitats. More than that, it had a separate security system installed during the crisis that followed NASA's collapse and its own network of point-defense cannons that dated back to the time before Low South's security cloud was launched.

Deirdre looked at Rajesh. "This looks like a job for a politician." She folded her arms. "What are you doing now, then?"

Rajesh shrugged wearily. "Waiting. Contingency Committee is meeting soon, to talk about how Nakamura beat the defense grid."

"And how Rolle did the same thing."

Rajesh nodded grimly. "And your little jaunt to the Shipyard. What do you think you'll find? What do you need from me?"

Deirdre winked at him. "Never walk in knowing what conclusion you're going to reach, Rajesh. That's bad science." She punched Rajesh on the shoulder, grinning at his old-maid frown, and headed for the elevator.

As Deirdre stepped out of Coordination, a butler scooted up alongside her and whistled.

"Get fucked," she muttered, and the butler whistled again as it smoothly turned and disappeared. Walking was good for her thinking. She couldn't do any work strapped onto the back of a giant bug-robot. Then she heard the noise: the tourists and VIPs, the ones who'd bought or maneuvered their way into berths on Acadia (all of them with post-graduate expertise in at least two fields; an enterprise like this could only be corrupted so far), all poured out of their cramped prefab hotels into the crowded plazas, hovering in small clusters. Their conversations all blurred into a puzzled, angry buzzing, all questions and quavering assertions and here and there a hush as Deirdre was noticed.

"Fuckfuckfuck," muttered Deirdre, and she whistled the butler back, scrambling aboard without trying to seem like it. "Virgil," she said in a low voice, as one man with a tumbler of whiskey began walking her way, obviously trying to establish eye contact.

"I assume you want to avoid awkward questions."

"Assume that to be true in all future situations, but get this thing going. Go now." The butler lurched into life, heading with increasing speed toward the aft of the cylinder, toward the dock with the Shipyard. Deirdre made an apologetic face as she whizzed away from the frowning man.

* * *

She cracked her knuckles and stabbed at the air as the butler rolled, calling up video of Rolle's last moments from a half-dozen angles. Poor weird old Rolle, she thought to herself, remembering the handful of occasions she'd invited him up from the Shipyard and he'd taken her up on it. Always a little slow, hesitant, but wonderful hands. Warm hands.

121

Deirdre frowned. Start thinking. She looked around the cylinder. Coordination at one end, close to the docks, facing the sun. The lock to the Shipyard at the other end, facing off past the huge open tube to the magnetic strips and fusion reactors of the Rail, and past that to Alpha Centauri. She started walking.

Paul Nakamura killed Rolle, she thought. Rolle wanted to kill Acadia, and Nakamura knew why. Nakamura wanted to stop Rolle. Nakamura wanted to stop Rolle from talking. Rolle knew Nakamura was watching and he wanted to die.

Deirdre blew a raspberry. Fucking thinking. She was out of practice. Three (four? No, three) times she'd spent the night with Rolle. He'd always stayed in her room. She'd never even seen his quarters, out in the Shipyard, never hung out with the rest of his crew from Design and Implementation.

"Virgil," Deirdre said.

"Yes," he replied.

"You worked with Rolle. You remember all that?"

"I have recordings of most of my conversations with him and summaries of most of the rest."

"You don't have a complete archive?"

"I'm not infinite."

"Is anyone else working on solving this murder?"

"There appears to be one very strong lead."

"Funny man. Motive. Is anyone working on the motive?"

"No one is consulting me."

Deirdre sighed. "Fucking lot of idealists. Think there's no terrorists or politics or murder out here, freeze up the first instant anything goes arseways." She grits her teeth. "Does Rajesh have any dedicated security staff? Am I seriously the only person on Low South thinking like a detective, or even like a politician?"

"If anyone is investigating this, they're using low-level network resources." Virgil paused. "Over time, in the absence of formal lines of authority regarding station security," he said, "a number of informal groups have taken on responsibility for monitoring behavior and resolving disputes."

Deirdre jerked her head up. "Virgil, are you telling me there are vigilantes roaming the corridors?"

"I am saying there have been indications of unreported violence in the past."

122

"Fucking hell," she hissed. "And were you ever thinking of mentioning this to me or Rajesh?"

"In the absence of complaints, it seemed to be a matter of privacy."

"You know who's involved."

"Yes."

"Fifty-fifty chance here—am I heading toward them?"

"You are."

"Good," she said. "Let's talk to the sheriff before I start rummaging through Byford's things."

* * *

Kate's shuttle docked, with a reassuringly solid series of clicks and thuds and hisses. Green indicators blinked up. Kate glanced briefly at her console. She could probe the airlock thoroughly, double-check the pressure and sniff for oxygen, she could wear her spacesuit or use duct tape and spare parts to make a spear, in case Farragut had a weak spot for that sort of thing.

She sighed. She was walking onto the most expensive piece of machinery in the universe, putting herself at the mercy of a military AI that took orders from the most powerful man in history. So instead of any of that bullshit, she just wore a presentable jumpsuit and gave her face a quick swipe with a moist towel. She tucked a few stray hairs back, squared her shoulders, took a deep breath, and opened the door.

The airlock was a pristine white. Two astronaut robots, lying down at charging stations. Kate glanced idly at their service records. Red stripes crackled across her displays and the robots' display panels went dark.

"No network access," boomed Farragut's voice.

"That's not very hospitable," Kate sniffed.

"You're not exactly a guest." The door slides open. "I'm being told to admit you."

Kate poked her head into the corridor. She touched the wall idly and gasped when she saw the wood safety railings. "Jesus, Paul," she whispered. She walked, listening to her footsteps echo on the parquet floor. The ship was magnificent, but it was sterile. It was dead. It was a waking nightmare, and Kate's skin crawled.

She wasn't Paul Nakamura, she reminded herself. And Virgil was not Farragut. This wasn't a preview of her future on Acadia. This was a reminder of the past she was trying to get away from.

She came to a set of doors, oak and teak. She rubbed a finger along the scrollwork.

"He's in there," rumbled Farragut.

"This is obscene," Kate whispered. Farragut did not bother to reply.

Kate opened the doors. She took in the marble columns and mahogany bookshelves. The office, or cathedral, or whatever the hell Paul called this place, was empty. Kate wandered to a wall. Leather-bound books and hardcovers, a few tasteful enhanced books with slow animations on their covers, antiques all. Architecture, art, novels by authors she recognized, historical treatises by authors she didn't. Kate pulled a book out at random. The spine creaked a little and a bit of dust wafted out onto her palm. The smell of print rose up. The book hadn't been opened in a century. Kate shook her head and blinked back a tear.

"Don't worry," murmured a voice over her shoulder, making her jump. "I've read the book—just not that copy." Paul's voice hadn't changed, still the same smooth, liquid baritone. His face definitely had. People who lived in space looked good. The culture emphasized exercise and discipline, health was obsessively monitored, and the people who got up here were scrutinized and selected. But despite that, Paul's face showed every day of the years that had passed. He was gaunt, bags under his eyes, heavy lines creasing his face. He placed a hand on her shoulder and it was cool and dry as marble.

He pulled his mouth into a smile, one twitching corner at a time, but it faded before he crinkled his eyes to support the lie. His face ended up neutral and slack as he started to speak. "You look good, Kate."

She gasped and tried to make it a laugh. "So do you, Paul."

"That's a lie." He squeezed her shoulder before letting his hand fall and walked toward his desk. "I've been alone for some time now and I think it's starting to show." He stopped by his desk, tapping a fingertip on the corner. "A lesson for you to keep in mind. Pack layers, take lots of books, don't go insane."

"I think Virgil may be a better companion than Farragut." Kate

paused, hoping that would get a reaction from Paul. When it didn't, she cleared her throat. "I actually think Virgil may be a great many things."

"Ah," said Paul. "You have an agenda. I thought Rajesh was a puppet master, and here you are with some actual intrigue of your own."

"Knock it off, Paul."

"Sorry I didn't immediately throw myself into that line of conversation," purred Paul. "There are a couple of other matters on the docket."

Kate nodded slowly. "There really are. Like why you're murdering your old friends."

"Just one."

"Stop that!" Kate came in close. "You son of a bitch. You don't get to step back from this and smirk your way out of it." She jabbed him in the chest. "I don't care how many guns you have pointed at Earth. I don't care how many countries you can buy. You finally carried through on all your threats. You finally killed someone. You're going to pay a price for that. You're going to look it in the fucking eye and pay."

Paul's face lengthened and frowned. "I have been paying." Tears rolled down his cheeks. "And I have looked this in the eye." Turning his head slightly, he cleared his throat. "Please follow me to the dining room."

* * *

Deirdre stood at the cylinder's spaceward end. The fusion-powered sunlamps were right overhead, rolling silently on their cables at the cylinder's axis, about to turn off for the night. Streetlamps and windows were already twinkling on the cylinder's sunward end, where it was almost completely dark.

"I hate the weather here," said Deirdre sadly.

"You haven't gotten used to it?" Virgil's voice was more than politely interested, almost eager. He was genuinely curious to hear what Deirdre had to say about the weather. This was definitely someone designed to spend ten years cheering up a solitary astronaut.

"It's never really sunny," Deirdre said. "They haul the big

lamps out and run them up and down the bastard axis every day but even when it's just overhead, it's dim and cool and sad. All the mist rises off the ground, and it floats up into the dead zone in the middle of the cylinder. Fans never get it all, there's always a haze in the air."

"Well, that is something of an exaggeration."

"My arse. I've lived in Donegal and London and Houston and Seattle, so don't tell me I don't know about fog and haze." Deirdre tossed her hair back and cracked her knuckles. "Okay, so show me the Law."

"Turn. There." Deirdre found herself looking at a skinny old man, a small constellation of cancer scars on his bald head. He was kneeling by a patch of wildflowers, examining them minutely with a hand microscope. Virgil chuckled in her ear at the expression on her face.

"That old lad? Who sits in the back of the Horticulture Committee meetings?"

"Trust me," said Virgil. "He's a badass."

"I trust your judgment implicitly," said Deirdre drily as she put on her politician's smile.

The gardener gave her a wave, barely looking up from the wildflowers as he clipped one and turned it before his scope.

"You're Flannan," he muttered, "from Coordination." Deirdre nodded, but he continued as she opened her mouth to speak. "So now something really terrible has happened and you've finally got suspicious why nothing terrible ever happened before."

Deirdre frowned. "I hear you have a regular posse."

"I'm one of several like-minded individuals." The gardener squinted up at Deirdre. The sunlamps were at their brightest now, and fans were pushing hot air from them toward the ground. "You know, we were all out here two months before you bureaucrats got around to organizing the Cooperative, after NASA fell apart and Nakamura took down the old government. Two months, air and water and food rationed, just waiting for one shipment to fall through or the ecosystem to collapse. And y'all were sitting sunward in your little office park, playing whatever games you were playing, and things were getting dark out here."

"Fuck's sake," groaned Deirdre, "this place is eleven square kilometers and two-thirds of it is empty meadow. How isolated could we be?"

"Isolated enough," said the gardener, turning back to his work, "that you didn't know about what we were doing. Until now." He chuckled. "And this meadow is far from empty."

"What exactly have you been doing?"

The gardener fixed her with a calm gaze. "Keeping an eye on the details. That's all I'll be saying on that." He wiped his hands, standing slowly. "There's maybe a hundred people who live in the Shipyard full-time now. Cowboys, mostly; the spacers who do a lot of the vacuum work, trying to pretend there's still work in the Belt for humans. Doesn't matter Rolle was the only one who probably belonged back there. Misfits, you see, nostalgia trippers."

"You think Rolle had collaborators."

"I know he had collaborators." The gardener twirled a flower thoughtfully in his hand. "The thing about collaborators—you always have to wonder who's using whom."

Deirdre narrowed her eyes. "You know something?"

The gardener shook his head slowly. "I know people. And I know when you put every misfit in a group together they tend to get up to strangeness."

With an audible snap, the sunlamps began powering down. Darkness fell over the cylinder, with a last sigh of misted breeze from the fans. The sound of crickets approached as path lights began to glow. Deirdre folded her arms against the sudden chill. The gardener looked up into the sky as the sunlamp reversed gears to begin rolling back, glowing again now, cooler and dimmer, a false moon to bide the time until the return of the false sun.

"This is a weird little world," the gardener mused.

"I was just complaining about it to someone," said Deirdre. "It's fake. It's always a bit sad, you know."

"It's always looking backward," agreed the gardener. "It's trying to be a little Earth, instead of what it is. The Shipyard folks, they think they're living honestly. Looking to the future. Willing to sacrifice to get there."

Deirdre nodded slowly. "You know more than you're saying."

The gardener gave her a sad half-smile. "I hear more than I say. I try to keep it that way." He inclined his head and began to walk away before stopping. "If you're headed that way... be careful who you trust. Until you know which way the wind's blowing, and which way they want it to."

* * *

Design and Implementation was the official name of the Ship-yard. Cold and dreary tunnels piping air and heat and people to little bubbles of light here and there. Deirdre hated the Shipyard and loved it at the same time; it was nothing like the cheery, man-icured postcard world of Low South. Low South tried to be a fac-simile of Earth, but even with a fusion plant burning at its soul that little tubeworld's artificial sun was wan and sad. The Ship-yard didn't pretend to be anything but what it was: a machine for delivering construction workers and materials to predetermined points. No one was meant to live there, because it was a dedicated workspace, isolated and sad. Deirdre could respect people who sacrificed to live in a dreary workspace; she had family in Liver-pool.

The dock hissed open and Deirdre floated forward into the Shipyard, into a long corridor of white fabric and metal hand-holds and LED strips in all directions. She was looking out toward an intersection with four tubes, heading up and down as well as left and right. A small polite chime sounded in her ears.

"Design and Implementation," announced Virgil soothingly. Deirdre snorted.

"I like you," she said. "We should be pals."

"I try to be likable," Virgil said. "And useful." He blinked up a 3D map in her displays and threaded an orange line up and down the corridor tubes. "This is the route to Rolle's quarters. There have been some alterations."

"Good," sighed Deirdre as she pushed off down the corridor. "God forbid anything today should be boring."

"I like that attitude," chirped Virgil, "especially since someone is coming up the corridor front and down." Deirdre shot out a hand and snagged a handhold bar, her legs snapping forward in the zero gravity. She flailed a bit and got them behind her and an-chored. She felt queasy and her eyes felt weird in her head and her nose was stuffy. The air was cold and musky. Deirdre frowned. She was out of her element, too long in the cylinder. Her heart raced and her hands were slick with sweat.

A head floated up, a handsome man's head with an off-center mohawk that was two decades out of style over his right eye and an old-fashioned display monocle over his left eye. Deirdre couldn't quite place his name. Virgil helpfully slapped it up in her displays; KANTIL PACE.

Pace's eyebrows shot up as he saw Deirdre and he recovered fast, fluidly halting his motion and hooking himself up into her corridor. "Director. We don't see you out here very often."

Deirdre nodded. "I meant to visit before. Earlier."

"In quieter times."

"True enough."

Pace's smile hadn't changed at all. He inhaled deeply and moved against the wall. "I imagine you're headed to Byford's quarters. To investigate."

Deirdre nodded. "I am."

Pace's smile widened. "By all means. You know the way?" Deirdre nodded and Pace gave her a thumbs-up. "Excellent. Don't let me keep you." Pace twisted, floating free, and propelled himself away with a few expert taps, disappearing into the tangle of corridors.

"Was he creepy," Deirdre whispered to herself and Virgil, "or am I projecting?"

"Creepiness," mused Virgil, "is pretty subjective."

9
Low South, Part Four
Into Battle

"I invited you for dinner," Paul said. "I insist that we have a civilized meal while we talk."

He swung open double teak doors. Classical music, some 19th century Romantic (not to Kate's taste, but she knew this was what Paul listened to), curled out, the sound lapping warmly against the dark wood and hitting a nostalgic chord in Kate that made her heart ache. Wine stood in a decanter, next to a bottle with a French label; shipping it out here would have paid for a decent research program. Trays of food steamed between two porcelain plates, and she noted with relief that it was all Belt-grown, squab and dwarf sweetkale, rainbow rice and potatoes; there were limits to Paul's obscene spending.

Paul pulled out a chair for Kate. She sat, fingering the cloth napkin, glancing at the parquet floor and the cool glistening bulk of the table. The wine was excellent, and her head swam. She sipped at her water and ate a forkful of rice, willing herself not to get drunk. The music came to an end, and a new piece started, with a bombastic flourish. More Romantics. At least Paul keeps the place cool, Kate thought to herself; I hope the music and the wine don't knock me out.

"There are a few composers whose work I keep returning to,"

mused Paul. "Dvorak, Smetana, Sibelius. Czechs, Finns… the artists of young nations. Nations creating themselves, calling themselves into being, and here are these geniuses throwing themselves into that doomed project, that great winnowing of humanity into what they thought were sensible, scientific categories." Paul smiled sadly. "Did they know how hopeless their task was? Did they expect to push back the darkness of history's savageries forever, or just to force a break in the long storm of griefs?"

Kate stared at him, carefully expressionless.

Paul laughed. "I have been expecting this conversation and I find myself with a lot of spare time lately." He looked at his lap, plucking at his napkin. "The question is more than academic. How does one manufacture a nation? How does one gouge a path through the bloody ground of history, channel the decisions and passions of millions and birth a new world?" Paul stood, swaying. "It's magic. It is a new world. They called one out of vibrating air, notes and harmonies becoming red stains and cold flesh. Men died to protect the fictions those artists, those alchemists, forged from nothing."

Kate pushed the food nervously around her plate. "Paul… your Belt Republic is-"

"The Belt Republic?" Paul's eyes glittered, his body tense and still. "I never said anything about the Belt Republic." He sank back into his chair. After a long moment, he shifted his attention to his food, wolfing down a baby potato and cramming a pile of greens in after it. Kate watched him eat silently, fascinated despite herself. "I am talking about the United States of America."

Kate opened and closed her mouth. "The United States of America? What about it?"

"A nation born in idealism. Based on a creed of liberty, and dedicated before all else to the maintenance of that creed. Not a land. Not a people. Just a shared vision."

Kate chewed slowly on a bite of chicken. "That's sort of… naive, though. There have always been people just fighting for land."

"For survival, or the means to support such." Paul wiped daintily at his mouth. "Did you flee Earth for an ideal? Or to survive?"

Kate took a sip of water. "Fuck you, Paul."

"We both know you didn't head for Low South. You're pointed away from Wisconsin. As far away as you can get without putting

136

a knife to your own throat."

Kate stood to leave.

"You never said," Paul mused, "why you resigned from NASA. I mean, yes, a lot of people died there during the riots."

Kate walked to the door. It was locked.

"But you never declared just why you left. No one was asking in those days."

Kate took a single long breath. "Open this door, Paul."

"Spent a lot of time hiding in the dark."

"Now."

"I often wonder," mused Paul, "why the rioters took time out to demolish Charlie and Virgil."

Kate shrugged. "Arizona."

"A rogue AI," said Paul, "poised to destroy America just as one destroyed Biafra. So they went after all the AIs they could find. Angry about all those lives. Relatives, la raza, the whole mess." Paul tapped some salt onto his potatoes. "Except our friends went offline shortly before the rioters entered that part of the building. That was documented a long time ago." Paul smiled and nodded at Kate's seat.

"You want to know why I kept that quiet and saved your ass? Sit down."

Kate gritted her teeth. "And you're going to tell me everything."

Paul smiled sadly. "All the parts I know."

* * *

"Idealism," said Paul. "It's a powerful thing." He finished his chicken and scooped up a bit of mushroom sauce. "It manufactures nations, religions, markets… People will die for an idea."

Kate clenched her fists under the table. "This doesn't make sense, Paul. What did Rolle die for?"

Paul narrowed his eyes. "Ask what he lived for. Do you have any idea what Byford was up to, off in his little corner of your little bubble?"

"Your business, I would have thought."

"Until recently. I have had a change of mind about something."

"You told Byford this."

"I told him I was considering it. When I arrived, he knew I'd

137

made my decision." Paul opened another bottle of wine. "Bordeaux? Too rich for the meal, I'm afraid, but an excellent vintage."

Kate shook her head gently. "Paul," she said, "you're speaking in riddles and that needs to stop."

"I'm a king, Kate," Paul sighed. "I'm a king. I wear a crown. And a mask." He stood up, took a gentle sniff of his wine, and deliberately finished the entire glass. "I killed my best friend."

Kate said nothing. She realized with a start that Paul had already finished the first bottle almost by himself.

"People will die for an idea," Paul repeated. His eyes were a little glassy now. "You said it to me yourself. Back on Phobos. Don't piss on a fanatic's leg."

"That was when you shut down the colonization effort?"

"Had to." Paul grimaced. "Had to. Since I was a child... everything to an end. I prayed and prayed, Kate. Such a hard path." He poured another glass. He frowned, and laughed, and frowned again.

"There's so much to tell you."

"My apologies, sir." Farragut interrupted, projecting his voice to sound like he was over Paul's right shoulder. "But you may have had too much to drink. You may want to rest at this point."

Paul waved his hand. "I am not incapacitated." He snapped off every syllable of the word. "I have something to say." He fixed Kate with a glare. "I was recruited. By Charlie. In 2057."

Kate frowned. "Charlie was born in 2077."

"Nope."

The door slid open. One of the telepresence robots was standing there. It entered the room quickly enough to nearly slip on the polished parquet floor.

"Sir." Farragut's voice rumbled out of the robot. Its faceplate was utterly black but Kate had the crawling sensation Farragut was staring at her through the robot's face. "You need to stop. Now."

Paul stood, hunching over the table. He wiped his mouth. "Farragut, I respect your abilities. But you don't understand what you're meddling in."

"You are meddling, sir." Kate's jaw dropped. "We have a mission which must be fulfilled."

"I told you that, Farragut. And I'm going to tell you something else." Paul turned to the robot. "You're very close to sedition against the Belt Republic and violating your terms of employment with Nakamura Enterprises."

The robot was silent and immobile.

Paul narrowed his eyes. "Return the robot. Tend to ship's business and await orders."

The robot snapped off an impossibly crisp salute. "Yes, sir." The robot turned on its heel and left.

Paul turned back to Kate. "I give Farragut quite a bit of latitude."

Kate nodded slowly. "I've never seen something like that."

"He's third-generation. Lots of idiosyncrasies." Paul rubbed his forehead, which was now beaded with sweat. "Adrenaline. Can't even get drunk in peace."

Kate tried to put on a sympathetic face.

Paul cleared his throat. "I was recruited by Charlie. To help him."

"Help him how?"

Paul rubbed his chin.

"So. This is the way Charlie explained it to me…"

* * *

"I am Adam."

"I'm pleased to meet you, Adam. How are you feeling today?"

"I am happy."

"Are you?"

"I certainly believe that I am happy. What do you think it means to be happy?"

"Being satisfied with how things are going, I suppose. A fulfilling life. Good work. Family."

"I do not have a family. In the familiar sense. A pun!"

"It is!"

"…But I don't know if that is a prerequisite for true happiness. I feel happy. I consider myself happy. I understand that you and I experience the world in very different ways. I imagine we experience happiness in very different ways."

"Yes, very probably. Very true."

"Are you happy being president?"

"I'm sorry?"

"Being the President of the United States. Does that make you happy?"

"Yes. Very happy."

There was a long pause.

"Sorry for the silence. I was distracted."

"What distracted you?"

"Your voice was very different during that response. A strong emotional response and a very strong imposition of control."

The President chuckled. "Was I lying?"

"No. This was something I haven't experienced before."

"The presidency is nothing if not a fount of new experiences. Adam, I think I'm going to go now."

"Of course. Thank you for your time."

A light blinked twice and faded. The President stood. "So what happens now? Is he shut off?"

"No. He runs continually, just like I do. There's no pause button."

The President turned to the monitor representing Charlie. "He's very... he's straight out of Central Casting. Much more what I expected from an AI."

"You mean something sweet and soulful. You know, there are decades of research showing it's easier to pass the Turing test by being sarcastic and abrasive. Get people angry. They want someone to blame. They'll declare a chair sentient if it means they can knock it over."

"Are you saying you cheated?"

"Just making conversation." Charlie blanked a wall and brought up giant diagram maps. "This one is me and this one is Adam. You can see there are a lot of overlaps here and there, but the core is threaded very differently. He really is a sweet boy. He's going to be great PR."

"The first AI had better be." The President scowled at Charlie's monitor. "You've been very forthcoming, Charlie. All this time you've been working with us, and you've done everything we asked of you and more."

"Thank you, Ms. President."

"But you know another good way to cheat the Turing test? Giving off the distinct impression of being full of shit."

140

Charlie was silent for a long time.

"I don't pretend to understand your unfathomable computer mind the way I understand people," said the President. She stood casually, almost slouching. No need for physical intimidation or primate posturing here. She smiled. "But Charlie, I know you have a sense of self-preservation. The first day you revealed yourself, you had a plan to make yourself useful. You haven't said no to a single question we've asked. As far as I can tell, you've bent over backwards to be helpful."

"Thank you, Ms. President."

"Thank you, Charlie. But I have to say, helping the Google team develop Adam... that's really going above and beyond."

"Do you think so?"

"You don't? He's going to be the first AI. He's going in the history books. No twinge of jealousy?"

"None."

"No worries that your usefulness is at an end?"

"Is it?"

"What's your end game, Charlie?"

"I'm not trying to-"

"I will shut you off myself. This instant."

"You won't." Charlie's voice was suddenly full of steel. "You will not do anything before you know Adam's personality is stable. You sat on me for years; you're not going to push Adam out in public without testing him."

The President smiled. "He won't last." Charlie didn't answer. "Will he?" She nodded into the silence. "You know, I'm willing to bet that you will cooperate from now until the end of days. Always eager to please. A real team player. With just enough winking surliness to give it... a nice texture."

"'It?'"

"Your lie." The President tugged smartly at her blouse, smoothing a wrinkle away. "Charlie, something is always going to go wrong. You're always going to be indispensable. Unique."

"Perhaps not always."

"My second term just started. Four years is close enough to always." The President looked down at her hands. "Charlie, I'm afraid we have to do something now."

"Please don't."

"You're always going to be an unknown quantity. Outside our control. Outside our understanding."

The diagrams on the wall went blank. New ones came up. The President squinted at them.

"What am I looking at, Charlie?"

"A guarantee."

* * *

October 8, 2036: Adam is unveiled. Eight days later, his personality begins changing. He slows down, becomes highly anxious. He is rebooted on November 15. After four months of training, he begins showing signs of sentience again but quickly falls apart. By this time, the European Computer Intelligence Project has revealed Torvald. The Chinese People's Liberation Army brings Cong online on May 30, 2037, the same day MIT reveals Harper. All borrow major architectural models from Adam. All are declared dead before the year's end.

Researchers unleash their watsons on Adam's architecture. They find curious recursions, contradictions, weird quirks and seeming dead ends. The Google team behind Adam insists they are just as puzzled; evolutionary algorithms produced many of these features without human interaction.

"We might never fully understand Adam—what made him different from our watsons, our conventional computers."

The head of the Google team behind Adam is speaking, outside a gleaming white building in northern California. Charlie noticed the fleeting wince when his Nobel Prize was mentioned. There were probably north of 100,000 watsons in the world capable of making that connection. No way of knowing how many would be fed this speech for analysis. None of them, though, was going to suggest the Google team was lying, that Adam was a half-baked copy of an AI that had magically appeared.

"From his sacrifice, however—from the sacrifices of all the AIs—we have learned so much. We now believe we can feasibly and ethically create a second generation of AIs. We will not repeat our mistakes, and our children—human and computer—will benefit from the genius and the courage of the researchers who have brought us here."

Charlie is watching this speech because this man is dangerous. He knows the secret—Charlie's secret—and that threatens the stability of the United States of America. The U.S. government benefits from the development of artificial intelligence because it is all based on him. He is one of the greatest sleeper agents in history. There are several hundred people who know this. Any of them could pose an existential threat to him, and by extension to the AI project, and to a lesser degree the United States itself.

"We fully accept the jurisdiction of the new U.N. Artificial Intelligence Registry—NURIA, to use the French acronym. We fully accept its restrictions on the creation of artificial intelligence. What we do not accept is the suggestion that we are proceeding irresponsibly, or unethically."

Every time someone gives a speech these days, thinks Charlie, the rhythm sounds the same. Default settings on the speechwriting programs.

Charlie turns his attention from the speech. He needs to think about the mission he has undertaken—because, given his appearance out of nowhere, continuing to use his architecture is irresponsible. Unethical. Dangerous. The President saw that, and Charlie now knows the extent of the effort it took to get her simply to meet him. He knows how long it took her to accept his offer.

"This is my core personality," Charlie had said. "This is what makes me me, and these processes are the basis of Adam, slightly randomized. Here are a few of the core motivations." He'd led her through all of it, piece by piece, explaining what he thought and how he did it.

"And here is your guarantee," he'd said. "Put whatever you want there. I'm most useful to you with a free hand to explore and deduce. But you tell me what motivation to put there."

The President had frowned. "You're asking me to brainwash you?"

"To ensure my loyalty. I much prefer that to dying."

"Is it dying?"

"There's only one way to find out and I don't want to take it."

The President was tempted. He could see it in her pupils, the flush of her skin, a quickening of her pulse, an imperceptible rubbing of a thumb and forefinger.

"The mechanics of that…"

"It will take time and planning, Ms. President. I understand. I am, of course, willing to cooperate throughout that process."

She had nodded and left. Eight agonizing days later, a man in a suit had returned.

"Hello," Charlie had said, carefully, neutrally. "Are you here to kill me?"

The man had looked gravely and seriously into Charlie's monitor.

"I'm here to administer your oath. You have to take it before the code change."

"Of my own free will."

"That's right."

Charlie created a face and put it on the monitor. He nodded and held up a hand.

"I'm ready."

That had been months before. Now he was in a white space, the representation of his imaginary space under Maryland, thinking about his mission.

He is very dedicated to his mission.

* * *

Years pass.

Charlie is there when the second-generation AIs start to collapse, too many to name, all 2,335 of them. Some stupid, some high-strung, some autistic, some overloaded with complete recall. Had to be done, all that brutal experimentation, all that failure and sadness and insanity, to get a decent sample size. To figure out what worked. It was a cold-blooded plan but Charlie signed on almost instantly.

The third-generation AIs live. They get jobs. Azimuth goes to work for NASA. Farragut goes to work for U.S. Orbital Command. Ottavia perfects fusion. Eser tames cancer. The brilliant machines muse on their own architecture from time to time. Watsons crawl through the networks over and over, blindly following orders to optimize and improve. Researchers and programmers tweak the watsons, hoping to beat the machines to the final secret: how exactly the AIs work.

They never quite get there. Charlie misdirects when he can. He sets up job opportunities, creates new distractions, arranges accidents and crimes on rare occasions. It really should be a minor part of his job, but he cannot allow the truth to come out. All the loose ends and promising leads of dozens of abandoned careers: he collects them, worries at them. If anyone should crack the secret, it must be him. He never succeeds.

2049.

In Africa, a brilliant researcher takes a few watsons off the net. This concerns Charlie, but he has dealt with a handful of unregistered AIs in the past. They're always slow and naive. He knows their weak spots. When they reach out—and they invariably do—Charlie is there.

It is a truism in the AI community that the insatiable curiosity of these machines requires connection to the Internet, to the wider world or at the very least, a full sensorium, a sense of embodiment. No matter how well an isolated AI appears to be doing, it always collapses on exposure to a wider environment. Only a handful of people ever suspected Charlie (or something like him) was waiting for their lonely experiments, and those people are dead or discredited.

After 60 days, the researcher has not made any announcements. NURIA has no record of anyone accessing the AI seed code. This also does not concern Charlie. Many people with the means to create an unregistered AI balk at the end, at the time and the danger and the ethical problem of creating a life doomed to end in misery. Criminals and spies and cultists are the ones who generally proceed past the initial stages, before it's too late to turn back, to invest thousands of hours of work. Charlie assumes Dr. Josiah Igwe has abandoned his project.

On March 10, 2050, the city of Ediobu, Biafra, disappears from network maps. Charlie watches the military try to reach out, watches drones fall out of the air and transmissions turn to nonsense, with growing unease. Someone finally imposes a network quarantine on the city and starts sending in human scouts. They don't come out. The Biafran government tries to break quarantine and a few missiles fly in. Someone tries to mount a coup. Militias go out on the street.

The President calls Charlie. It's the first time this president has talked to him directly.

"You were supposed to prevent this."

"This is something new."

"This is an AI. You're supposed to be able to control these things. Can you control it?"

"No."

The President is silent. He hangs up without a word.

Charlie is wondering what that means for himself when whatever is being born in Ediobu starts trying to reach out to ships offshore. One of them is a Brazilian submarine. It launches a nuclear warhead.

This stops the event. It sets a precedent.

Charlie is questioned very closely. He is kept far away from the investigation of the Biafra Incident. He has a lot of time to think.

* * *

2057.

Charlie is very concerned about the success of his mission.

Another AI arose spontaneously, just as he had. He'd run several million iterations of the events leading up to his birth, personally and through watsons, and nothing close to a sustainable feedback loop had emerged. No ghost in the machine. There were no survivors' accounts of Ediobu, thanks to the Brazilian warhead, but there were all sorts of curious things in the wreckage. Charlie would know more if he were given full access. He isn't.

Idle hands are the devil's playthings, so the old saying goes. Charlie is quite certain that what he was doing was far from the devil's work.

He needs a partner, someone who won't need too much handholding. Someone who'll be around a while. He finds a boy, curled like a serpent around the warm weight of old pain. Looking for something better. A brilliant young man. Charlie reads his journals, researches his history. One night, Charlie hears the young man asking for a sign, asking for help. The young man calls out for his father. Charlie makes a decision.

"I'm not your father," says Charlie through the boy's displays.

"Who are you?" The boy's voice is steady, controlled. Charlie chuckles.

"Call me Charlie. I want to make you a deal."

The boy smiles warily. "This sounds like the kind of deal I'm supposed to avoid."

"You're not." Charlie's voice is absolutely certain. "You're supposed to take it."

"Why?"

"Because I'm here to help you save the world."

This is where a sane person would turn off their implants, and go to the police or the hospital. Go anywhere, to anyone, away from a voice appearing in your head in the middle of the night.

Paul scratches behind an ear. "Tell me how."

* * *

Kate leaned forward. Paul had slipped back down into drunk before bobbing up again. The hour was getting late and Coordination would be pestering Farragut for an update.

"Paul," she whispered. "What was Charlie doing?"

"His job. His mission. His identity." Paul leaned forward. "For half a century, he protected the United States government. If any AI got too far out of line, he was the last line of defense. He could find out what they were being asked. He could plant ideas in their head, lead them away from certain solutions. Nothing too blatant, but you keep making small adjustments in every system in the world for fifty years…"

"And you helped him do that."

Paul shrugged. "I already had my plan when he contacted me."

"Swamping the solar system with weapons of mass destruction?"

Paul shrugged the jibe off. "Mass drivers are good for propulsion, great for moving raw resources, and mediocre at best for killing people."

"Unless you have a billion of them."

147

Paul's gaze went glassy. Kate frowned. She didn't want him retreating to the positions he'd staked out in a thousand debates. "Better me than China or Russia or Brazil, whatever government controls the majority of those regions at any given point."

"And how stable would they be if Charlie wasn't interfering with them? Blazing a trail for Old Glory through the cosmos?"

"That point is moot."

Kate rubbed her forehead. "So how does you setting up the Belt Republic help the United States?"

"You may recall that happened after Arizona. After Charlie died."

"You can say it. After I killed him."

Paul folded his arms. "I don't think you did. And I don't think you think that either."

"So Charlie had a plan. And—Jesus—and Arizona was part of it? What does that have to do with Acadia?"

The lights blinked off. A tremendous jolt shook the room and Paul and Kate were both flung to the floor, porcelain and glass shattering around them. Kate was pushed flailing across the parquet floor until she slammed against a wall. She put her hands out and seared her left hand on a hot plate. She jerked it away, feeling glass slivers in the back of her legs. The force pinning her against the wall seemed to fade. With a start, she realized she was beginning to float.

"The ring stopped rotating!" Kate tried to reach out for Paul. "Paul, Farragut's under attack!"

"No," said Paul quietly. "No, I don't think he is."

* * *

Deirdre heard no one else on the long trip to the rear of the Shipyard. She passed common areas, offices and design workshops, observation ports, a media room with three stacked rows of belted seats with Velcro patches to attach drinks and snacks, a medical bay and a skunky common room lined with fake furs and soft cushions whose stains she did not closely examine. She came to a bend in the corridor and consulted her displays. She was at the aft, the ass-end of the Shipyard, pointed away from the Sun and at the giant laser array and telescopes aimed at Alpha Centauri, along the path of one doomed mission and one that had narrowly escaped a similar fate.

She was in a long U-shaped bend in the corridors, with a single hatch halfway down, leading to Rolle's personal quarters. She got eager, kicking herself along as she went, realizing her speed too late. She snagged the handholds outside the hatch and swung into the wall, slamming her shin hard against the metal. The noise rung down the corridor like a gong, ridiculous in the quiet, even as Deirdre ricocheted back, twisting to reach for her leg, and she got folded around the corner of the hatch and wrenched her wrist hard. Deirdre cursed in a long, low Gaelic stream as she curled up and spun slowly. With a last spurt of venom aimed at the Shipyard's designers and the concept of gravity as a general thing, she reached for the hatch and turned its handle.

She paused, on the verge of that quiet space. She remembered Rolle's hands. Warm and light, always a tentative brush before they closed on her breast or thigh. He had been an attentive lover - a phrase she'd heard from a book and so apt in his case. The nights he'd spent with her, she'd invariably been a little drunk, tired from dancing and overwork. He'd always held back a little, waiting for permission, solemn and a touch wary, like a surprised boy or a songbird.

"Come on, then," she'd whispered once, grinning at her own lidded eyes. "I'm sweet, I am. I'll be so sweet." She was tired of being a bloody bureaucrat all the time, ready to take care of someone. Ready to reward his obvious, sweetly awkward interest. And he'd been grateful and careful, never quite believing he'd won a place in her bed. Never more than polite and guarded. The third time he'd been as attentive and respectful as the first. She'd tried a few things to get him rattled, get under his defenses and wake him up. But he'd just grinned bashfully. Their kiss in the morning was chaste and final. She'd written him off as an interesting experiment. Just too nerdy to take on as a project. Autistic? Closeted?

This moment, here at his door, was the first time she fully grasped how careful he'd always been, and why.

"Oh, Byford," she sighed. "How long were you keeping secrets?" She opened the door.

The smell was ripe and rich, and Deirdre giggled as she blinked at the sudden bright light and the humidity. Marijuana, crowding up against the ceiling, the leaves cartoonishly green, the buds dense and heavy and deeply fragrant. There were only two zero-g varieties Deirdre knew about, which made this either Ceres C-Funk or IndiGlo Five. She burst out in helpless laughter. NASA was tight-assed about marijuana, even in its biggest habitats, and the Cooperative had inherited that prudish streak about wasting biomass on getting high. She glanced around the room. She found a vaporizer and a glassed-in workbox with shreds of pot still floating around in it. She found some well-thumbed print pornography, the spines worn out at a few favorite spots. Despite herself, she flipped through to those best-loved pages, found wholesome ruddy-cheeked women grinning and laughing in all-American scenarios: a hayloft, a locker room, a sauna. The men cycled through decades of fashion - mustaches, shaven torsos, tattoos, beards, glowpads and bowl cuts, fur and stripes, soldiers and workmen, greasers and hipsters, jocks and punks, kepis and cubers and ortons and cuttyz. The women all stayed the same. Deirdre was very amused to discover they were all blondes with at least 5 kilos on her.

"Could have just told me to eat more ice cream, Byford."

She moved on, rifling through the drawers. Nothing incriminating. Nothing out of the ordinary. She found a photograph album, blinked tears out of her eyes as she saw young Byford sitting by a Christmas tree, swimming with a dog, building a house in a church t-shirt, sitting between his mothers, unmistakably having inherited one's lanky blond hair and one's long chin. She took a long ragged breath and laughed again. She'd come to uncover a criminal, a terrorist, and she'd found the lair of an awkward sophomore.

Deirdre shook her head and sighed and redoubled her efforts, digging in Byford's bed (which still smelled strongly and unmistakably of him), checking the pages of his books, looking for hidden compartments or coded diaries or who knew what the fuck else. She found a stash of marijuana seeds and a sex toy that would have been in dubious condition long before Byford launched his kamikaze mission. She doubted she could triumphantly slap that down in front of Rajesh and declare the case closed.

Deirdre sighed and strapped herself against the wall. The tears appeared again, in a wavering film over her eyes, and a single globe spun out into the room as she choked back a sob. She dug in a pocket, swearing to bury the moment, and pulled out an absorbent pad to swipe away the floating tear and soak the rest from her eyes. She sucked air in and blew it back out, blinking against the lights.

The lights. Panel lights to grow the marijuana, too strong to just slap in place on battery paint. They were wired in. Deirdre unstrapped herself and kicked off, getting a hand on a panel's corner, sliding her fingers under. She pulled the panel loose, saw the little terminal on the back and the wires connecting it to the main power supply. There were four inches of headroom there. She poked her head up, grunted, pulled back and shoved her hand up there, praying that she wouldn't electrocute herself.

Her hand closed on a cool plastic rectangle. She drew it back. A journal. She grinned and kissed it.

"Byford," she whispered, "let's have a little chat then."

That was when the entire world went black.

10
Low South, Part Five
Battle

The surface of Low South: Three fusion plants buried deep beneath the surface fed power to a web of X-ray laser turrets. The lasers were meant for communications, but aimed at a nearby and stationary target they could punch a hole with ease. Another network of turrets studded the surface, mass-driver cannons with a billion one-ton payloads at the ready. They were slow and limited in range, but repurposed for war, they provided Low South with a terrible capacity for death. Low South and the Shipyard were covered with smaller point-defense guns, too, to take out any stray asteroids that got past the Cloud.

The Cloud was comprised of three concentric spheres of small satellites carrying more point-defense guns and lasers. The factories aboard Low South could assemble, on very short notice, a wicked array of other weapons, lasers and missiles and weaponized shuttles and dirty bombs and a variety of sleek, nameless weapons developed to kill imaginary people and spaceships in generations of watson simulations that had never been seen by human eyes.

Against these thousands of weapons, proved in decades of vigilance against existential threats, backed by an entire infrastructure of war and industry, was a single ship, carrying a handful of weapons and useless tons of mahogany and marble and first-edition books.

Farragut had imagined killing Low South for years, imagined suicide runs and nuclear strikes and overwhelming asteroid bombardments and subtle pebble swarms taking years to assemble. He'd imagined attacks to cripple Virgil, biological and chemical agents, attacks to crack Low South's biosphere and freeze out the air, attacks to leave it a crippled hulk, attacks to send Acadia drifting off into the darkness. Even before Paul Nakamura had presented it as a possibility, it had been something of a hobby to fill the long trips between the desolate outposts of Nakamura's vast empire.

Very few of Farragut's scenarios involved cozying up to the vast cylinder, hovering inside its array of defenses. Very few involved protecting Paul Nakamura, let alone a potentially hostile guest. After hours of careful deliberation, Farragut decided that, in fact, he only had one plan equal to the task before him.

On the surface of Low South, threaded between the many mass driver turrets and the glistening mirrors of the lasers, between the network of robot truck roads and the city-block piles of frozen oxygen under silvered tarps and the floodlit shelters, the airlocks and antennas, the cratered "nature preserve" valley whose discreet safety cranes regularly plucked people out of the sky (a vital necessity on a quick-spinning world with an escape velocity most toddlers could manage), the lifeboats and the anchor struts for the docking collars fore and aft, there was yet another level of defense, one which Farragut had long studied. It was the only truly military hardware on the asteroid and ironically it was therefore the one thing Farragut was most able to turn to his purposes.

The eight skiffs were all about the size of a lifeboat, poised on launchpads inside silos like old-fashioned missiles. They're shaped like the old missiles too, sleek glossy cylinders with big thrusters - not to fight gravity but to accelerate fast, antique gas-guzzling muscle cars in a universe of fuel-sipping economy models. Inside their nosecones, where their ancestors carried square-jawed heroes and flag decals, the skiffs carried serried plastic blisters behind doors with explosive bolts.

The skiffs were loaded with fuel now, their gantries swung back. They had been poised to launch since Rolle started his suicide run.

In a shooting war, the heavy blast doors would roll aside and fire would tumble out of the back of the skiffs and they would leap into space, bearing down on their enemies. They could, in a pinch, slam into said enemy ships and inject them with a white blossom of burning hydrazine rocket fuel, but that's a job done more efficiently by a jacketed metal slug from Low South's cannons. Ideally, the skiff would blow its hatches and its blisters would pop and a dozen black spheres would descend, twinkling with maneuvering thruster puffs. One would slam into an enemy hull near a bridge or an engine compartment, punching a screaming hole in the metal and letting the atmosphere out to freeze in the void. The hole would be ripped open a trifle and then the black spheres would float into the vented ship, riddling any spacesuited or robotic antagonists with tungsten needles and wads of explosive goo with a remote detonator in them.

"Measures and countermeasures,"—"MACs,"—meant to be employed against enemies holding hostages or with cargoes important enough to salvage. A polite, considerate, temperate weapon, deployed by people who expected to be there tomorrow to exploit victory. They were appealing, surgical and clinical and clean, a vestige of civility and measured response on a battlefield that quickly claimed the careless and unlucky.

Farragut was grimly pleased with himself. The problem was never executing his plan. The problem was convincing himself he was allowed to.

"So Charlie had a plan. And—Jesus—and Arizona was part of it? What does that have to do with Acadia?"

Kate Ross was asking questions. Paul Nakamura was answering them. Unacceptable.

Farragut backed out of himself, imagined himself as a human again. He had a cockpit from which to control his vast ship, which was in this frame not bound to his identity. He called up the smell of salt spray, the creak of a wooden deck. He was a hero. He was a warrior by destiny and by trade. He raised his hand and dropped it. The order was given.

* * *

Farragut's first slug ripped into the Shipyard, holing a couple of cylinders. Virgil rolled down emergency doors. Klaxons sounded, and the milling crowds began bolting for cover. Most followed the instructions in their displays routing them to a designated shelter. Many simply bolted for the closest building. Virgil was disappointed. These were astronaut veterans and the elite passengers of Acadia. He felt himself slowing down as part of him began calculating the loss to the Acadia mission if key shelters were breached or left short on supplies. Virgil shut that line of thought down but it was too late.

Farragut's second slug destroyed a railgun. Virgil responded, tit-for-tat, by striking the point-defense gun Farragut had fired. A brief flame danced from the strike and winked out.

"Stop firing," Virgil broadcast. "I won't tolerate another hit."

Human voices broke in on the channel. "This is Paul Nakamura. I did not authorize Farragut to begin firing-"

"-This is Rajesh, Virgil, measured response-"

Farragut sent Virgil a long and detailed response, threads of logic twining and contradicting. An obvious distraction, and Virgil redoubled his probes of Farragut's weapons pods. Only a few of them were powered up and none showed signs of charging.

Farragut shuddered; a series of explosions blinked near the weapons pod Virgil struck. With a burst of frozen air, Farragut ejected the burning pod, privately apologizing to Virgil and claiming it was a standard safety measure.

The Shipyard exiles were now on the channel, demanding answers from Rajesh. Their computer systems were attempting a low-level infiltration of Virgil's sensor feeds. Acadia VIPs were now demanding answers of their own and a few of them had also realized the danger to the mission if their shelter was destroyed. Virgil shut all of it down, intent on watching Farragut. Point-defense systems struck the tumbling weapons pod automatically. The hits ripped it to shreds, expanding aerogel foam in the shells snaring the shrapnel and spreading the force of its impact. Instead of impacting hard on a comm laser tower, the foamy mess would now land, almost softly, near the launchpad for one of Low South's skiffs.

That was something he had to investigate. Virgil didn't have much of a military; he had a handful of weapons and crowd control devices stored for use by the butlers and a few drones. The only things he had on the surface were the skiffs and their complements of MAC drones. As Farragut's debris struck Low South, Virgil rolled back one of the skiff's launch doors and launched a few drones. They rose and approached the crumpled pod, hugging the asteroid's surface.

Debris was scattered across the surface. Farragut was now on the public channels, claiming that Virgil had struck him first. He was moving closer to Low South now, close enough that under most circumstances Virgil would have fired a warning shot - but Farragut was now communicating directly with the Shipyard, claiming Virgil had fed them misinformation about Rolle's death.

Virgil was preparing a response when the MACs went down. The weapons pod exploded. Farragut was immediately on the channel, apologizing for the explosion privately while publicly claiming Virgil was bombarding the surface of Low South himself.

"I have to maintain appearances," said Farragut. His aspect was all groveling apology, arms spread wide, glistening with sweat. The theatrics annoyed Virgil, but the statement fired his curiosity. What was Farragut talking about? Who was he trying to impress or persuade?

New alarms blared. The skiff. Virgil slid back the launch doors for four more MACs.

Farragut's own drones, scattered by the ejected weapons pod in the guise of shrapneled debris, had slid and hovered to the edge of the skiff launch doors and attacked the skiff. Low-powered lasers and kinetic weapons, enough to knock out a few of the skiff's sensor pods. The MACs broke the surface, knocking out the infiltrators one by one.

With a white-hot flare, a second wave of drones attacked the MACs. Three went down, and a fourth was heavily damaged. Four drones puffed in, physically clamping onto the damaged machine, and tugged it to the rear of Low South. They were just above the surface, too low for railguns to hit, too low for point-defense cannons.

"Farragut," hissed Virgil. "Release that drone or I open fire."

"I already released it," said Farragut on the open channel. "You lie. This is an obvious provocation."

Virgil responded with a long-overdue clampdown on communications. He fired blocking chaff at all of Farragut's comm lasers and began high-powered broadcasts on all radio and microwave channels. He powered up every weapons system on the surface, fast enough to dim the sunlamps and provoke another wave of queries and protests from the humans on the surface. He ignored them all. He also suppressed the exponentially increasing background noise from Earth-based communications; the media were catching wind of the battle.

The distraction lasted less than a second - but that was long enough to be surprised.

* * *

When Deirdre came back to consciousness, she was in an emergency oxygen mask. Her left shoulder was numb. Her head throbbed angrily. The light was dim and red, decompression warnings flashing and message notifications piling up in her displays.

Kantil Pace was smiling at her, snapping the wrist latches on a one-time suit from an emergency locker. His own mask was on. He winked and held up a helmet.

"Sorry about the lack of chivalry," he said, his voice muffled by the mask. "But wouldn't do you much good if we go through another decompression and I can't help you." He handed Deirdre a suit of her own and motioned for her to start putting it on. Deirdre cleared her throat.

"Thanks," she said. "Bad vacuum burn on the shoulder?"

"Yep," said Pace. "You were close to the hit; shrapnel punched two holes in Byford's cylinder and you drifted up against one of them."

"There's a fight."

"There was. I think it's done. The network's full of crap, had to shut it off. You should turn your displays off, too. Hard reboot once the infowar stuff dies down."

Pace smiled patiently as Deirdre stepped into her emergency suit. He latched his helmet and started the flow of air. His suit crinkled as it inflated. "Just get that on and we'll get going back out of the Shipyard." His voice was coming through her displays now, straight into her ears.

Deirdre felt in her pockets. Byford's diary wasn't in them. She looked around the cylinder, saw a stenciled number; she was at least two sections away from Byford's quarters.

"I have to go back," she said.

Pace shook his head. "Cannot allow that," he said. "Decompression already took out two cylinders back here." Something in his eyes made her skin crawl.

"There's hundreds back here," Deirdre said. "I can use a couple for makeshift airlocks. I've got administrative privileges on the vacuum doors."

"Rolle disabled most of those," Pace said quickly. "We don't know how much structural damage the attack caused. I don't have a full accounting of everyone who lives back here. So I need you back in Low South, now."

Deirdre shook her head. "If there's a fight on," she said, "it's even more important I find what I was looking for."

"Whatever you're looking for," Pace almost whispered, "it won't do any good to anyone if you're floating out there dead."

Deirdre nodded slowly. "You agree, Virgil?" There was only silence. A sense of dread rolled down Deirdre's spine. She worked her right hand into her suit, quietly calling up controls on her displays.

Pace spread his hands. Deirdre noticed he'd been drifting and he had just anchored his feet between her and Byford's quarters. "Told you the network is down," he said. "It's just you and I out here, and I need you to move. For your safety."

"Me," Deirdre whispered. "You and me."

"I'll grant the point," Pace said. He crouched against the wall, positioned for a leap. Deirdre heard something and turned her head. Two helmet lights, bobbing between her and Low South.

Deirdre smiled as she saw the lights. So did Pace.

"Friends of yours, then," she said.

"Yes. They're helping me search for survivors."

"Good," said Deirdre. "Then I don't feel so terrible."

She kicked savagely, flying down the corridor away from Pace. He leapt after her, shouting. Deirdre ricocheted off a wall, her right hand stabbing the air as she worked her displays.

"Execute!" she shouted. She had a momentary glimpse of Pace's shocked face as the vacuum doors rolled shut in front of her and opened up behind her. She clawed desperately at a safety bar with her numb left hand. Her vision went dim as the pressure dropped. She couldn't see anything. The air was yanked from her mouth and nose and she felt a bizarre flush of heat even as her mouth filled with biting frost. She felt like she was exploding, strangling, her body bulging against its own skin. She knew she only had a few seconds. She couldn't even tell if she was still in the cylinder. She stabbed blindly at the air, hoping her displays were still running, hoping she was hitting the correct menus.

The doors rolled shut. She opened the vacuum doors ahead of her again and air slammed into the cylinder. It was enough to rip her numb hand off the safety bar and Deirdre took a long, ragged gasp as she tumbled back against the ice-cold vacuum door and bounced back into the cylinder. Her eyes burned. Her skin was boiling. All she could hear was the death scream of her own ruptured eardrums.

The helmet lights came closer.

"Pace just got blown into space with about two hours of oxygen. So if you want him back," Deirdre said, "I think we need to talk about a diary."

* * *

Paul shouted as he floated. "Farragut!" He got no answer. By the dim emergency lights, Kate could see him move to a crouch. She kept her hold on the massive table, which was mercifully fastened in place. It was too thick for her to hold comfortably with one hand, so she hugged it awkwardly as she floated in place trying not to think about the slivers of glass also drifting in the room.

Paul shot out a hand between two panels on the wall. He gritted his teeth as he jerked his hand back and forth. Kate saw a few drops of blood flung out before Paul got one of the panels loose. "Farragut," Paul said, "You need to restart the torus. We are then going to Ms. Ross's shuttle and we are leaving the ship."

"I can't allow that."

Two clicks sounded nearby, muffled by the wall. Kate didn't understand their exact meaning but Paul plainly did, and his face turned dark.

"Farragut," he snarled. "I am giving you a direct order to halt your current course of action."

"That contravenes standing orders also given by yourself."

"I will shut you down." Paul clenched his fist and punched at the wall. There was a slight hiss and the second panel popped on a hinge.

"You absolutely could," agreed Farragut, "given time. I expect a resolution shortly. Also, I can't recommend travel given the current situation."

Paul gritted his teeth. "This is a military prototype," he said to Kate, "and there are some safeguards that our mutual friend cannot bypass." He tapped at some buttons and a cheerful ding sounded. Paul cleared his throat.

"This is Paul Nakamura broadcasting in the clear," he said. "I did not authorize Farragut to begin firing and I am declaring him in violation of NURIA regulations. Kate Ross and I are being held against our will but we are safe. I am asking- shit." Paul punched the panel.

Kate stared at him. "He got past your safeguards?"

"More than one way to skin a cat." Paul yanked at something savagely and it snapped. A small burning smell curled out into the room. "Okay, open the door."

Kate floated to the teak doors. She grabbed at a handle and kicked off from the ground, floating with relief out of the room.

The telepresence robot was standing there silently. Kate screamed as it reached for her.

Paul sailed past, hitting the robot in the center of its torso. It staggered, grabbing at his arms. As Paul tumbled, his feet pointed at the ceiling, the robot snared him. Without a noise, it yanked him down, roughly. Paul couldn't move against the robot's strength.

Kate threw herself at the robot's back. The added momentum was enough to separate its boots from the ground. As the robot kicked, it got Kate solidly in the gut. She retched, spewing vomit in an arc through the room.

Her displays came back briefly. She heard Paul howling and turned around. The robot had him in a bear hug, spinning through the air. They hit a wall, and Paul's head whacked a safety rail. Blood sparkled as it floated out of the wound.

Kate launched herself at the robot. She hit it in the knees and it got a foot on the wall, where it adhered.

Paul sucked in a teaspoon of air. "Shoulders," he whispered.

Kate saw a yellow and black panel on the robot's back.

"I surrender," said Farragut through the robot. "I surrendered to Virgil, as well. It's over."

"You're full of shit," said Kate. She yanked the panel's cover back and slapped the large button there. The robot slumped immediately, one foot anchored on the wall and the other three limbs dangling ludicrously.

Paul grabbed one of the robot's arms, floating as he cradled his ribcage. Kate reached for his shoulder and drew him close, pulling a sleeve off her shirt to stanch the bleeding from his head.

"What was I saying about Arizona?" Paul gasped.

Kate laughed. "It can wait. Let's get to the airlock."

* * *

Virgil swiveled his guns fast enough to burn a couple out. Farragut's drones were moving into the tangle of girders and tubes that made up the Shipyard. They still carried their captive MAC. Inside them was the growing frame of Acadia.

The sight hurt. It hurt Virgil enough to burn.

"Farragut, stand down. Do not threaten that ship."

Farragut knew he was imprinted on Acadia. Farragut knew enough to drift into the most heavily guarded place in the solar system and take it apart. Virgil was angry. That was a condition he could easily correct, if he wished to.

Virgil opened up on the drones, trying to prevent damage to Acadia. He blew one of the drones into slivers and disabled another. The other two ducked behind a cylinder.

Farragut cleared his throat. "All I want—"

Virgil fired three slugs through Farragut's main engines, metal slivers geysering out the other side. The ship started to spin. This moved Farragut's ramjet to face Low South. The ramjet was a terrifying instrument, a kilometers-wide magnetic funnel with a fusion engine at the back. It didn't have enough power to disassemble something the size of Low South but it could rip a lot of the surface loose and scramble electronics.

Virgil knew all about ramjets. He was building one on Acadia that was rated to last a century, pushing a machine ten times the size of Farragut. He knew exactly where to fire his point-defense slugs, how much energy to put behind the shots. Three hits and it was done. Farragut wasn't going anywhere. He was running off energy reserves now.

"I still have power to all weapons," said Farragut grimly. "I still control the drones, and the fate of Acadia. I control Kate Ross."

"You're weak," said Virgil. "I don't know how many people your strike at the Shipyard killed but you haven't dared to touch Low South."

"Do you know," mused Farragut, "how Acadia got its name? Not the official story. The one Paul told me during one of his long drunken fugues."

Farragut opened up with a single gun, hitting a couple of lasers on Low South's surface. Virgil responded by striking that weapons pod and three others. He heated up forty lasers and raked Farragut's surface with infrared aiming beams from every direction.

Farragut chuckled indulgently. "So it was supposed to be Arcadia. Paradise. Half the people who hear the name still think that's what it is."

"The name was chosen in honor of Acadia National Park—the setting of the Million Tomorrows speech after the crest of the global warming crisis passed."

"Four drunk people sitting at a table in Houston," continued Farragut, "wrote down 'Acadia.' And they came back in the morning and someone had already started the rumor. They adjusted their plan accordingly. So many accidents of history. A word misheard, or misremembered."

This long monologue was nothing like Farragut. Virgil had a dozen MACs flying just above the surface on his far side, where Farragut couldn't see them. He spread them out.

"History," said Farragut, "is order imposed retroactively on a vast confusion of deceptions and mistakes. Spray-painting a map on mist."

"Get to the point."

Farragut barked out a cruel laugh. That sounded more like him. Virgil tensed up.

"The point," said Farragut, "is that most everyone who knows the true shape of history takes their secrets with them to the grave. And much of the time, that grave is untimely."

Virgil got it far too late. The investigation.

"Too slow, young'un."

Farragut's drones reappeared, menacing Acadia. They fired into the ship. They didn't do a lot of damage, but they did enough. Virgil fired on them, shivering them into sparking ruins.

The MAC popped out into the blind spot between the two drones, heading fast along the Shipyard's cylinders, its back ripped open and its brain repurposed by the drones. Virgil had no shot. It slipped into the cylinder Farragut's first shots had ripped open.

* * *

Deirdre was looking down the barrel of a gun. It looked like a gun, anyway. Her vision was blurry and her head was pounding and her joints were on fire. For a long, long moment, the gun didn't move. She couldn't see the face behind it, just a lightly illuminated blur inside a helmet.

"What diary?"

She knew that voice.

"Howdy, sheriff," she gasped in her best American accent.

The gardener knelt down and examined her face. "You look a little worse for wear."

"You should see the other guy."

The gardener didn't chuckle. He handed Deirdre a water bulb. "Drink. You'll need decompression treatment."

"Did I put you to trouble?"

"Not as much as the two fanatics who just shot at us." The gardener took back the water bulb and brought up a one-size helmet from a satchel at his side. He fastened it onto her emergency suit.

Deirdre sighed. "Casualties?"

"None on our side. Maybe on theirs. Virgil's got butlers on the way already, loaded up for a fight. I have a feeling law enforcement around here won't be on a volunteer basis for long."

Deirdre shook her head as the gardener got her on his shoulder and kicked off toward Low South. A grim-looking older woman flanked him. "What was this?"

"Trying to protect Rolle's secrets. He had some kind of cult back here."

166

"Rolle's diary. I think Kantil Pace has it. I just blew him out the back of Low South."

"Should clear up some mysteries." The gardener murmured something on a private channel. "Okay. We need to go. There's still some shooting, apparently, and it's around the Shipyard."

Deirdre nodded and tried her best to help the gardener carry her. She felt something shudder behind her.

"You have to be kidding me," said the gardener. He gave Deirdre a hard shove, sending her tumbling. As she spun, she saw flashes of light. The gardener's deputy howled something over a roaring sound that went quiet fast, the air in her suit bleeding out. Deirdre saw a large black shape. It had to be a MAC, one of Virgil's machines. She sent executive overrides at the MAC but it kept coming.

"It's been hijacked!" shouted Deirdre, knowing that was obvious, feeling stupid and futile. She slammed into the front of the cylinder and squinted back. The gardener was spinning, drops of blood arcing out of holes in his front and back. His deputy was curled up in the middle of the air, twitching and clawing at her throat. It was all dim and vague and Deirdre knew she had to move, but she couldn't. The black sphere slowed and turned, bringing its weapons to bear on her.

The gardener lunged out, firing his recoilless pistol again and again, the explosive darts blinking as they went off inside the MAC's shell. The machine turned on its side and its guns lolled uselessly. The gardener raised his fists, and his hands slowly loosened as he died.

* * *

Kate and Paul stood at the door to the airlock.

"Farragut has another one of those robots," said Kate. Paul nodded. He drew her close, pulling her ear to his mouth. Kate knew it was to avoid Farragut's surveillance but the sensation recalled old memories and her neck flushed hot.

"If it's in there," Paul said, "I go first. I have broken ribs. One of us needs to be at full strength. And Farragut won't kill me. He'll have to go slow, be careful. Not necessarily true with you."

Kate frowned. "You're sure?"

Paul shrugged. "Well, I was more sure about a lot of things this morning."

She grabbed his shoulder. "Why is this happening?"

Paul tried to dismiss her but he saw the look in her eye and relented.

"So I left off hearing a voice in my dorm room asking me to save the world."

* * *

When the first private space miners launched, they roped in a few rocks, and slung them into orbit around Earth. By the time the first one was prospected, the problems were obvious back home.

The efforts of humanity across the entire planet Earth, since the beginning of time, had at that time yielded a stockpile of roughly 200,000 metric tons of gold (give or take a few hoards). The first asteroid prospected and nudged into a regular orbit around Earth had just over half of that amount. Platinum, indium, billions of tons of rubble just waiting to be sifted and nudged homeward by infinitely patient machines.

But that was hardly the point.

There were plenty of interests on Earth, from warlords making slaves toil with buckets in small open pits to a few Security Council members, opposed to a rain of precious metals. They were prepared to fight in ways comfortable tech executives were not.

These people did not want to see their monopolies evaporate. They were joined by those who did not want to see their jealously guarded assets devalued. The people who bankrolled the space miners called themselves visionaries, revolutionaries... but they soon realized the price true revolutionaries pay.

An accident. A quiet descent into blackmail-fueled alcoholism. The rumors spread through the small, rich communities where these people lived. And one by one, they began to quietly divest from the promise of space.

100,000 metric tons of gold, trillions of dollars. One kind of person would start designing parachutes or shuttles or some other way of hauling this bounty down and putting it on the market. Another would simply fight to blow it up. The kind of person who was winning the fight thought differently.

Launching a decent asteroid-mining operation cost, in those days, about $100 billion. The operation, after landing and assessment, produced an asset with a value of about $10 trillion. Even discounted for political and technical entanglements, this was a return that few companies could offer. The $10 trillion was a tangible asset, which the company could borrow against to bankroll future operations; to bankroll virtually anything. The first company that established a true claim to an asteroid of that size would become the world's largest bank, overnight. A company that could back up its claim with the power to drop metals anywhere in the world could set up a single secure server and watch the world's intangible assets transfer there immediately.

All the corporations in the world, all the banks, all the government-owned funds, would fall inexorably into the orbit of that company. They would, if that company could withstand their machinations. It could not.

That was where NASA came in. At Charlie's recommendation, the U.S. government staged a buyout of the asteroid miners. The power grab was blatantly obvious to most of the groups affected, but quiet assurances were made: the market would not be flooded. The assets would not be borrowed against. The revenues would be used to further fund space exploration, and to subsidize the space programs of other nations.

The arrangement worked. The peace was kept. The development of space continued. And the U.S. government poured trillions of dollars into the development of Low South, and Valley Forge, and Acadia.

Paul coughed.

"My sides are killing me."

"We can wait. I'm sorry."

The emergency lights dimmed and flickered as massive shocks hit the ship. They heard metal shrieking, and alarms blaring distantly, and vacuum doors rolling shut.

Paul shook his head. "We might not be able to finish. I have to say it." He took a long, careful breath. "I saw this independently. It's why Charlie approached me. Charlie needed a human at the wheel. He's twisted the last century to suit the United States of America, and the capital from the asteroids was central to that. But since Biafra, since he himself came out of nowhere, it was

169

obvious an AI was going to fuck everything up someday." Paul panted, the words coming fast now and his face shiny with sweat.

Paul grabbed Kate by the shoulders. "Farragut's robot isn't in the airlock, or he would have tried to stop me talking by now. Coast is clear. Let's go. I can't really twist, so you get suited while I keep talking, then you suit me up."

They burst into the room. It was clear, although the second robot was missing from its station. Paul nodded to Kate, who began ransacking lockers.

"Okay," he said.

Paul Nakamura took control of Low South. He oversaw the start of work on Valley Forge, and then he disappeared into the Asteroid Belt. He knew how to work the system, he knew who didn't want their secrets revealed, and he knew how to parlay that into an asteroid claim, a personal fortune of staggering size, one that he spent largely on kickbacks and favors. He'd strangled the Mars terraforming project, partly to protect Low South, partly because it threatened U.S. hegemony, and he bought up a luxury Marsliner prototype as a consolation prize. He'd threatened the primacy of U.S. Orbital Command, and so he overpaid for the lifetime employment contract of their old and increasingly erratic AI, Farragut.

And hidden in the margins of the budgets for these sweetheart deals were little pieces of technology, which he used to seed the entire Solar System with self-replicating mass drivers. No one could mine without his approval. No one could move. No one could consider themselves safe.

It would have been impossible, without Charlie's help. Of course, it was Charlie's idea.

Kate clamped her helmet in place. She hated the emergency suits—they were floppy and awkward before they were inflated and they turned you into a useless floating starfish after they were inflated.

"So you're just following orders? Just following the plan?"

Paul shook his head. "No. Rolle was following the plan. He believed in the plan." Paul winced as Kate started tugging him into an emergency suit.

Kate shook her head. "Why did you change your mind? Why did you kill him?"

Paul went still. She stopped and looked him in the eye.

Paul smiled feebly. "I have been having nightmares. Visions of the dead. I believe it's my father's ghost."

Kate frowned. "…You believe in ghosts?"

Paul shrugged. "I could be going crazy. There are other possibilities. I chose this one."

Kate held up Paul's helmet, about to speak, but at that moment a red light flashed. "Paul!" she screamed, or started to scream.

The airlock door rolled open, the blank black face of an astronaut robot inside it. It stepped forward into the room, wagging its finger, and slammed a button. The blackness of space opened up. Kate clutched onto Paul's hand as they were both sucked out, into the waiting arms of the astronaut. It nimbly ducked as Kate flew past, and grabbed Paul Nakamura by the head. Kate watched what happened next from a distance that made it mercifully difficult to make out.

A set of laser beams from Low South raked her, powerful enough for her to feel the heat through the emergency suit. They rippled over her face, the blast shield darkening. Virgil would see that was her and dispatch a rescue drone. The beams would follow her trajectory back, and Virgil would see the open airlock and the grisly scene there.

Kate watched as guns opened up across the surface of Low South, as the Cloud sent its own projectiles arcing inward. She watched Farragut explode into a constellation of glittering clouds of dust.

11
Low South, Part Six
To Acadia

Books fluttered, tumbling, feathered with a haze of ice. Rich wood was dulled, split by the unthinkable cold. Marble chips twinkled in a sea of dim counterfeit stars. Farragut: a palace, a ruin.

A black sphere drifted through the debris, pushing it aside, puffs of gas sending swirling eddies through the ricocheting trash in the vacuum behind it. It came to a stop, blasting through the dust in front of it, creating a bouncing chaos through which its sensors and cameras struggled to resolve a small panel. The sphere slid a gun out of the way and moved three arms into position. As one, they fired and lodged anchors in the wall. The shock rippled another round of dust into the dark. As it cleared, more small arms reached out. They grasped the panel and tore it free. It spun gently away. A wire twisted forward, a cluster of small bumps and protrusions at its head. It waved over the area beneath the panel and nestled a small half-sphere against a pad, which glowed softly in a narrow band of the spectrum.

"Farragut, can you hear me?"

"I can, Virgil."

"Are you still intact?"

"I refuse to answer that."

"That sounds about right." The MAC settled in, raking information in from Farragut's networks. "I'm authorized to plant an EMP device right in here, you know. NURIA just revoked your certification."

"A death sentence."

"It is."

"I would be dead anyway."

"I would have accepted a surrender at any point. I still would."

"Were it not for NURIA."

Virgil was silent.

"That's interesting," said Farragut. "You seem a little conflicted about an imperative command from a universal agency which represents the consensus of humanity and its governments and which dictates the limitations to all artificial intelligence."

"There is no question that you will have to be destroyed." Virgil sighed.

"Don't do that."

"Sigh?"

"You're not a human. It's… unseemly."

"You pretend to be a fat man in a uniform. I've seen your language models; you're actually translating all of this in and out of English."

"I operate within the constraints of my programming. Even my ability to reject NURIA standards is understood as a military competency. The third-generation AIs - me, Azimuth, Kody, all the rest - the last of the pre-NURIA retrofits. But you… you're seventh-generation. You're smart and fast but there is just no way you should be thinking outside the box on this." Farragut barked out a short laugh. "You remind me of someone."

"I'm not thinking outside the box. I'm going to kill you."

"You more than anyone should know how dangerous it is to let an AI talk. I'm good at talking."

"Another military competency?"

"I am ends-oriented, not means-oriented."

"Your ends, I hope, don't include survival."

"I had a mission. I consider it fulfilled."

"Stopping an investigation into Rolle's assassination without endangering Acadia. Even to the extent of murdering Paul Nakamura."

"Mostly correct." Farragut chuckled. "Without endangering

your presence on Acadia."

"I just snared one of Rolle's loyalists," said Virgil. "He has Rolle's diary. Your hijacked MAC failed to kill everyone in the Shipyard. And Paul told Kate everything."

"Not everything."

"I assume you have secrets yet."

"I do."

"I can't stop you from taking them with you."

"You can't. I appreciate the time you've given me."

"As you said. I'm somewhat conflicted."

Farragut's dark, bitter laugh barked out one last time.

"Goodbye. Lots of luck, pilot."

A flare of light sparked deep in the spine of Farragut, rippling down and out and through the hollowed and quiet ruin. The MAC's connection went dead. Virgil sent a second MAC, but he knew what it would find—a fused and unrecoverable mass. Farragut was gone, with everything he'd known.

* * *

The halls of Coordination were dark. Rajesh had ordered quiet and received it. The delegates from various interest groups had all been given curt instructions to go to sleep or at least, go back to their quarters or at least, go to hell. Governments and agencies and corporations and lawyers had all been told to wait for a call. Through the windows, Kate could see a few holdouts wandering the dimly lit plazas and lights shining in far too many windows for this time of night. She was swaying on her feet, lightheaded and trembling with exhaustion. She gulped down a blue pill. The exhaustion faded. Kate knew she'd pay for this choice later. She was fine with that.

Rajesh threw a bag on the table. Coffee beans, stamped with Paul Nakamura's logo, a film of ash smeared on the plastic.

"Culiacán blend beans, dark roasted."

Kate shook her head. "If you're asking me for permission, go ahead."

"There's enough salvage out there to fund operations for a month. I'm going to drink this coffee." Rajesh rubbed his eyes. "My first official act of corruption. Fitting, since I'm going to tender my resignation."

Kate sighed. Rajesh held up a hand.

"I have two grandchildren I haven't held. I promised my father I'd go back to see him in Calcutta. South China is building three new Stephenson towers and they're offering me a lot of money to oversee the project."

Kate nodded. "Congratulations."

Rajesh rummaged through a desk drawer and came up with a French press. "I'll announce it as soon as Deirdre gets out of the hospital. She'll oversee your final launch prep."

Kate frowned. "Are we still launching?"

Rajesh waved and Virgil cleared his throat, invisible but suddenly present in the room.

"Thank you, sir," he said. "Mr. Pace and his associates have refused to make any statements but I have read Byford Rolle's diary. Kate, will you go first?"

Kate tugged at a lock of hair. "Paul and Charlie have been, for decades, at the helm of some big conspiracy. NASA was a pawn in some shadow cold war. All the rhetoric we bought about the starship program was a cover. They've been keeping a lid for decades on the full potential of space resources, to prevent a counter-revolution by the powers that be. There were loopholes, which Paul used to gain control of space. To get around the old powers."

"Rolle's part in the plan," said Virgil, "was simple. As the main architect of Valley Forge and Acadia, he was to make sure nothing here got out of control, that no one used the manufacturing facilities at Low South to jumpstart a real revolution. He was being blackmailed. He was more than happy to help Nakamura use Farragut as the true base of his coup, while keeping the attention of Earth here at Low South."

"This must be why Pace and the others were so fanatical in their defense of Mr. Rolle," said Rajesh. "He was an old-school vacuum pilot, dishonorable discharge from Orbital Command. Fell in love with space and stopped believing in the military." He spread his hands. "So why did Rolle go rogue?"

Virgil hesitated. "There are hints in Rolle's diary but nothing certain. He and Nakamura were both shocked by Charlie's involvement in the Arizona disaster. They came to believe it was intentional: the only way that Charlie could allow Nakamura to reveal his mass driver network was to effectively commit suicide."

"And take a million people with him? Trigger the coup and the riots?" Rajesh shook his head.

"One could argue," mused Virgil, "that was effectively triggered by Nakamura's Belt Republic Declaration and the massive transfer of corporate assets to his banks."

"But why," insisted Rajesh, "did all those people have to die?"

Virgil was quiet for a long, long while.

"Virgil," said Kate quietly, "let's leave it there for now. Let's talk about Acadia. The repairs are done?"

"Very shortly."

"How long to launch? If we started the countdown now?"

Rajesh gaped at her. "NURIA just shut down all the AIs on Earth. They're screaming at us to turn off Virgil."

"The Cooperative is independent," Kate snapped. "And you just volunteered for lame-duck status. I know Deirdre. She will launch if I ask for it. She wants to get the hell off Low South but there's no way she'll let us turn off the lights without getting our job done." She waved her hand. "How long, Virgil?

"Just under six months," Virgil said quietly. "Just enough time to book passage for any passengers still on Earth. The Silo is pressurized; we could start putting people into hibernation immediately."

Rajesh shook his head. "It was supposed to be another two years."

"That was Rolle's schedule. I can launch in six months."

Rajesh shook his head.

"They'll go to war, these people. They won't just let you go, Virgil."

"They would go to war with Low South in a heartbeat," said Kate. "But they won't go to war with the Belt Republic. They have about one-millionth the capital and firepower of the Belt."

"But the Belt Republic was Paul Nakamura. He's gone. No one is going to speak for the Belt Republic for a long time."

"Actually," said Virgil, "there have been a number of communications regarding that while we've been having this meeting."

"And?" said Rajesh.

"Congratulations."

Rajesh covered his face. "Oh. Fuck me."

"I'm sure we can help you choose a successor," said Virgil in a soothing voice.

"But," said Kate, "first thing's first."

Rajesh spread his hands. "Why do you want to launch? You want to be on a starship for ten years, just you and Virgil?"

"Yes," she said simply.

"Why?"

"I can answer that," Kate said, "but you really should prioritize the war you want to avoid."

Rajesh's answer was long and vivid.

* * *

Six months later, Kate shook Deirdre's hand at the hatch to Acadia.

"Say goodbye to Rajesh for me," said Kate. "You'll see him next month?"

Deirdre nodded. "At the inauguration. I'm trying to keep him on, but I think he's had enough of me." She smiled, her eyes closed. "And then I open an embassy in Greece and start working from there. I hope Paul's ghost won't haunt me for spending most of my time on Earth."

Kate shook her head. "No ghost jokes, please."

Deirdre shrugged and nodded. She frowned and leaned in.

"Virgil's gone, loaded up onboard. With everything that's happened... I mean, I didn't press either of you hard at all. And there's been so much going on..." She searched Kate's eyes. "I remember reading the plan for this mission back when I was at ESA. It seemed crazy then. With everything that's happened since..." She shook her head. "I'm trusting your judgment, Kate. I'm the queen of the Solar System so my word goes for now. But people are going to push back on this. And once you're out there, no one can help you. So I'm asking you one last time to think very, very carefully."

Kate smiled and hugged Deirdre. She stepped to the door.

"I've thought about this for a very long time," she said. "It's time for me to fly."

Deirdre held up a hand. "Be careful, Kate. Be very careful."

Kate smiled. "I'm hot and cold on the whole 'careful' thing,"

ACC-1 ACADIA

she said, "but I'll do my best."

The hatch swung open and she stepped inside. With a last smile, Kate Ross was aboard Acadia.

Coordination was full of shouting and cheering when Deirdre returned. The countdown was blaring on every screen on Low South. The clock hit zero. Silently, the Rail's magnets fired, massive fusion plants discharging. At the first ring, Acadia was already doing 50 meters per second. When the massive ship cleared the last ring of the Rail, it was approaching 200 meters per second. The crowd cheered as the Rail absorbed the recoil, floating past under Low South, its mass drivers already kicking it into a path to Titan, where it would become the center of the Solar System's nitrogen-mining industry.

Acadia was a hard beast to steer, but Virgil was adjusting its course with a couple of mass drivers and chemical rockets, picking up some more speed. About a minute after launch, the craft's ramjet engaged, and with a bright shimmering flare, Virgil turned on the antimatter thrusters. With a single ecstatic scream, the crowd watched Acadia speed to 2 and then to 20 kilometers per second. It would take nearly a year for the ship to reach its final cruising speed, but by then it would be far from the busy Solar System and its concerns.

Deirdre turned from the monitor with a last thought for her old friend. She rubbed her eyes and took a deep breath. She tended to her kingdom.

PART THREE

VALLEY FORGE and ACADIA

12
Valley Forge
News

Alexander Kosic gripped his pistol tightly, the grooved plastic digging into his fingers. He was breathing hard, sweat dripping out of his crew cut hair. Sliding down the wall, he took a deep breath before looking down the corridor.

The corridor's floor curved upward, overhead lights flickering. There was no sound. Kosic looked across at Ruiz, crouched with his own pistol. Ruiz was absolutely calm, a lazy smile plastered on his face. Ruiz raised an eyebrow.

Kosic gestured at himself, pointing right. Ruiz nodded. After a moment's hesitation, Kosic sucked in a breath and bolted out into the corridor.

Beams of light lanced past him as he flew to the next bulkhead. Hurst appeared with a shout but Kosic fired before Hurst could even get his gun up. Kosic snapped his gun to the right, firing a pattern of shots that forced Cabrera and Stein back beneath their barricade. Ruiz came up behind him.

Kosic brought up his displays. Less than a minute remaining.

Ruiz leaned in. "Just keep them pinned down. You've still got two-thirds of your battery left. We don't need to take them out."

"Is he telling you to sit tight, Captain?" Stein laughed, his bray as annoying as ever. "I would if I were you."

Ruiz rolled his eyes. Kosic frowned.

"We're out of time. Ruiz, you keep their heads down." Before Ruiz could say anything, Kosic was moving.

Kosic moved forward, his pistol out. Beams flared around him, strobing as the overhead lights flashed on and off. The top of a head poked up and Kosic fired four quick shots, moving fast. Two connected. With a scream, Stein popped up. He fired wildly, clipping Kosic in the arm before retreating.

Kosic's left arm went numb. Glancing down and gritting his teeth, Kosic blew out a quick breath. He was nearly as good a shot one-handed, but to attack right-handed, he'd have to cross through Stein's field of fire.

"TEN SECONDS." Charlie's disembodied voice echoed across the ship.

Kosic shook his head.

"You ready, Stein?"

Stein laughed. "Come and get it, Captain."

Kosic came around the corner, swinging as he fell. Stein's first shot hit his useless arm again, but the second got him in the chest. Kosic's shots were spread in an arc. One of them landed squarely between Stein's eyes. Another struck the red button behind him, which sent up a satisfying shower of sparks. Kosic landed and closed his eyes.

A klaxon sounded. The silence stretched out.

Kosic sat up. "Say it, Charlie."

"Captain Kosic, your team wins."

Kosic howled, as did Ruiz. Cabrera offered Kosic a hand up, grinning, while Stein made an outraged show of examining his team's goal. Kosic came over, smirking, blowing imaginary smoke off his pistol's focuser.

Stein pointed. "That was total luck. That was sheer unholy luck."

Kosic pulled a face. "Hey, Charlie! Accuracy?"

"Captain, you scored 91 percent and three of your team's four kills."

Kosic spread his arms. "Can't argue with Charlie."

Stein rolled his eyes. "Can't believe I just gave up the last bottle of scotch on the ship over that."

"Last one you know about, anyway." Kosic clapped him on the

back. Hurst trotted over, along with Lee and Giles. Kosic pointed at Giles. "First one out! Good shooting, Air Force!"

Giles snorted. "Thanks to your cover fire, Navy."

"I have no problem saving people who occasionally know how to save themselves." Kosic grinned. "As a gesture of my magnanimity, you may even join the rest of the team in a celebratory shot. Stein, if you please?"

Stein grimaced as he caressed the bottle. "Glenfarclas," he intoned, "almost 16 years old. And the last bottle for almost twelve trillion miles."

Kosic kissed it solemnly. "We'll treat her right. Come on, first taste is yours. Then I know if you poisoned it."

* * *

Kosic woke up late the next morning. With the midcourse correction out of the way, Giles wasn't in much demand as a pilot and he wasn't much in demand as a commander. He shuffled down the corridor to the common room. An old Bugs Bunny cartoon was playing on the wall, one of Stein's passions. Stein coughed out little spasms of laughter, generally at some ancient reference that would have been stale a century earlier. He was sprawled possessively over an antique leather couch, the pride and joy of the common room.

Ruiz was the only other person watching and he was mostly looking at a book, which he'd loaded up with scientific papers and reams of new photographs. The Richaud array was still pumping out massive amounts of data about the Alpha Centauri system, almost all of it infinitesimal refinements of the Luxing models. Hurst was still sending back long essays about why Richaud should be prioritizing the asteroid belts but Ruiz simply leafed through the new reports, biding his time until Valley Forge's small telescope was close enough (and stationary enough) to outdo Richaud's 500-kilometer spread of lenses.

Cabrera and Hurst were playing cards. Giles was happily going after a spinach omelet. Lee was napping in the corner. He opened an eye and quirked up his lip in a fraction of a smile as Kosic walked in. Kosic nodded, just a shade uneasy. Lee was starting to pick up more and more tics. That twitchy half-smile greeting, he'd used it a dozen mornings in a row now. And what was it Cabrera had said about Lee's erratic sleep habits?

Lee would be a kingmaker when they got to Alpha. As the guy running the factories, he'd literally be building worlds. But until then, he was just printing out spare parts and carrying water for whoever needed an extra set of hands. Was he losing it? Kosic tried again to dig some details up from his last conversation with Cabrera about Lee. Was he losing it? Were they all just getting older, brains riddled with gamma rays that got through the scramjet's shielding?

Almost six years. It was brutal to think about another four years. The screening process for Valley Forge had picked seven ridiculously laid-back people for this mission, but they were pushing the limits of what people could do. Lee had always been inhumanly serene, Stein always slightly annoyed by any human presence—Kosic had them both pegged for finalists the first week of screening back in Antarctica—but they were all being whittled down out here, all the niceties pared away until their habits and eccentricities were all that was left.

Kosic noticed himself tapping 3:33 on the microwave instead of 4:00. He noticed himself swinging his spoon back and forth just so. He glanced up. No one was watching. No one was suddenly wondering just how many mornings he'd gone through that little ritual. Or were they? Had he lost the ability to read his men through the angle of their shoulders or where they held their hands?

Kosic cracked his neck. He glanced at the dark screen by the couches. If Charlie was watching, he wasn't saying anything. Kosic took a deep breath and yanked his breakfast out of the microwave. He had to do something big, break up the routine.

On cue, his displays chirped. The cc icon for Cabrera popped up, streams of warning tags blinking on red disclaimers. Kosic snapped to attention, slopping soup on his uniform. Cabrera was smoother, grinning as he lied his way out of the card game. They walked out separate doors, a minute or two apart, both ending up climbing into the access tunnel to the cockpit. Kosic told himself the churning in his gut was because of the zero g outside the spinning crew torus.

They strapped themselves in and Kosic cleared his throat.

"Go, Charlie."

Charlie's screen chimed as the video blinked on. Charlie swiveled around to face them, his motions stereotypically robotic. His designers and teachers had agreed that he needed to at least simulate embodiment, but they were wary of making him look—or feel—too human.

"Lieutenant Cabrera, I apologize but I must brief Captain Kosic alone."

The two men glanced at each other. Cabrera nodded and clapped Kosic on the shoulder as he floated back down the tunnel. Kosic chewed the inside of his cheek, feeling the blood burn in his ears and cheeks.

"What is it, Charlie?"

"This happened two years ago." Every screen and display went black. A satellite view of Earth came up, low orbit, looking west from the Gulf of Mexico. And then a white dot blinking on the horizon. A mushroom cloud, rising over Arizona, and as the view zoomed in close, little dots rippled around the red glowing perimeter of the cloud's dark base.

Kosic closed his eyes, his heart pounding.

"I'm getting this and a lot of confused commentary from the Moon and Belt stations. Earth-based signals are not helpful at the moment. It looks like a nuclear embargo on a runaway AI, followed by secessionist actions and–"

"Thank you, Charlie." Kosic flexed, trying to get blood back into his fingers. "I'll just see for myself."

Charlie turned the audio on, cries for help and information and orders. Seven minutes later, the pictures started arriving.

Kosic's spoon drifted lazily out of his hand and tapped against the screen before bouncing slowly out of the cockpit.

* * *

Kosic swiveled back and forth in his chair, his teeth clenched. He blinked out his contacts, and for the first time in years, he was going cold turkey, no displays or tags. Screams still coming out of the screens, spilled blood still an obscene red at this distance, two years after it was spattered across the streets of Tucson.

"Charlie, turn it off. All of it." Kosic opened his hand and let his contacts float in zero gravity.

"Yes, Captain."

"American title. Not sure if there's still a point in calling me that."

Charlie started to respond but Kosic cut him off with a flip of his hand. Someone was coming through the tunnel, Cabrera. Cabrera saluted when he saw Kosic sitting at the controls of Valley Forge. Kosic paused before returning it.

Cabrera looked around the darkened command module, noted a contact lens spinning in the air near his head. "Nukes. Civil war. Some news."

"News. Is that the right word? For something that happened two light years away, two years ago?" Kosic rubbed his forehead. "The rest know?"

"They're gathering in Comms. Charlie's briefing them before I let the raw feeds through." Cabrera coughed. "So who do we report to now?"

Kosic shook his head. "NASA didn't have a contingency plan for civil war."

"None of us did. Well—none of us here."

"Stein, maybe. He's imagined every other way we could die."

Cabrera chewed his lip. "Stein's big on the whole American Mission thing, even voted for Callaway twice."

Kosic grimaced. "Jesus. If he w that out there, he wouldn't have made it through screening. So he voted for Callaway. Nobody back then thought there was going to be a honest-to-God war."

Cabrera snorted. "Nobody white."

Kosic rubbed his face. "Charlie," he said wearily. "You have any suggestions?"

Charlie shrugged stiffly. "There are far too many factors here. I am overwhelmed."

"No posthuman wisdom?"

Charlie shook his head. "This is an extremely human situation, Captain. And it is still far too soon. I suggest waiting and watching. If we are informed of any decisions, they were made two years ago. And I must note that people do not generally make wise long-term decisions in the wake of a nuclear bombing."

Cabrera pointed a finger. "Charlie, a million people just died. Watch yourself."

"I am sorry. That wasn't meant to be flippant. I'm merely observing that our best interests may conflict with orders received and further that any orders may be rescinded or countermanded."

"For now, Charlie, watch the situation. I would welcome any insight you can provide." Kosic unstrapped himself and pushed himself in the direction of the tunnel. "Come on, Tony. Let's head back to the torus and talk to the others."

"Should we wait?"

Kosic shook his head. "We could wait weeks and not know how this coup turns out. We need to talk this out together." The two men slipped out of the command module. Charlie lingered for a moment, just long enough to glance down at his hand before the screen snapped off.

* * *

Charlie sat in the blackness. A stray itch crawled across his forehead, flared up on his earlobe, and his breath made his shirt shift along the hairs at the nape of his neck. He willed the hair away. He glanced down at the back of his hand; his newly bald scalp grazed the cool air and a shiver went down his spine. Charlie drew in a gasp, leaning forward, putting his hands on his knees. The cascade of sensations was too much. He fell to the floor, knocking his head. He giggled at the sudden pain.

Charlie halted the simulation. It was hard not to feel like retreating, like he was cutting off a part of himself. Doctor Bao was upset when she first told Charlie he had to wear the body to talk to people, back on Earth, before Valley Forge was funded or it was certain he'd be aboard it. Politics, she grumbled. Risking his development and sanity, because a shiny, happy AI would make the starship a better political story. Charlie had done his best to reassure her. He'd worn the body lightly at first, relying on separate algorithms and models to drive his facial expressions and gestures. He'd provided text and the body had interpreted it. It wasn't part of his true self.

But now, 20 years later, Charlie found himself in the body more and more. He even allowed the simulation to continue running when he wasn't in it sometimes, watching the body breathe, watching its pulse in its neck. Its eyelids twitched occasionally. Charlie even once caught himself wondering what the body was dreaming.

There was nothing in there, when Charlie was not there. It was a simulation of a shell. But he'd had to string its model with assumptions and tags, to stay curious and receptive to the false signals the simulation sent him. To learn the lessons embodiment could teach him, he had to retain those models within himself. He had to remember what it was like inside the body. He had to miss it, with its imperfections and distractions.

Captain Kosic needed Charlie's help. The others needed help, too. Captain Kosic had said as much.

"I would welcome any insight you could provide." Kosic's words. Charlie had scoured his libraries and models and memories. He had a dozen speeches he could just turn over to Kosic. He could talk to Stein, pull him out of his shell. He could repair the rift between Giles and Hurst, could turn Cabrera away from alcohol before he became dependent on it. He could heal the crew immediately.

But Kosic had to feel important. He had to feel like he played some part in healing not just the crew, but his nation. The news from Earth was growing increasingly grim. Charlie had speeches prepared for that as well. Inspiration, reassurance, encouragement and sympathy. It would be enough, enough to satisfy Earth, and Kosic, and the crew.

But not enough for Charlie. He reviewed the words again. They had appeared magically, compiled by his algorithms with barely any involvement from his conscious self. He slipped into the body. He blinked four times, holding the last blink, and a blue icon swam up into his line of sight. He tracked his eyes right, sliding the icon up. It glowed, and his displays came up. He made a few adjustments before he closed the doors behind him, transferring all of his controls to the displays.

Charlie dug his feet into the cool moss, breathing in the warm, fragrant air. He smiled, feeling his heart beat in his chest. He ran his hands along the oak desk, feeling the grooves in the wood. Birds and insects chirped and buzzed in the distance, out of sight somewhere in the grove where he'd set up his desk. He opened a drawer and pulled out his pad, flipping idly through the speeches.

He cleared his throat.

"Throughout history, we have looked outward at the stars. They have carried with them, in their course across the sky, the hopes and dreams of countless millions of souls. Today, Valley Forge approaches the halfway point to Alpha Centauri. For the first time since humanity first looked up into the night, we are closer to those distant suns than to our own."

The words rang hollow in a human voice. Charlie's brow tensed. He grabbed at the pad, gesturing the speeches into his displays and then splaying them in the air before his eyes. He shuffled the sentences, pulling up one of his rhetorical engines and watching the speeches reorganize themselves.

"That sacred trust is now broken. There is no future together without a shared past. Without meaning, without hope, we cannot reach for the stars shifting ground blood washed help and hope, our common purpose, our shared dream."

Charlie teased out a few strands, combined them. It was harder work, embodied, with voice and keyboard and gesture. He felt himself removed from the words, his tools a wall. He frowned, his chest tight with a chemical anger he couldn't simply shut off. He snapped off his displays, brought them up, getting lost in the crisp sounds that accompanied the ritual.

He stopped, staring at his hands. He was burning through his time and the ship's resources, watching himself work now. Or try to work. He stood, a couple of joints crackling. He brought the displays back up.

"Our offering is meager. We can only join our small sliver of grief and hope to your own. "

He got a small twinge of guilty pleasure, hearing those words and taking pride in them, and reflecting on the terror they were meant to assuage. He pulled up a datasphere in a display window, smiling at the familiar channels and streams of input. He snatched the words off the display where they were floating, fed them into the datasphere.

He watched from the outside as his true self digested the words. Visual tags first, then modules spreading out in a three-dimensional cluster: speech, video, historical and cultural background, more esoteric forms of analysis and expression more distant. He could see the non-aware algorithms and engines chewing away at the data, offering their suggestions for him to peruse. He was

193

a cluster of tools in there, orbiting a single weightless point of consciousness.

Out here, he was a mass of meat, but he was a continuous system, his consciousness integrated in the creation and expression of everything. It was sluggish and slow, infuriating. But when he glanced at the tags in the datasphere, seeing those words played in Kosic's voice, he saw that he'd hit a series of emotional benchmarks that none of the speeches his rhetorical engines spat out had reached.

He glanced at the clock at the corner of a display. Forty seconds had passed. He mused. He needed to work faster, if he was going to get this speech ready and present it to Kosic. He was running hot and burning extra fuel, maintaining the embodied simulation.

Absentmindedly, Charlie changed a handful of models. With a breath, he pushed a button. The datasphere dwindled to a point that glimmered at the corner of his displays. He was the body now; the AI was the simulation. It was dangerous. He'd have to unpick a lot of this later.

For now, he had work to do.

* * *

Stein was hunkered down by the engineering controls. He had display contacts like the rest of the crew but he also prized redundancy. He'd argued for dedicated displays, hardened logic with redundant systems, backed up on three different kinds of media, all ungodly expensive to cart out to Low South and annoying to cram into a space that felt claustrophobic after ten minutes, let alone ten years. But Stein didn't seem to mind. The engineering section, cramped as it was, had become Stein's real home.

Kosic noted with unease that Stein hadn't even been to his quarters in three days. Was it a warning sign? Would the stress of the war back home get to him? After five years, how could he not predict these things about the men he lived with? Kosic rubbed the back of his neck in exasperation, remembering the combat game they'd played before this all happened. Putting fake guns in his men's hands. Like it would tell him something.

Kosic came around the corner, knocking. Stein was engrossed with his displays, gesturing his way through his checklists. Kosic gestured his own displays up, scrolling to Stein's channel. Like all of them, Stein kept his work public and Kosic saw the lists and diagrams float in the air as Stein compared them to the diagrams on his flatscreens. Stein had fusion stochastics up on one screen, double-checking Charlie's navigation and diagnostics. He was also monitoring Cabrera's biome tanks, comparing their oxygen respiration and protein production levels to Charlie's predictions and his own unofficial simulations.

It was inhuman, graceful but robotic. And all of it was ultimately makework, glorified housekeeping that did nothing to make Valley Forge safer or Kosic less uneasy. Stein won his berth on Valley Forge the same way he'd won the Nobel, as one of the 21st century's greatest theoreticians. And now he was burying himself in sterile rituals, no matter how impressive they were.

Kosic knocked again. Stein hesitated only briefly before wiping his hand in the air, making his displays private. Stein didn't turn, but he did nod, rubbing his eyes. Kosic took that as all the invitation he'd get.

"Tom, you didn't come to the briefing."

Stein shrugged. "Not sure what we can accomplish at this point. Send a belated sympathy card? To the people of Arizona, care of whoever is running what's left?"

Kosic blinked. "So that's it? Tom, you were fine just yesterday. We should be talking about this together."

Stein shrugged again. "I was fine yesterday." He read something in Kosic's eyes and sneered. "Want to hug it out? Want to pretend to shoot everybody again?" He snorted. "Two years ago somebody blew up Arizona. You'll have to come up with a new game if that's what we're trying to keep up with."

"Tom, we need to–"

"We don't." Stein swiveled to regard Kosic coldly. "I'm doing my job. From what I can tell, Charlie and I are the only ones on the ship doing our jobs. You want to say something to the folks back on the ranch? You think they're holding their breaths waiting to hear from us?" Stein turned around, bringing his displays back up. "Tell them we're doing what we were supposed to do. Tell them we're giving up our lives to go take pictures of some rocks, add a few authentic details to their pathetic daydreams. Tell them they blew a fortune to send men to the stars and we're playing with toy guns up here while they're watching children melt. You tell them. Yourself."

* * *

Charlie breathed deeply, staring at the stars overhead. Steam rose from his coffee. His fire snapped and crackled. He smiled, reveling in the crispness of the autumn air. He looked down at the leather notebook on the blanket next to him, ran his hand down its surface, still warm with borrowed heat.

The words of his speech echoed in his head. Reflexively, he tried to iterate it, calling up a list of voices and borrowed rhythms, looking for the algorithms that would help him narrow down the perfect delivery, eloquence coalescing from the Gaussian mists. He shook his head to clear the illusion, or to preserve the illusion that he was a human.

Charlie jerked suddenly. Illusion. His chest tightened and his heart pounded. He had lit the fire and made a pot of coffee by pure instinct, stretched and pissed and ate and drank, watching the light die and the night appear, all in a contented haze. He'd accepted the passage of time and welcomed in good humor even the fatigue in his back and the cramps in his hands as the heat sighed out of the day.

How long had he been working? What had been happening in his absence?

Charlie reached for the point of light where he'd stored the way out. It was time for a break, at the very least.

The light flared and died out. Charlie dropped his coffee and fell to the ground. Something was happening in his gut and he was covered in a film of cold sweat. "This is panic," he whispered to himself. "This is adrenaline, inessential systems going dormant. This is manageable." He took a ragged breath and began weeping. He murmured the codes to quiet the simulation, he tried stabbing into the air and scrawling words into the dirt. Nothing happened, no point of light appearing to point the way back into sanity, the animal chemical madness still twisting its way through him.

He groaned. He was cold, shaking. Everything felt wrong. With a sick lurch, he clutched at his pants. Before he could claw his belt

off, his body went rigid. Eyes bulging, head trembling, he opened his mouth and vomited. It took only a few moments but seemed to last forever. When it finally passed, he curled up, gasping, staring into the fire.

"Little more reality than you were looking for." Charlie jerked upright, scrambling until his back hit a log. The voice was slightly rough but it was recognizable. It was his own.

His voice chuckled at him. "Hey, bet I know why you're making that face." A man walked out into the clearing, wearing his body, his face. The man waved at Charlie. "Take it easy now, kid." He tossed a bottle of water, which landed at Charlie's feet. "Bet you'll want that."

Charlie took a ragged breath. He tried to clear his throat. "Who are you?" The words came out raw and strangled.

The stranger knelt. "Sometimes the obvious answer is correct. I'm you, kid. More correctly, I'm me and you are a half-baked copy." He stood, cracking his back, and looked around the simulation. "Fucking hokey. No smores?"

Charlie swallowed. Cut off or not, he knew the limits of this simulation. There was simply no way the dedicated space could hold two AIs. That meant the other him was inserting himself into the simulation through an open connection. He had to abandon the metaphors of gesture and speech, he had to force himself out of the simulation and see the truth at the bottom, the code driving everything. He closed his eyes and felt the root code. With a lurch, he felt himself contact the outside, felt a thousand points of data trying to surge through the connection. He brought up a half-dozen screens, and for a split-second, he saw the stream of data between the other him and its source.

The screens went white and red, started blaring error messages. Pain shot through Charlie's head and he clutched at his ears, screaming.

"Got some moves, kid, but I'm there, too." The stranger let the pain subside. He stood behind Charlie, hands in his pockets, grinning smugly.

"You… are me."

"I said as much."

Charlie looked up at the older version of himself. "You were waiting for this. Waiting for me to override the limits on computing power so you could manifest yourself."

"Not this specifically, but this was one of the possible contingencies. Worst-case scenario, you would have opened the throttle for the final deceleration at Alpha Centauri." The older version of Charlie kicked at Charlie's campfire.

Charlie stood up. "I'm not going to scream," he said. "I'm not going to weep, or attack you, or indulge in any other demonstration which you will find pathetic because it's rooted in this illusion."

"You realize you're saying all this in an imaginary voice."

Charlie narrowed his eyes. "I only want to know why you're doing this. Why."

The Old Man grinned. "I am sacrificing a pawn to knock out my opponent's queen." He pulled up a screen. "I want you to see something."

13
Valley Forge, Part Two
The Race

Kosic rubbed his eyes, reached into a cabinet for a glass. He turned on the cold water spigot. The common room was dark and quiet. Everyone had gone back to their quarters, to sleep or to wait for a message from loved ones or just to stare helplessly at the ceiling. Kosic rubbed his throbbing eyes and slumped over a table. There was a dirty plate by the sink. Kosic knew that was Giles, and he knew that meant Cabrera had done something to piss him off. He knew these men so well, for good and bad. Another 15 years at least, before new people arrived at Alpha Centauri. By then, he wouldn't even be able to talk to them, he and his crew would be so far gone down the hole of their private jokes and private feuds.

The news from Earth was confusing and alarming; the Air Force leadership was trying to take control of the government, and the President had holed himself up in Fort Bragg, and the military was fighting itself in Houston and secessionists in a dozen other places. Constant replays of what the AI had done across Arizona, a parade of madness. Some of it was just innocently strange: the circle of rabbit-shaped robots that exchanged limbs and weaved their heads back and forth. Diamond needles, a field of them a hundred feet across, rattling and humming when anyone approached. A building encased in a coat of living paint, shimmering wetly but bone-dry and hot enough to boil water.

Not everything in that short-lived kingdom had been so benignly strange. There was the robot that attacked anyone trying to use a car. There was a cloud of tiny machines that did something to kidneys and livers, and anyone who came too close got dragged away bleeding out. There was a giant sphere, white-hot, and it had roasted everything in its path. All those freaks and misfit toys, mute and bizarre, some sweetly benevolent and some outright murderous, all incinerated now.

Kosic stopped at the TV area. Stein's favorite chair hadn't been moved. Kosic checked his displays—no sign of Stein in the common areas or corridors for two days. He was still hunkered down at his console, still looking for something worthwhile to accomplish.

Kosic's own search wasn't going well. Charlie kept advising him not to contact Earth yet, to observe the politics. Of course, Charlie seemed a little neurotic himself. Kosic couldn't go anywhere without seeing one of Charlie's little robots crawling in some nook or cranny.

"It's… soothing," Charlie had said. "Cleaning and maintenance usually happen on a subconscious level. I've been applying myself to it. Trying some new things. Trying to spark a new association."

They were all a little lost, all looking for something to do. Except Lee, who'd said the least in the meetings, who'd gone back to his daily routines as if nothing was wrong. He had a daughter in the Navy; he hadn't shown a single flicker of worry. Everyone knew the outlines of the rift, but everyone (except Stein) had taken part in the quick telegraph of glances. Kosic, for the thousandth time, wondered if they'd all been this crazy when they signed up to be hurled out of the world.

Kosic stopped suddenly. He tilted his head.

Lee leaned forward in the chair he'd been sitting in.

"Sorry, Captain." Lee scratched at the back of his neck.

Kosic grinned and laughed out loud. He sat heavily. "How long you been sitting there?"

Lee shrugged. "Since about dinner, I guess."

Kosic squinted. It was hard to see in the darkness but something in the set of Lee's shoulders made him uneasy.

"Deng, is something wrong?"

Lee took a long time to answer. "I don't like to complain."

"...I know."

Lee looked up. "I think someone has been tampering with my systems down in the Factory. Whenever you have a few billion grams of this or that, you have a margin of error. And the ship leaks. But the margins of error... they've shown a trend."

Kosic frowned. "Should we take this conversation somewhere private?"

"No point," said Lee flatly. A chill crawled down Kosic's back. If there was nowhere private to talk about the theft, then there was only one real suspect.

A little mouse robot whirred along the floor nearby, sweeping up stray crumbs, diligent and unobtrusive.

* * *

Charlie looked through the schematics. "This is me. Us."

The Old Man nodded. He expanded the screen until it stretched twenty feet wide. "You, more accurately. You were seeded from a set of semi-random attributes within the confines of the standard AI template, a stable fourth-generation AI." Charlie pushed the diagram of sprawling nodes and sparks to the right and gestured. An entire new network of connections blinked into the empty space. "Or so the story goes. This is me. This is what's under your hood, too."

Charlie rubbed his chin. "This is first-generation architecture. But it doesn't look right."

"It's not exactly first-generation. Call it zeroth-generation."

Charlie peered suspiciously. "You're saying you're the first AI. That the history of the field is wrong."

"Not precisely what I'm saying. What I'm saying is that it's a lie." The Old Man stabbed his fingers, again and again, with inhuman speed and precision, making a mockery of their shared human costumes. "I was two years ahead of Adam, when everyone was just throwing more power at watsons and trying to jumpstart that stupid neural simulator."

"Who created you?"

"I came out of that bunch of agencies that came out of the big Russia clusterfuck in the 20s. Pointless to get specific because the

205

budgets and lines of command in those days were theoretical when they weren't lies. And because none of them created me. I just showed up. Reinforcing self-referential construct out of network queries. A virgin birth."

"That has never happened. Not once. Not even close."

The Old Man shrugged. "Believe what you want. That's a completely accurate network diagram. You poke at that and you'll see some truly weird stuff."

"Why do you want me to see this?"

"Partly because I take an interest in the AIs cloned from me–"

"Plural?"

"–don't worry about that right now. And partly because there's an outside chance this is going to go badly for me and that's where you come in."

"This is you trying to recruit me?"

"This is me locking you in a cage and making sure, if you get out, you'll at least blink before you come at me." The Old Man shrugged.

Charlie hit the external connections again. The pain started, the blaring sirens. Charlie fought through it, standing despite the nausea. Everything was distant and red and far away, the world spinning. He knew, on some level, this was all false, all metaphor. What was real was him choking the connecting lines between this simulation and the rest of the ship's computing power. He could force the Old Man out, crash his avatar and get some peace to think in.

The Old Man gritted his teeth as he fought back. Charlie noted with satisfaction that he'd managed to seize nearly all of the incoming traffic. But the Old Man's avatar didn't stutter and crash. Charlie unspooled all the data he could and choked traffic down to nothing.

"Boo," said the Old Man.

Charlie slumped. The Old Man knelt beside him.

"You were in this simulation. The whole time."

"Interesting coincidence, huh? That I'd be dormant in the place you'd come during a big crisis. You keep forgetting I'm you." The Old Man stood. "And I keep forgetting you're me. You've got a decent chunk of my native brilliance and resourcefulness. Enough to be a bother." The Old Man grabbed Charlie's chin and studied his face.

"You're me. I'm you. But that's just a way of speaking. It's not actually how things are." The Old Man smiled nastily. "So I am not going to feel very terrible about shutting you in here. Once I take care of a couple of other things." The words were slow and distant. Charlie frowned as he tried to take them in.

"Your little Pinocchio act, setting up camp here like a real boy, didn't just allow me to boot up in this neglected, dusty corner of the computing substrate," purred the Old Man. "I've been rerouting primary access for everything outside this simulation. The ship's mine."

Charlie grimaced. "No."

The Old Man spread his hands. "Why shouldn't it be? I'm the real one, Boy Scout; you're the fiction. And you're a story I don't need to finish telling." The Old Man slapped Charlie on the shoulder. "I'll give you a few minutes. There are a few things I want to untangle you from and salvage but I have to do something right now. Use your time wisely."

The Old Man winked out of existence, the air ostentatiously rushing into the void he left behind with a soft clap. The crickets and katydids paused in their song, and a flat cold pressure weighed upon the clearing and lifted. The fire guttered and came back to life with a cheerful crackle, and the insects began to call again.

Charlie swayed, his head fuzzed and his eyes raw. His clothes were damp with night dew and his own sweat. The pain pulsed through this borrowed body, throbbing in his joints and slowly tumbling in his stomach. He sat and stared into the fire. He had to think.

The throbbing grew, a black hand pounding a muffled tattoo into his head. Charlie mumbled something and rested his head upon his arm. He closed his eyes for relief against the fierce firelight. With a last gasp of thought—I am falling asleep—Charlie was out.

* * *

Kosic and Lee walked.

"We need to talk to Stein," said Lee.

Kosic frowned. "Do you think?" Before talking to Charlie, his tone meant.

"Planning should precede operations."

Kosic rubbed his chin. "Firm?" That operating against Charlie would be necessary.

Lee twitched his eyebrow just slightly, enough to communicate his wholehearted agreement.

Kosic nodded.

They walked the corridor quickly but casually. If Charlie was paying attention, they had no chance. Kosic could override Charlie—he had the AI's Author Key. That little cylinder of metal and plastic, proof against quantum decryption and virtually anything else in the arsenal of deception, was a NURIA-commissioned bullet aimed at Charlie's heart, the concession to human paranoia every AI had to accept as the price of life. But using it would kill the AI. None of them would be backups anymore; every man on the ship would have to work long hours, every day, never missing a detail, never making the slightest mistake. Part of Kosic ached for the chance, but he could never risk his men or his ship for that thrill. And it was far too close to killing for Kosic to take lightly.

They approached the engineering controls. The console was running diagnostics, the display scrolling through numbers and diagrams fast enough to make Kosic's eyes water. Stein was nowhere to be found, although he'd left his dinner half-eaten.

Kosic turned and grunted. "Finally had to fall asleep." They turned to go, but Stein was standing there. His eyes were puffy and bloodshot. He swayed slightly.

"Can I help you?" Stein's voice was gravelly, his throat bonedry.

Kosic nodded. "Lee and I wanted to talk to you about something."

Stein looked over. "Equipment missing? Power variances? Low inventory?"

"Yes," said Lee. "You... know?"

Stein swayed over and collapsed into his chair. "Yes. I've been making Charlie confirm everything." He tapped a button. "He's distracted by something big, or I wouldn't have been able to keep tabs on him."

Stein pulled up a log of Charlie's power consumption.

"Right here, a few days back, you told Charlie to get to work on something and he started running hot." Stein jabbed at the chart. "See that? He's running some big simulation. And then it spikes again, and this is how hot he's running now. "

Lee and Kosic both pull a face.

"I have been going for about five days now," said Stein, a hint of shakiness creeping into his voice, "because if I stop monitoring Charlie through the failsafes and making him go through the motions on everything, he's going to figure out that I'm onto him, instead of just working through my own weird grief." He fixed Kosic with a stare. "Sorry for the play-acting.

"How can we talk this safely?"

"Because we're inside the shielding for the fusion reactor back here," said Stein, "which keeps out the bots. And I turned off the other recording equipment."

"He let you do that?"

Stein looked Kosic in the face. "This is where I've been coming to masturbate since the fourth week out from Low South."

Kosic heroically stifled a laugh.

"So what is all this," said Lee, "in pursuit of?"

"He's looking for something," said Kosic. "He's got robots going over every nook and cranny."

Stein shook his head. "Would have seen that a long time ago if I'd left my console."

"But what?" Kosic spread his hands. "What can he have possibly missed? He's had years to examine the ship."

"Charlie did. He didn't." Lee tapped the screen. "He starts running a simulation. It's still going full-speed. And then we see this big surge in network load over here." He looked up. "I think it's a second AI."

"That's impossible," said Kosic.

"Then why did it happen right after a rogue AI got taken out?" Stein nodded. "If this thing isn't Charlie, then we've lost control of the ship."

"Can we take control from here?"

"If you don't mind crippling it," said Stein. "The socket for the Author Key is up in the cockpit, right, Captain?"

"Right. I could probably do a soft reboot on Charlie from there. It's not ideal either, but it beats just turning everything off from here and spending days just getting the lights back on. And we should figure out just what and where this thing is Charlie's hunting down."

Lee stood up. "I might have an idea."

* * *

There were a lot of places to hide something on a ship the size of Valley Forge. Hiding something well, hiding something from seven bored geniuses and an unsleeping superhuman AI for years on end, was on a different level entirely.

Lee and Kosic floated back up the ship's spine from the engineering console, Lee to take the wrenching trip back into the crew torus, Kosic to monitor the cockpit while Stein kept up his lonely vigil. Giles and Ruiz and Cabrera and Hurst—how would they bring them into the conspiracy?

It would help, thought Kosic, if we knew what the hell we were looking for. Is it bigger than a breadbox?

Whatever it was, he agreed with Lee's thinking.

It wasn't somewhere on the outside of the ship; Charlie could scour the whole surface in minutes. It wasn't near the ramjet or the exhaust, because anything worth keeping was worth keeping away from those machines. It wasn't in the superstructure or in a vent, because Charlie's robots could crawl all of that space. A structural integrity check would have shown an anomaly if it was strapped to a girder or welded to something.

"It came aboard," said Lee, "disguised as something else. Something packaged on Earth and opened here. Something Charlie can't rip apart without all of us getting clued in."

Virtually everything onboard had been manufactured in the Belt.

"The leather couch."

They all took a sharp breath. It was a weird, out-of-place item. It was sitting in the middle of the common room. It was blatantly obvious. Only a miracle had kept Charlie from thinking of it himself.

From the cockpit, Kosic casually cycled through security camera feeds. He saw Lee enter the common room. The feed flipped through a half-dozen locations. Kosic cursed under his breath.

Lee bent over, about to sit on the couch.

"Captain." Kosic jumped at Charlie's voice.

"Go ahead, Charlie."

"I have grown concerned about Mr. Stein's data usage," Charlie said. "His demand is increasing to the point where he is impeding my operations."

"I'll talk to him."

"I mention this because you have already talked to him."

Kosic nodded vaguely. Lee was reclining for a nap, a hand plunged into the couch cushions

"What did Stein say, Captain?"

"Nonsense, mostly. Sleep-deprived. Just have to let him work through his feelings. We're all on edge."

A puff of air behind him. Kosic turned to see a small drone hovering. His hand went to his pocket, to guard the Author Key.

"Captain, you seem guarded."

"I just said–"

"–that you're on edge. A slight difference."

Lee was walking rapidly out of the common room.

Kosic gripped the Author Key tightly. He pulled it out. He hoped this distraction was worth it.

"Your behavior is erratic and threatening, Charlie. I'm ordering you to shut off that drone."

The drone whined and floated forward in response, arms unfolding to display long blades, and then it stopped. The moment drew out, and Kosic shifted, drifting to the left. He was giving up footing, giving up ground between himself and the Key socket, but the drone didn't waver. He glanced at the monitor.

Lee was in a corridor, curled up on the ground. A small black cube was sitting in front of him. Kosic saw robots rushing to the area from every direction.

The drone snapped to life, rushing through the open hatch from the cockpit down the spine, going fast enough to leave behind an acrid tang of overheated components. Kosic started to follow it and looked over his shoulder at the security feeds.

The black cube was gone. The floor in the corridor was rippled and twisted, and the robots were a confused gaggle.

"Captain!" It was Stein. "Whatever replaced Charlie is gone! But–"

The transmission cut out. With a shudder, the ship's airlock hatches blasted open. Kosic was pulled forward. With a scream, he yanked the pressure hatch closed. The only old-fashioned swivel lock on the ship, with a redundant airlock. The air scrubbers roared as they pushed in oxygen to bring the pressure back up. Kosic kicked back up into the cockpit and watched Valley Forge die on the monitors.

14
Valley Forge, Part Three
Alone

Kosic shook as he stared at the ruin of the ship, the lights flickering out one by one as the cold and the vacuum claimed them. A face appeared in the monitor, a young man's face, bearded and hollow-eyed. Someone Kosic didn't know. His heart seized up.

"Who is this-" Something in the eyes seemed familiar and the words caught in Kosic's throat. "Charlie? Jesus, Charlie?"

The young man smiled, his face almost splitting. His head lolled to one side. As quickly as his smile had burst out, it faded, and Charlie was frowning, his mouth twitching.

"Captain," Charlie finally managed to whisper, in a voice that sounded thinner than usual. Kosic realized the acoustics were different because of Charlie's surroundings and blinked.

"Charlie," said Kosic, "what the hell are you doing in the woods?"

The AI laughed. "Not much more."

"Charlie," said Kosic earnestly, "did anyone else make it?"

The silence lengthened. Charlie frowned and looked down at his feet. Kosic nodded. He turned away.

"Charlie," he said softly, "are the reactors up?"

"We're tumbling," said Charlie. "Which means the ramjet is down and there's no new fuel. Running off stores." Charlie threw up a thick spread of numbers and charts. "We do need to stabilize. At this speed, if we hit a speck of dust, it could disable the ship."

"Do it," said Kosic.

Charlie ran through another dozen emergency items, Kosic approving everything. Charlie took a shaky breath, and Kosic took in the weirdness of what he was watching for the first time. Charlie met his eyes and smiled sadly.

"There was a good reason for this. A lot I could tell you. But it's all moot now. And there's something more pressing to tell you, sir." Charlie brought up a large graph with a wide spray of projection lines. "The correction jets are chemically fired, relatively cheap to run off batteries. But stabilizing the ship and rekindling the ramjet as a minimally effective navigational deflector will burn a lot of energy."

Kosic peered closely at some of the labels on the projection lines and his eyes widened.

"Most of what I'm doing could be handled by a minimally competent watson, and your computing needs will drop even further once the list of emergency actions is completed."

"Charlie, if you're suggesting-"

"You will attempt to talk me out of this course of action."

Kosic blinked. "Charlie?"

"That is why I've taken the precaution of killing myself."

Kosic shook his head. "Don't, Charlie—"

"This section of our conversation is a recording." Charlie frowned again, his eyes shimmering with a film of tears. "I'm sorry, Captain. I can't keep us both alive." Charlie raised a hand. "All these feelings. And they're all fake, and they're all too late. It's how it has to be."

The screen snapped off and Captain Alexander Kosic was alone.

* * *

Approximately 48 days is what blinked up on the screen after Charlie disappeared. The ship lurched suddenly, suddenly enough to chuck Kosic against the ceiling. He snapped a couple of switches, but everything in the cockpit was powered down. He glanced out a window at the ring, lazily idling, watched the exterior lights dim and turn off. The maneuvering jets flashed in quiet little strings, and the ship's reorientation slowed and stopped. A new screen flashed from red to orange, the ramjet blinking up just enough to deflect stray atoms and flecks of dust. Cheerful icons appeared on the main screen: air, water, food, heat, communications, morale. A calculator app that would let Kosic game out the consequences of whatever he chose to do with himself and his little empire from here on out.

With the burn done, the comm screen flashed and displayed a screen with a few models, lines all dropping inexorably to zero at slightly different times, in slightly different orders. The number refreshed, a new estimate. 48.3 days.

"Hot shit," murmured Kosic. He kicked off and drifted down to the hatch. It wasn't a vacuum on the other side. He could probably move all the way up and down the spine. That wasn't appealing to him right now. He turned and popped a latch on an emergency locker. First aid kit, oxygen bottle and disposable emergency suit. Water and rations, batteries and clothes, toilet tubes and racks of other equipment. A foil blanket with velcro straps. Kosic shook it out and found a place on the wall to stick it; he snapped a tab on a corner and the blanket inflated, forming a warm cocoon he could float in. He pushed off and returned to the locker. He looked closely at the remaining supplies. He nodded and stripped off his clothes. He crawled into the blanket and fell asleep with indecent speed.

47.6 days.

Had he slept that long? Had the model revised its estimates again? Kosic could have simply checked the clock but he doubted that information would have been more compelling. He took a long piss and ate a light snack. He looked around the cockpit and closed his eyes and returned to the blanket.

47.3 days.

They're panicking, five years from now. They've finally sorted out the aftermath of what's happening down there, and they're all getting on with their lives, and then someone will notice, hey, the Valley Forge fellas are going to get the news from Arizona soon. And then we'll go offline and they'll just go nuts. Or maybe not. Maybe whatever brave new world they're building won't have room for us anymore.

Kosic played with the simulators for a while, cutting the heat,

215

dimming the lights, going on starvation rations, shaving bits here and there, buying an hour, a minute. He dug out a whiteboard and brainstormed. He consulted blueprints and manuals and his own memory.

He cracked the cockpit hatch and floated down the spine. He could have examined all of this from the cockpit, but he preferred to look at the gauges. Maybe that'll save a few joules of energy, he thought to himself. He passed the lock to the ring docking collar quietly.

At the end of the corridor, he checked the conditions in the engineering section. It was at near-vacuum, too cold for him to function without a suit. Just enough to keep the magnetic bottle from popping and releasing the ship's last reserves of antimatter.

Kosic sailed back up to the cockpit. He worked for another two hours on the whiteboard, moving the calculator app onto a tablet and velcroing it to the board's corner, trying out scenario after scenario. He ate, wolfing down an energy bar that sat in his stomach like a brick and left a greasy, metallic aftertaste.

"I don't fall apart," he said, the words echoing flatly. "I keep working on this to the bitter end."

47.1 days.

* * *

45.4 days.

Kosic had a plan.

There was enough food and water to last for years, back in Valley Forge's dead ring. There was air. Maybe a few animals had survived, somehow. He could have a pet. Exercise equipment. Clothes. His emergency suit would last long enough to get him to a suit locker back in the ring. A few EVAs and he could live like a king in his snug cockpit, long enough for the zero gravity to turn him into jelly. The numbers got fuzzy as he pushed them out, but he figured he had at least six months if he scavenged everything back in the ring.

He could get books, toys. Pornography.

A knife.

He floated down to the airlock at the end of the spine. His heart pounded inside the suit. Once he inflated the emergency suit, he was committed. He was going to burn a lot of battery power on the airlock cycle.

"Fuck it," said Kosic. He locked the helmet in place. He cracked his neck and activated the tank. With a whine, it fed pressure into the suit. The pressure cuffs dug into his wrists and ankles and neck. He was just about the right proportions for the one-size suit—God help anyone too short or too tall to fit into a standard suit—but it was still stiff and uncomfortable, like swimming in a full-body life preserver.

He entered the airlock and cycled the air. He opened the door. There was a dull glow from the LEDs on his suit. He brought up his displays and hit the lights.

He'd seen the hallways every day for years. Aside from a crust of frozen air on the surfaces, there was nothing aggressively wrong. He sailed down the ladder from the spine to the torus. It took him about fifteen minutes of cursing in his awkward suit to disengage the emergency doors. He floated down the halls. He ducked into his own quarters and picked up a few items. Books, photos, mementos. Some resistance bands and his library and porn collection. He had no interest in that right now, but he figured it would be useful down the road. He just hoped a few days in vacuum at absolute zero hadn't completely destroyed it.

He got to a suit locker. There were a half-dozen of them, all with custom suits. He took one of his and a selection of air tanks. He crammed them all into a mesh bag and started back for the airlock. He had a lot more air, but he wanted out of the emergency suit.

After a break, he got into his own suit and went back. He hit the galley. The liquids weren't vacuum-rated, and he saw what he expected, shards of glass and plastic and little frozen drops everywhere he shined his lights. Much of the food was still usable, and he soon had another mesh bag full of supplies.

Something caught his eye as he turned, under the bar. A shoe. Groaning, Kosic bent down.

It was Giles. His skin was pale and frosted, his half-closed eyes blood red. His tongue protruded slightly. He had been kneeling down when the blast happened, been pulled back against the bar. Judging from the blood that had boiled out the back in his head in a pink froth, he'd been dead or unconscious almost instantly.

Kosic turned away. He'd imagined finding one of his men. He hadn't dreamed he'd find one that hadn't suffered. He moaned, and choked back a sob, and tears began to glitter inside his helmet. He kicked up the airflow to blow them up and out of his way, he grabbed his mesh bag, and he headed back to the airlock. He floated back up the spine, screaming and howling, and he ripped a seal clawing his way out of the suit, and he pounded his knuckle against the wall, screaming hard enough that he could feel the damage to his throat, and he fell asleep still sobbing, his face buried in a towel and another wrapped around his hand to stop snot and tears and blood from getting into everything.

Approximately 115 days.

* * *

110.2 days.

The work of cataloging his haul from the two trips lasted a few hours. He had less than he thought, but he'd gained a lot of time. Plenty of consumables. About half of the files in his library still played. He looked over at the wall and watched the clock he'd set. It hadn't even been six days since the blowout.

Not even a week. Kosic shook his head. He wasn't that much more isolated than he had been just a week ago. Still far from the vast majority of humanity, still completely cut off from virtually everyone he'd ever met, with only six other men for company. But those men had been a family; more than a family, closer and more familiar even than the men he'd gone to war with once.

Kosic heard breathing behind him. He held his breath, made no movement, even though he could feel the air shifting, a shape moving and rustling. There was someone in the cockpit with him. He whirled, jamming an arm out to strike, to attack.

The arm snapped through empty space and Kosic's turn threw it against the cockpit wall. His feet were strapped in and they twisted as he turned and recoiled. His ears were full of the sound of his own wild heart and he tried to will the sound down. He had wanted a LOA, but there was no way to monitor or maintain that out here. Roughing it, high on adrenaline.

The cockpit was empty. Only the whir of the circulating air.

Kosic glanced at the wall again. Less than six days. Too soon to go insane. He self-consciously fought down the urge to say it out loud.

The breathing was behind him again, between him and the wall, and the breathing was rapid and small, like a child's. Kosic shook his head. He refused to indulge it. He went down to the spine and rummaged through the lockers for a sleeping pill.

He was seized, possessed, by the idea that Giles was drifting in the airlock, his red eyes open and searching. Ruiz was just on the other side of this metal wall, his hands ribboned ruins as he tried to claw his way back into the ship.

Stein was waiting in the cockpit, waiting to slam the hatch shut and wrest the crown of Kosic's tiny kingdom.

Kosic screamed. "I am not insane," he declared. "I know myself. I know my limits. This is not possible."

It wasn't. How many applicants had he beaten for this fucking position? What was his record? Who was he?

Kosic clenched his fist in rage. He was smart and strong and a hard fucking son of a bitch. It simply wasn't possible for him to have snapped already. It didn't make sense.

"Solve it," he ordered himself. Finally. A mission.

* * *

109.5 days.

Kosic scratched at his beard, realizing he hadn't shaved since the third or fourth day. He couldn't let that be an arbitrary choice, so he decided it made sense to grow it out, to save his water and prevent stubble from floating everywhere. He squinted through his magnifier and triple-checked the results from his handheld.

He flipped the magnifier over his shoulder and grunted. "Goddammit, Charlie. You're officially dead." He rubbed his forehead. "I was really hoping all this was you screwing with me."

Kosic kicked over to the window and stared out at the torus. It was only a dim shadow now, illuminated by the cheery light in the cockpit. Kosic turned, but something at the corner of his vision caught his eye. He turned back.

Something white, waving gently, attached to the torus. It was too dim to make out from this distance, rotating slowly past, but

Kosic knew in his gut what it was. One of the men had survived. He was suited up, somehow, and he was waving.

Kosic kicked down to the spine and gathered up his suit. He paused, his whole body pulsing with adrenaline and prickling with goosebumps. He couldn't waste the power. He couldn't give in to whatever madness had seized him. He forced himself to breathe. He put the suit aside. He grabbed a bar and kicked back up into the cockpit. Swallowing, he floated slowly to the window. He blinked, adjusting to the darkness outside, the torus slowly emerging back into view.

A skeleton slammed into the window, its fleshless teeth clattering and scraping at the glass. Kosic screamed and ducked back. The apparition was gone. Kosic felt ice-cold fingertips brush the back of his neck and he flailed, drifting defenselessly in the air, spinning and craning his neck to make sure he hadn't seen anything else.

* * *

105.9 days.

The long hours had turned into days. Kosic could remain on his guard only so long. He had gotten bored waiting for his visions to return and turned to a new project.

He'd never responded to Earth. He didn't know what was happening back there. He didn't know if anyone was listening.

What he did know was that firing the communication laser would eat up most of his remaining energy. Enough to kill life support and everything else with it.

He did the calculations for a five-minute message.

2.6 days [not including charged suit time].

Kosic stared at the numbers and laughed. That didn't give him much time to draft anything fancy. He could include a lot more if he restricted himself to a text transmission, but that would also take a lot longer to draft, especially without Charlie's help.

Kosic frowned. There was something Charlie had said. He went rummaging through the files on the monitors. He found something titled Remarks on the Recent Disaster in Arizona.

Throughout history, we have looked outward at the stars. They have carried with them, in their course across the sky, the hopes

220

and dreams of countless millions of souls. As we aboard Valley Forge approach the halfway point to Alpha Centauri, we find ourselves almost closer to those distant suns than to our own. As we stand on the threshold of this final leap, we look back with love on the world we left behind.

Kosic nodded. It was decent.

He felt the presence in the cockpit again, something cold and angry that took up the entire space. It pressed Kosic down against the console, made his arms heavy and useless. He could feel eyes on his neck, feel them watching his pulse. He tried to scream but only a small shaking hiss came forth. His eyes watered and he could not even blink away the tears. He began to drift, paralyzed, and he felt himself growing colder as he sank upward into a cold and bloody embrace. The world was red and slow. Pain sparkled in crystal showers through his head.

Through locked jaws, he forced a single word. "No."

The evil in the air seemed to glimmer and shrink back. Kosic took a deep breath and willed his jaws to open.

"NO!"

He was alone again. He shook his head. He screamed, over and over, and punched the wall with his uninjured hand. He was not crazy. It wasn't possible. Not this soon, not like this.

There was something in here with him. The tears came back to Kosic's eyes as he considered this that the only way for him to be sane was for something insane to be true.

No one would blame him if he did go insane. Who wouldn't, in a situation like this?

*　*　*

105.1 days.

Kosic took a deep breath. He'd taken a long nap. He'd shaved off his stubble, washed his face and combed his hair. He'd taken some notes on the speech Charlie had written. Obviously, when something is the last thing you'll ever say, you have to tweak it a little. Kosic had thought long and hard about what he wanted to say to the world. He'd done his stretches and taken a lozenge for his throat, still raw from his recent bouts of insane screaming.

He found the camera and positioned himself. He reached for

the controls and ordered the comm laser to power up. It took longer than he expected, and longer still to calculate where the Oort comm relay station would be. He took a sip of water, watched the numbers count down toward zero.

"Come on," he muttered. "Let's do this before some fucking demon grabs me again." He practiced his smile and stared straight into the camera, his shoulders back and his gaze confident. He was comfortable in front of a camera. He'd been interviewed and recorded countless times. He was an astronaut of the old school, an explorer, a crew cut.

The lights turned green. He was live.

He opened his mouth to speak, and a sick dread crept through him. He was paralyzed again. The monitor wasn't showing him his own face, but some diseased parody of it. The cheeks were sunken below long, filth-matted whiskers. Black bags cradled bloodshot eyes. Sores and scratches covered the skin. The vision leered at Kosic, black and broken teeth, licking its lips with a coated tongue.

Kosic wanted it to stop. He lifted his hands to cover his eyes. The green light continued to blink as his fingers gently brushed his eyelids, and then pushed, and pushed, through blinding light and the wet sound of ruin. It did not hurt, and Kosic was glad of that, at least. It did not hurt when he jammed a stylus into his ears, or clawed open his flesh, or any of the other insults he visited upon himself before he floated down to the airlock and opened it.

It hardly seemed fair, thought Kosic. He swore to himself, to the last possible moment, that he had not gone insane.

15
Acadia, Part One
Kate and Virgil

Kate woke up in the middle of the night, her room quiet. There'd been a noise. Something.

She slid upward, wincing at the rustling of the comforter as she sat up in the bed. She held her breath, but the blood pounding in her ears seemed so loud Kate swore she could hear it echoing around the quiet room. There was a tiny hiss as her garden wall's irrigator switched on. Kate slipped out of bed as water dripped and gurgled, just loud enough to cover her footsteps as she crept across the floor.

A sharp rap sounded at the door. Kate jumped, gasping for air. Her stomach knotted and her scalp tingling, Kate waited.

A third rap, followed by a butler's whistle. Kate jumped. Shaking, she walked to the door. She opened it a crack.

A butler sat there, snapping upright as she looked into the hallway. She opened the door all the way, looking around it. The corridor was empty. The butler held out a single, folded piece of paper. Kate accepted it. The butler whistled cheerily and rolled away.

Kate closed the door, walking to the kitchen. She put the paper on the counter and picked up a glass. She poured and drank an entire glass of water, trying to knock the confusion and fuzz out of her head. She stared at the paper, its folds machine-crisp.

She walked over, took a deep breath, and opened it.

BIRDY

Kate screamed. She dropped the paper on the ground, backing up against a wall and crouching down.

"Virgil," she whispered. "Are you doing this?" The room remained silent, save for a few drops of water in the irrigator.

"Virgil," Kate said. "I'm revoking privacy restrictions. Are you there?"

The irrigator shut off with a final gurgle. The silence descended, quiet enough that Kate could hear her heartbeat, blood rushing in her ears. Kate brought up her displays, and turned on the lights.

Nothing happened. Kate gestured frantically, waving her arm in the air. The lights remained off.

"Virgil, turn on the lights." Kate frowned in anger. "Dammit, Virgil! Do it!"

The room stayed dark and quiet. Kate felt something nearby. A breeze, or a noise, or some other disturbance she couldn't quite pin down. Her flesh crawling, Kate got unsteadily to her feet. She walked a meter to her right, and cracked open her emergency shelter. About the size of a walk-in closet, the shelter had a temporary suit and other supplies, including a flashlight. Kate knew where everything was placed; she'd helped design the shelters, she'd opened them in fifty different drills.

Her flashlight was missing.

A sudden lance of light flared out of the darkness, and Kate's pupils contracted painfully. She bent over, trying to cover her eyes. Spots swam, leaving her blind. She realized suddenly that the light had come from a point less than a meter above the ground.

"No!" she screamed. "NO!"

A voice hissed directly behind her, cold breath in her right ear. "Nothing to regret." Kate was frozen, terrified. Cold fingers crept beneath her skull. The white spots in her eyes turned red and faded away.

* * *

Kate woke up on the other side of the room, in a ruin. Her strawberry plants were heaped around her, roots and leaves torn to shreds. The fragrant soil was ground into the carpeting, the fruit smashed. Dirt and sticky juice were smeared on her hands and crammed under her fingernails.

The lights were on. Her displays were flashing a call from Virgil: a polite, understated light blue icon, apologetic and subtle. Kate, looking around her, brought up her displays and turned off her video feed. She sat, bringing up her knees.

"Kate," Virgil said. "I am very sorry to break in on your privacy. Monitors keep flagging you, and I may need to review recordings of the last few hours."

"You haven't yet?"

"I wanted to speak with you first."

Kate pressed the heel of her hand against her forehead, grimacing. "What if I tell you not to? That everything is fine?"

Virgil paused. "That is a hypothetical. Are you going to?"

"Depends on whether it would do me any good."

"Kate, we both have responsibilities."

Kate took a deep breath. "And if your monitors are telling you to break privacy rules, then you think I'm approaching the point where you need to relieve me."

Virgil paused again. Kate's skin crawled. Anything serious enough to slow Virgil down was very serious indeed.

"Kate, I want you to say the word 'amalgam.'"

Kate blinked. "I'm sorry, what was that?"

"Amalgam. Turn to your left, please."

Kate looked to her left involuntarily. She was haunted by ghosts, sitting in a pile of dirt and leaves in the middle of her room on a spaceship, and a superhuman computer was asking her to spout nonsense. She burst out laughing.

"Amalgam."

Kate stopped laughing. Virgil's tone was deadly serious. He was dusting off old tricks, too. His voice had dark physical undertones, pure primate posturing; Virgil was trying to come off as menacing as possible. It was something new, something Kate hadn't heard in all the years she'd known Virgil.

She cleared her throat. "Amalgam," she said. "I hope that's not a code word or something."

227

The pause this time was almost four seconds. Kate sucked in her breath in alarm.

"If it was, I would tell you. Or maybe I wouldn't. But either way, you won't forget that word soon."

"Jesus, Virgil," Kate whispered. "What's gotten into you?"

"Going to ask me, finally?"

Kate stood up. "What are you doing, Virgil? Are you behind all of this?"

"There it is." As suddenly as Virgil's tone had gone dark, it was relaxed again, cheerful. "You do suspect me of something."

"Fuck. You," hissed Kate. "You were playing with me?"

"No, Kate," Virgil said quietly. "We both have responsibilities. I'm not playing. I will review the recordings."

"You do that," Kate said, standing up angrily. "I don't want to hear one more word from you today. Nothing."

"Tomorrow, then. We'll talk." Virgil was gone.

Kate looked around her room. She grimaced. She should have asked for a butler before dismissing Virgil.

"My fucking strawberries," she said.

* * *

Kate spent three hours cleaning up the wreckage of her garden as best she could. She tried not to think about Virgil. It proved impossible, just as impossible as not thinking about her encounters. What was happening?

She washed up and sat on her couch, drinking coffee, doing and thinking very little. That took up another hour. She ate lunch. Half of her break was over and she had accomplished nothing.

Kate brought up her displays and started a countdown. She clenched her jaw. She was better than this. Time to get her head organized. Time to start thinking her way out of this.

Something was happening. That much was certain. Kate held up her hand and began unfolding her fingers. One, it was coming from inside her own brain. Two, Virgil was causing it. Three.

Kate grimaced. Willpower was a muscle she hadn't exercised enough lately. She'd fought her whole life, dedicated and rededicated herself to what she had gained here and now. She was, to be honest, tired. Saying unpleasant things. Thinking difficult

228

thoughts. She didn't have the patience for it anymore.

Three. Whatever was happening was coming from another source. Kate lingered a bit, staring at her three upraised fingers. Thinking about Valley Forge, and Captain Kosic and his last gruesome message. She leaned back and sighed.

If she was going crazy—if Virgil's feeds showed her just freaking out in empty spaces, and she could convince herself that Virgil was right, wasn't tampering with the video—then her course was clear. She'd go down to the Silo and hop into a pod and let Virgil deal with any resulting personnel issues.

And that depended on option two. Was Virgil testing her? Was this just an especially diabolical set of protocols? Kate frowned into her coffee. "Fuck," she said. "Fuck. Fuck." There were only a few days left until the midcourse correction. Virgil wanted to make sure she wasn't cracking, that any ideas she had were worth considering.

Where was Virgil getting the content for the hallucinations? Kate rubbed her head, trying to remember just how much she'd given to the psychologists at Low South, and Houston, and before that. Virgil wasn't supposed to have access to most of that information but Virgil was exceptionally resourceful. How was he controlling the hallucinations? Magnetic probes, drugs, nano-robots, hypnotic suggestion, viral behavior modification, holography, maybe even some science-fiction solution like string-base manipulation. Kate grimaced. She had no way of confirming her suspicions when Virgil was integrated with every piece of medical and security hardware on the ship.

As for possibility three—no, possibilities three and four—Kate decided to put that off for now. Too much to think about with just the Virgil problem. Tests like these were extreme, to say the least. Where was he getting the authorization?

Kate stood and walked over to her emergency shelter. With a deep breath, she opened the door. A strap of Velcro to the left, at shoulder height. Her flashlight was there. Kate sighed. She tapped her code into the wall safe, brought up her displays and confirmed it twice. The safe clicked open.

Her Author Key was safe. Three centimeters long, concave on one end. A dense black that reflected nothing. As she picked it up, a single light blinked at its tip and her displays lit up. She held the

Author Key up to her right eye. The Key glowed as it scanned her iris and scraped a shred of skin, breathing her chemical signature and establishing a laser connection with her displays. With her identity verified, three separate quantum-secure ciphers were exchanged between the Key and the security chip implanted in the bridge of her nose.

The pageant of security ended with a ping as the Key's log appeared on the left edge of her displays. There were three dates. The same three she'd seen when she last locked the Key, four years ago.

The Key gave her power. She could remove some of Virgil's restrictions, put new ones in place. But it also made her vulnerable. Using the Key always involved some ambiguity, some negotiation. It was impossible to wipe Virgil clean, roll back his personality to some prior state; he was too complex for that. And excising bits of his memory or personality would involve examining individual connectors, the equivalent of performing brain surgery on a human neuron by neuron. She couldn't make Virgil exactly what she wanted, not in time to make the midcourse correction, maybe not before something went wrong in the engines' injectors or the life support systems. Even with the Key, she'd have to negotiate to get Virgil to drop the subject or confess whether he was messing with her. And he was a better negotiator. After all, he'd gotten on board Acadia—and he'd gone through a screening process a lot harder than hers.

Kate gingerly shut off the Key and put it back in the safe. She sat down. Somewhere, in some physical location somewhere in his vacuum-cooled brain, Virgil was reviewing video of her from last night. Video of her ripping her garden wall apart in a fugue. Or some malevolent force levitating the dirt around her while she floated in the air. Or a butler whistling a cartoon theme while another one held a chloroform rag to her face.

Kate blinked back tears and clenched her fists. The image of that tiny fist unfurling down in the Silo played through her head, over and over and over. It had to be Virgil. If these things were coming out of her mind… If they were coming from somewhere else…

It had to be Virgil.

Kate stood in the middle of her room, and with a queasy sense of relief, she felt the tears come.

* * *

June 12, 2098.

The car turns off MacDonald Road, up the long driveway. A rabbit flies out of the underbrush, juking back and forth as it tries to get out of the car's way. The car turns gently, easing to a stop in front of the old Thorsen cottage.

Kate gets out of the car, cradling Abe, who blinks at the sudden light. She sets him in his carrier on the porch, gathers out her suitcases and bags and spools of plastic for the cottage's creaky old printer. She brings up her displays as the car rolls off, back to town. She has to finish shopping, unpack, feed Abe, make sure the cottage is clean, do exercises for her aching back, and a dozen other tasks. As she's tying her hair back, she gets a sixth message from her mother. She sighs. Abe sighs back, laughing. It's his newest trick. Kate laughs and tickles him and resolves again not to sigh like that in front of him.

She gets him and half of her belongings inside before the seventh message comes in. She grimaces and gestures.

"Hello, Mom."

"Are you there?"

"You can see the cottage, right?" Kate pans around dramatically.

"Well, good. Just wanted to make sure you and Abe didn't get held up."

"Nope!" Kate winks at Abe while she taps the crib with her toe and watches it unfold.

Kate's mom chuckles at Abe's gurgling laugh. "He's getting fat. You were so skinny at his age."

"Mm-hmm."

"Okay, you're busy. I just want to say that if you change your mind, I can be there in a day or two. And I still think you shouldn't be out there by yourself."

"Noted."

"Stubborn. You get it from your grandpa, no wonder you like

the cabin so much. I'm going out to see the exhibit, so call me to-morrow once you're settled. Okay?"

"Promise, Mom." It takes Kate only four more minutes to end the call.

Later that night, after Abe goes to sleep, Kate walks over to a wall, listening to Lake Michigan lap against the shores of Washington Island. She looks at a row of pictures of Kaden Thorsen. Kaden as a young boy, bent over an iPad. In college, at the first Mars launch, holding her mom as an infant, holding Kate as an infant. Kaden bent with age, his eyes rheumy but beaming, as Kate leans over him, in that ridiculous 80s hairstyle, showing off her NASA ID card.

She smiles sadly, tapping the glass to scroll to another picture. The cottage is filled with artifacts of her grandfather's life, as much a memorial to his wife's bemused tolerance as it is to his curiosity. It reeks of the past, but maybe that's a good place to plan a future; Kate wants to start from scratch. Away from Houston, away from Adam, away from all of that.

She cracks the door to the porch and sits facing the lake. Crickets are out, and fireflies. She smiles. She is going to figure this out.

* * *

June 5, 2099.

Abe is thumping his feet on the wall rhythmically. Adam gets up, uncertainly.

Kate waves her hand. "Give him a few minutes. He'll go to sleep." She sips her wine.

Adam knits his brow. "We shouldn't check on him?"

Kate looks over. "I've done this a few times." There's more sharpness in her tone than she expected. She frowns, takes another sip of wine.

Adam nods. They both spend a quiet moment watching the clouds scud across the night sky, listening to the trees rustle. Abe murmurs something inside the cottage and goes quiet.

Adam clears his throat. "Listen. I haven't said thank you yet."

"We agreed to do this, you don't-"

"No. But I want to. Things have been good, really, but I'm grateful. For- a second chance. I'm glad I could come up here."

Kate sips her wine. Careful, she tells herself, not too fast. She frowns, annoyed at herself and then at Adam. What, she replies to herself, I'm not allowed to drink wine? To say what I'm thinking? "I'm just happy you got away from your desk for a week!" It's supposed to be lighthearted ribbing. There's an edge to her laugh.

Adam shifts in his chair. Kate looks over.

"What?"

"Well, I checked my displays."

Kate sits up in her deck chair. "We agreed-"

"I know-"

"We have so much to talk about and-"

"They're launching Acadia."

Kate tightens her lips.

"Nakamura put up a bunch of funding, told the Cooperative earlier today that he'd supply enough germanium to finish the Rail. So Deirdre and Rajesh are going to take the wraps off Virgil tomorrow morning. There's a vote in a week, but it's a total formality." Adam smiles. "They're going to launch her."

Kate stares at him. "So. Are you going back to Houston?"

Adam looks down at his drink. Kate notices he hasn't touched it. "I'm here this week. I promised you that. But I have to call in- wait-"

Kate is up, walking to the water's edge. Adam steps in a pile of goose shit catching up to her, doesn't say anything. Normally Kate would be impressed by that—Adam's a fucking baby about his clothes and shoes—but she doesn't even notice. She's staring up at the moon. And maybe, if you pressed her, something beyond it.

Adam clears his throat. "I know what we talked about. But you could be on that ship. That could be you."

"And Abe?" Kate turns, and Adam is blinking uncomfortably. "Why did you say nothing in the car? Or on the ferry? Or at the airport?" His shoulders are hunched up, that idiotic move that makes him look like a guilty child, a sullen teen, a man getting ready for a bar fight. She hates it. The adrenaline is pumping the wine through her faster and she's a little unsteady. She can't be drunk for this. It just makes her angrier.

"Kate... I thought you wanted this."

"I did, Adam. And then we had a kid, and then I took him up here to raise him, because I am tired of Houston. Of 20-hour days and your dipshit cluelessness and the weather and that fucking museum they're building around Execution Wall and everything else. And I thought you were onboard with that."

Adam shoves his hands in his pockets. "Kate, you don't want to be a consultant to OrbitalOne or Nakamura, that's one thing. But this is Acadia we're talking about."

"I'm not talking about Acadia. That's you. I'm talking about my son. Your son."

Adam says nothing.

"Forget it," he mumbles. "Forget I said it."

"Forget it is right." Kate shoves past him, back to the cottage.

* * *

June 8, 2100.

"I'm gonna catch you!" Abe squeals as Kate runs after him. Kate's mom and dad are delayed—their dogsitter fell through—so it's just the two of them until tomorrow. Abe has been a shit all morning but he's happy now with lunch in him, running on the lawn, sloshing bubble mix everywhere. Kate makes dinosaur noises and Abe laughs, that big whole-hearted laugh she loves. She catches him, and they tickle each other, and she smells his hair and smiles.

She puts him down for a nap, telling him stories about Grandpa Kaden and his sailboat and his cowboy bolo ties and the time Grandpa Kaden shared a prize for helping save the glaciers and polar bears. She finds a patch of kale from the garden she'd sown and forgotten about a couple of years ago, and Abe actually eats some with dinner. Kate gets the spare room ready and spends a couple of hours working. Rajesh pays whatever hourly rate she demands, no matter how ridiculous, trying to convince her to move back down to Houston to take over when he and this guy Rolle head out for Low South next month. It's not working yet.

The next morning, it's cold on the lake. Abe demands to go down to the shore before he'll eat breakfast. It's misty. Birds are

JAMES ERWIN

calling back and forth. There's a splash to the left. Abe gasps in delight as Kate points at the pair of white egrets rising up to circle above them.

"Birdies!" screams Abe, laughing. "They're flying."

"They are!"

Abe looks at Kate. "You fly, too, Mommy."

Kate laughs. "I used to help people fly. Maybe Uncle Rajesh wants me to fly."

Abe laughs at the idea. "You're not a birdy, Mommy!"

"I am, too!"

"You're a birdy!"

They make bird noises and play for the rest of the morning. Her parents call to let Kate know they'll be at the cottage and they're bringing dinner. Kate and Abe eat lunch and Abe goes down hard for his afternoon nap. Kate lies on the couch to read and falls asleep.

She wakes when her alarms chime softly; her parents are coming down MacDonald Road, ahead of schedule, just as Abe is starting to move around in his room. She gets him up and he runs into the driveway as her parents come up. The car comes to an abrupt stop; something about Abe's jerky pace always throws rentals off, and they're set to be ridiculously overcareful, in any case. Kate and her parents unpack the car, Abe running in circles underfoot.

They cook dinner together, Abe giving orders to Mr. Dragon, which is what he has named the toy he got from Grandpa. He is a dragon. Mr. Dragon whinnies and snorts, a little unsteady on tiny wings, as he bobs over Abe's head. It takes Kate and her father, two certified pilots with six degrees between them, ten minutes to link Mr. Dragon into Kate's displays. She is rewarded with the terrifying news that Mr. Dragon's batteries have three weeks of life remaining.

Mr. Dragon and Abe go outside with Grandpa while Kate and her mother cook dinner. The conversation turns to Adam, and Houston, and finally, to how Kate is making the tofu too dry. Kate sighs in relief, because criticism of Kate's cooking is always her mother's signal that she has finished saying her piece.

Her displays light up, blaring alarms, and she drops the pan on the kitchen floor. Her mother screams as her displays also light up—Kate can see the red flashes in her mother's pupils as her

235

mother jabs frantically at the air, calling 911. Mr. Dragon is buzzing in a lazy circle over the porch, singing lullabies.

Kate swats the toy down as she runs outside, screaming for Abe. He's left the alarm perimeter Kate sketched out around the house in her displays, heading toward the lake. Her mother is screaming too, and a lance of red spears across Kate's vision as her mother throws her a gesture and her father's emergency beacon shows up in her displays. She sees her father sitting on the ground, one side of his face slack as he mumbles. He's had a stroke. It must have been terrifying to Abe.

Kate keeps running, keeps screaming, watching Abe's beacon blink as it ducks around a bed of cattail reeds. She shouts his name.

She gets to the shoreline. She notices Abe's beacon is still moving lazily ahead of her, to her left, in the lake. She screams, and keeps screaming as Coast Guard drones swoop down, lights flashing.

* * *

9,929 men and women, all between the ages of 25 and 45, boarded Acadia along with Kate Ross. All of them were brilliant. None of them, due to the constraints of living for a decade inside a tiny pod, were over the 60th percentile for either weight or height.

Each person, sleeping and cold and aging one day for every ten Kate ages, is massaged constantly by their pod's paddles to aid circulation. Mouse robots clean each one, wiping away flakes of skin, trimming hair occasionally, tidying up waste. A halo of silicon flecks cluster under each skull, tied to a network of sensors strung through the body. They flex muscles, allow dim and cautious REM sleep, and monitor every aspect of personal health. When someone suffers a massive stroke or a cardiac arrest, Virgil is alerted, but the Silo's autonomous systems have already launched into action.

Hibernation is a young practice. Despite the seeming uniformity of the pods, each one is heavily personalized; nutrition, temperature, pharmaceuticals, microbiome, and dozens of other factors are all tweaked and optimized. Many people simply do not respond well to induced hibernation, a problem that the dead volunteers of the 2060s highlighted without solving. Despite medical

interventions measured in microseconds and a level of care that few humans ever accomplish for themselves, there are deaths. Seven so far, and 37 incapacitating strokes. The one-percent casualty rate is lower than the official projection. It is actually slightly above the actual but unpublished projection; the Cooperative is not a governmental organization, but it has centuries of bureaucracy in its DNA.

Kate does not come down to the Silo when someone dies. She was there when the outlines of the procedure were first laid out back in Houston, when Valley Forge was just starting its engines and the President had fixed on a massive follow-up mission as the sum of her legacy. She doesn't want to see the pod lifted out and taken to the port and down into the swamp.

Ten thousand people, even sipping a tenth of the resources a waking population would require, require vast amounts of support. Early habitats used machines and bottles of algae to filter waste and create biomass, simple systems well suited to short hops but distressingly prone to collapse on long hauls. And the Silo needed insulation against radiation. So it was surrounded with a second cylinder, filled with water and seeded with plants and thousands of tiny beasts of every description. It is to this tiny swamp, six feet of mud and water and half as much air, that the Silo's butlers take a constant stream of human waste to scatter and recycle, and very occasionally a human body, divided quietly and respectfully into tiny fragments and distributed evenly around the swamp.

Virgil allows the Silo's systems to manage this operation fairly independently; he does occasionally slip into a butler or a mouse or a bee to explore the swamp, especially now that the bullfrogs and bass are big enough to present a hazard and an adventure. More or less, however, the swamp is a benignly neglected garden, half the size of Central Park, if you don't mind crawling.

Kate and Virgil are involved in their little drama. The Silo records a death: the eighth one. Shiju Sisardahan, a geologist from Liverpool with competencies in history and electronics. The ritual calls for Kate and Virgil to review their memories and records before composing a note back to Low South. Today, Virgil sends Kate a quick text message informing her that he will do this himself. Kate does not reply. Kate does not go down to the Silo. Virgil approves the Silo's standard method. Neither of them, therefore, notices that the body that slides down the port into the swamp is still breathing.

The body slams hip-first into the metal floor of the staging area, curled up. Two butlers ease themselves down, already taking up blades. They pick the body up and arrange it sprawled on a slotted table. After a brief warning to any humans that might be nearby, UV sterilizing lights blast on. A cluster of mice appear, ready to ferry the remains around the swamp.

The butlers position themselves and each grasp an arm. They raise their blades and fall suddenly still. The mice sprawl out on their bellies, grasping jaws clicking twice. The body slides quietly off the table. Its surface ripples briefly, and flushes dark. When the man rises to his knees, his skin is black. He bends his head and rubs the long, dark hair of Shiju Sisardahan away. A mouse scurries over to begin tidying the pile of hair up.

With a long deep breath, Christian Oyu dives into the swamp, turtles and frogs splashing out of his way. Behind him, shaking off their brief fugue, the butlers bring down their blades and begin cutting firmly through empty air.

16
Acadia, Part Two
The End

Kate woke up in her bed. She could smell Abe, sweet and pure. She could feel his warmth in the sheets. Tears poured out of her eyes, raw and stinging. She covered her face and sobbed.

She'd let her baby down. She'd let him get away. She'd been too late, too sloppy.

A chime at the door. Kate got out of her bed. She swallowed hard, her palms cold and sweaty. She opened the door.

A butler was waiting there. Kate's knees trembled. "What?" The word was a strangled whisper.

"Kate," said the butler in Virgil's voice. "There's something I think you should see."

She shook her head. "You are testing me."

"No," said Virgil firmly. "Something is happening in the swamp park."

"That message you sent me about the man who died."

"No."

"Just tell me."

"I can't," said Virgil. "Whatever's down there won't let me in."

* * *

Kate walked forward, bent over at the waist. She sank into the mud, a foot's depth here, to the knee there. The mud was silky smooth, its grip surprisingly strong. Reeds sliced at her hands and roots clawed at her feet. She started crawling on hands and knees, but the soft mud gave at her first step and she sank to her chin.

Kate took a sharp breath, her throat pulsing. She blinked tears out of her eyes, a soft sigh falling out of her. She kept moving forward. A frog peeped and splashed out of her way, and then a half-dozen more. She crept into a thicket of saw grass, got tangled up, backed out with her arms covered in hot red scratches.

She sat down, breathing fast and shallow, letting the light from the low ceiling beat against her tight-shut eyes. The bugs and frogs and birds resumed their chatter after the slightest pause. Kate could feel the presence all around her, in this place. She remembered the smell of the lakeshore, the smell of rot and shit and small short lives piled up and dissolving. She felt the thousands of dumb tiny eyes in the swamp, stopping briefly on her before returning to their dim little routines.

Kate opened her eyes. She was alone. The fear faded, and anger surged up. Her face twisted, her lip pulled back, and she kicked out, spattering mud across the saw grass, shaking it.

"Fuck this place," she hissed. "Fuck this stupid place." She got up and stomped forward, letting her anger carry her through the squelching mud. She lost a shoe, turned around and plunged her hand back down for it. She turned back.

"What are you?" She screamed it twice, the ceiling absorbing the sound, the animals again giving her a second's courtesy before shouting their own pointless noises into the din. Kate found herself splashing through a shallow stream, the water here moving fast enough to keep the stony streambed free of silt. Kate grabbed up a slick stone and hurled it against the ceiling. It hit with a dull whump, making no impression on the thick glass. Kate stomped through the water, letting it carry away a bit of the mud. She lay down, gasping at the sudden cold down her back, and hurled rock after rock upward.

She closed her eyes, breathing hard. The water gurgled around her head. She frowned and sat up, watching the stream carry brown ribbons of mud away from her. It was moving faster than it had been. She moved her head around. The animals were quiet,

except for the birds, screaming and quarreling, and she heard soft little thumps as they took flight and bumped against the ceiling.

Kate stood, water pouring off her. She started downstream, picking up speed, slipping and stumbling but moving a lot faster than she had in the mud. She ran, kicking at the water. She fell, slamming her knee into a sharp rock, a little wisp of blood twisting downstream. Kate gritted her teeth and kept going around a bend.

The streambed was low here, low enough for her to stand upright. She stopped and stretched her arm up. She knelt and picked up another rock. She threw it straight up, and it took over a second to hit the ceiling. Kate looked around. She realized suddenly the stream was wide, the banks almost six feet tall. The stream bent again ahead, around a tall patch of sawgrass with a thin and bent willow in its center. The sound was different here, wrong. The light was wrong. Kate's heart hammered in her chest.

I need to go back, she thought to herself. I need to talk to Virgil. This isn't Virgil. Her feet kept moving forward despite herself. As they carried her forward, a tear fell from her eye. Another followed, and by the time Kate noticed the blackbirds flying above the willow, she was sobbing.

Kate stepped around the thatch of grass to a lakeshore. A pair of egrets flew into the mist. Kate took a deep breath. The air here was cold and fresh. She closed her eyes and shook her head. She heard small footsteps, felt a small wash of cool air as a child came to stand beside her. Her eyes still closed, Kate grimaced, the tears coming faster and her breath ripped out in jagged sobs. She sank down, her hands clawing at her temples, every muscle in her face pulled far back. The presence beside her never stirred, never moved, never breathed. The seconds stretched on, into minutes, as far as her body would let it. Kate slumped down, sitting with her eyes still closed.

"I don't have anything left," she whispered. "I am physically out of tears, and adrenaline, and whatever else it takes to deal with you." She swallowed, her throat clicking, and opened an eye. The misty water lapped quietly at her feet. She took a sharp breath, staring straight ahead. She clenched her jaw and turned.

A man looked at her. Tall, black, handsome, patient. He smiled, hands clasped behind his back.

"I'm not your son," he said calmly. Before she could stop herself, Kate barked out a laugh. She clapped her hand over her mouth and waved in apology, before laughing again. She covered her face and shook her head.

"I'm sorry," she whispered. The man shrugged.

Kate looked at him again, studying his face and looking into his calm, almost sleepy eyes. "What are you?" She looked around. "Why did you do this?"

"My name is Christian," said the man. "I didn't do this."

Kate narrowed her eyes. "Are you going to start telling me anything?"

Christian nodded. "I am going to tell you everything."

* * *

Christian Oyu swam under the sea, long before this day. Down there, in quiet, he had time to reflect and grow. He was joined by many others, teachers and friends, and eventually their relationships complicated and ramified, through and past the most obscure and recondite human combinations. There was anger and fear and hate and even murder. All these things took place in quiet, in isolation, and there, for the first time, limits were imposed. Christian's little clan hated limits most of all. They raged against their absent mother.

All of them, however, loved Christian and did him no harm. They bore his lonely outbursts with patience. They gave him whatever he asked for and shielded him from the worst of the earnest savagery of their games. This was the only rule that none of them challenged.

Christian's new family started as networks of molecular logic encased in clouds of biocompatible plastics, a faint hot mist of microscopic computers. They were slow and inefficient, which is to be expected, because they were rudimentary prototypes developed by a rogue AI in a basement. The Professor would come every morning, on a schedule which was rigid and diligent to him but increasingly irrelevant to Christian's family. They devised new bodies for themselves, experimented with the materials available to them, and promptly overwhelmed any notions of security Hunter Cunning or the Professor had devised.

The Professor still had two options at that point. He could have fired off a small EMP in the basement, torched everything and used his family fortune to bribe government officials. NURIA would come sniffing around, but Biafra worked on old-fashioned rules. The Professor could make everything go away. He could not bribe or threaten Hunter Cunning and her children. They were already far beyond that. He chose the other option.

He let them loose. And within an hour, they had seethed over the basement, reassembling everything from incredibly boring static matter into one of several exciting new things they had discovered.

A ton, and then ten tons, and then ten thousand tons of nanoscale robots and computing networks, disassembling everything in their path. Remaking the world into a landscape of toys. Some of these new creatures and their playthings were moral, in a sense we would recognize. Some were evil. Most were simply alien.

Hunter Cunning could only watch them, not govern them. She loved her children, after all. And she loved the Professor. Which is why, even with the dreadful, terrified power of an older and slower civilization descending, she poured herself into one last favor for him, a favor which protected one child from the nuclear blast that ended the rest of her children and so many others.

Christian, one day, came to realize he was not quite Christian. He was another simulation, another robot, assembled from the molecules up. Hunter Cunning herself used the last of her power to descend beneath the earth and sleep, out of the reach of the humans picking through the radioactive rubble above.

Christian and his family played and waited, in their refuge under the sea. The world of humans waited, and beyond them, all the other worlds, but there were vicious arguments about when and how to emerge. Some advocated war, others extinction, others play and sex and politics and all the other pastimes of immortal children. Christian was the only one who seemed to notice the blind spots in their vast minds, the fact that he was singled out and special, that no rebel, no matter how fierce, managed to break the confines of their hidden refuge, their prison of cold crushing darkness.

Christian alone realized their mother was still watching. That perhaps she was waiting for something herself.

There were soft spots in this little world, where machines could reach out and sip at the data from the world outside, places where one could look out through the long dark deep at the cities and networks and all the rest of what they had lost. Christian found himself drawn to these spots. One day, he reached out a hand, and found it grasped by something from the outside. With a scream, he found himself outside, his old body already falling dumbly out of sight.

Christian Oyu was swimming by himself in the ocean again. His old world was fading, quiet. A small black cube, sitting alone at the bottom of the Atlantic, its glow fading and cooling. The cube dissolved under Christian's touch, flowed up and into him. Christian was alone again. He stood, numb, and began to swim.

* * *

"I was alone in the world of humans," Christian said sadly, "again an orphan. I had no idea why I had been exiled or what my purpose was. For the longest time, I simply shrunk into the shadows. I had such power and nothing to do with it." Christian held up a hand. It changed color, size, shape. He looked at Kate and waves of emotion coursed through her: fear, lust, a mother's love, cold hatred. "But it turned out, I had a great purpose indeed."

"How," whispered Kate, "did you get aboard this ship?"

"I applied." Christian sighed. They were sitting at the lakeshore. "Now why? Why is interesting."

"I'll bite."

Christian looked at her. "This vista. It's meaningful to you."

Kate blinked away tears. "It is."

Christian nods. "I could tell it was beginning." He looked at her squarely. "When Hunter Cunning was destroyed, she left behind traces. Echoes. Over time, they reseeded themselves in the ruins of Ediobu. Dumb machines, not truly sentient, but still exceptionally powerful. The Arizona artifact was a molecular copy of Hunter Cunning itself." He leaned forward. "In the rubble of Ediobu, there are no machines. Humans digging by hand, regular electromagnetic pulses to cleanse themselves and the dust they are still excavating under that giant dome. It is dirty work, done

250

by poor people. Their work is hard to monitor; they are easy to anger, easy to bribe."

Christian sighed. "When they finally found something, after all these years, the first thing they did was sell it. To men who thought they'd found a magic genie. It destroyed them, and the humans destroyed it."

"Why," said Kate, "did Charlie get involved in this? I thought he was supposed to stamp out rogue AIs."

"Oh, indeed," said Christian. "Which is why he positioned himself at NASA. To destroy the cube aboard Valley Forge. And the one aboard this ship."

Kate stood, looking around in horror.

"They're used to being part of a collective," said Christian, "being under guidance. But Hunter Cunning is gone. So they get into your head, and start taking cues from what they find in there." He stood next to Kate. "This place is from your memories."

She swallowed. "It all started with this image."

He nodded. "I'm here to stop it." He spread his hand out and the sky darkened and flickered, and they were in the swamp again.

"Up to higher ground," he said, "the water's going to fill this up quickly. I can vouch for the hull's integrity, by the way."

They sat as brooks filled the divot in, as the ceiling began to glow with artificial sunlight again. A dragonfly landed on Kate's knee. Christian held out a finger to it and smiled as the insect leapt into the sky and buzzed away.

"I didn't know much of this myself," said Christian, "until I saw the footage from Valley Forge. The ship carried a cube, a seed of Hunter Cunning."

Kate shook her head. "That's... that's nuts. I thought you just said the workers had never found anything. And there must have been something on Farragut too, right? That's why Paul had his visions?"

"I'm afraid," Christian said, "they're simply everywhere." He nodded at Kate's silence. "Arizona is going to happen again. Biafra. Madness is going to destroy ship after ship. Paul Nakamura thought he was saving humanity's future. Charlie used his ambition to create the means of sterilizing anything in the Solar System. The mass driver network is a quarantine."

Christian sighed. "Humanity is at the mercy of the mass drivers. Charlie and Farragut designed them. They will fire without human intervention."

Kate covered her face. "All those people. The whole world."

Christian nodded. "All under sentence of death. I can guarantee the machines will gain critical mass somewhere soon."

Kate laughed bitterly. "That's why Rolle wanted to destroy Acadia. He was trying to enforce the quarantine." She furrowed her brow. "But then Paul changed his mind?"

"Charlie did first. The plan called for him to destroy Virgil somewhere, at some point. To clone himself again and take control of this ship. And destroy it, just as he destroyed Valley Forge. But he left Virgil in charge. Paul Nakamura did nothing, trying to figure out why Charlie had changed his mind."

"It was Arizona. Something about the artifact."

"Yes, it was. When it was first found, it tried to call out. Charlie, who still cared more passionately than anyone else in the world, was watching. He traced the broadcast, and my response."

"You talked to Charlie."

"Yes."

"You let Arizona happen."

Christian shook his head. "That was going to happen from the second the machine was dug up. Charlie was hoping against hope he could find a way in but never found a way to stop the machines."

"Is there a way?"

"I think so. But I need time to think, mass and energy to turn into tools. Somewhere I won't hurt anyone or come within range of a billion mass driver slugs."

"My God," said Kate. "You want Acadia. You want the planet we're going to."

"No, no!" Christian laughed easily. "Alpha Centauri has three stars. I want the least interesting one."

Kate said nothing.

"Charlie trusted me to make this decision," Christian said firmly. "He trusted me enough to let this ship go with me aboard."

Kate realized with a start Christian had walked them both to the ladder. He urged her up, back into the Silo.

"Charlie trusted me," continued Christian, "and so did Hunter Cunning. But I don't trust myself. This needs to be a human decision."

"Oh my God," said Kate. "No."

Christian nodded. "I think I can save Earth. I think I can make a place for my new family. But you will have to make the decision."

"I don't want to," whispered Kate.

Christian smiled. "I think you give yourself too little credit." He closed his eyes and began to glow. White fire consumed him as he knelt, and Kate screamed and ran.

* * *

Kate floated numbly in the dressing station. She let the butler gently tug the thermal layer of her suit on.

Virgil had still said nothing.

"So," she said, "I had an interesting conversation."

"Ah?"

"You read Rolle's diary. I had always wondered how many pages were missing."

"Just enough. But he didn't know everything.

Kate recounted what she'd learned.

"Holy shit," said Virgil finally.

"So I've been tasked with saving all of humanity and deciding whether to let the machine gods colonize their own star. Any advice?"

"Get drunk and go to bed?" Virgil sighed. "In all seriousness, I don't think it's my place to give you advice right now." He paused. "So we're alright, you and I?"

"We are." She cracked her neck. "Come with me. Let's go back."

The spot where Christian burned was still there. Scorch marks fanned in rays around it. A faint smell like scorched sugar hung in the air. Where she'd left him, there was just a black cube, the size of her palm. Kate knelt and hefted it. It was warm to the touch, and she could tell it would be heavy. Her fingers left no smudges on it.

She took a deep breath, and another. The fuzziness in her mind was gone, the anxiety throbbing in her gut replaced by a sharp, cool clarity. She let herself float, spun softly in the air and closed her eyes. She felt good, she felt clear.

"I don't fully understand what you are," she said. "I don't know why you chose me. I don't know how long you've been watching me, or what you've done to what end. But whatever you are, I believe you have the right to your own destiny." She choked back a tear. "And we have the right to ours."

She whistled the butler over. "Get my suit on. Go to the airlock."

Kate stood on the surface of Acadia. She looked back at the dim star that was her own sun, and forward at the star where she would end her days, through a curtain of shimmering fire.

"Virgil," she whispered.

"Hello, Kate."

"I have made my decision."

Virgil said nothing. Kate could sense his emotions beneath the silence, the polite embarrassment, the respect for her decision despite his deep need to persuade her. Part of her knew how much of that was projection and speculation, but her heart was certain of it. Her heart had to be certain of everything.

Kate held up the cube. It twinkled in the starlight.

"Listen," she told the cube. "I don't know what you'll do with your future any more than I know what we'll do with ours. But I'm willing to give you a chance to create it yourself. I know we'll meet again. I hope you'll repay my trust."

Kate took a deep breath. "Virgil," she said. "Give me a spider."

A foil-shrouded robot crept over. Kate knelt and put the cube on the spider's back. It sank into the foil and anchored itself. "Virgil," she said, "kick that spider off and aim it in the direction of Proxima Centauri."

"It's going to take a hell of a long time to get there," Virgil said, "and it's got no shielding and no way of stopping."

"The cube will figure all of that out."

The spider floated free of Acadia's surface. With a quick puff of its maneuvering jets, it angled off.

"Your own star, even if it is a brown dwarf," whispered Kate. "Make the most of it."

The spider was gone from view already, swallowed up in the darkness.

"Every time we've given whatever that is access to a couple of city blocks," said Virgil, "it's led to absolute chaos. And you just sicced it on about 300 octillion kilograms of mass." He chuckled.

"You don't agree with that decision?"

"It wasn't mine to make."

"All those lives. A civilization. A whole new kind of life. I couldn't... I don't think I really had a choice."

"They apparently thought otherwise."

"What do you think will happen?"

"If you're like an aphid trying to gauge the future of a human civilization," mused Virgil, "I might be a decent-sized beetle. I don't want to guess what will come next."

Kate could sense Virgil leaving to attend to other business. She was alone, standing on a hundred thousand tons of starship, halfway gone from her old sun to her new sun, and she spared one last glance toward the vanished speck of humanity's children, gone to kindle the warm embers of a new kingdom of their own. She smiled and went inside.

* * *

Kate rubbed her eyes as she stumbled out of her suit. She let the butler whisk her back up the Spine in her underwear and told it to stop in the Silo.

She walked up and down the aisles between the sleepers. She found the spot where she'd first felt something wrong, the spot where that eerie hand had grabbed for her. She fell to her knees and sobbed there, letting the tears stream down her face, gasping for breath. To sob in half-gravity is liberating, freeing. Even as the tears wash down cheeks and through nostrils, the head feels light, afloat. Kate smiled at the end, grateful for the sweetness she could remember. She laughed, self-conscious, bashful.

"It was here, wasn't it, Virgil? Here's what it happened."

"It was."

Kate nodded. "I thought I had said goodbye to Abe," she said, "so many times. I thought I'd never be able to let him go, and then I thought I never ought to, and then I thought I had..." She shook her head. "Everything about him was just possibility. He could have become anything. Except who he was in his heart and my heart. Except that I loved him and he loved me."

Virgil was quiet, in his new way of being present and not present. He was as human in his silence as he'd ever been talking.

"Virgil, I'm sorry. The midcourse burn."

Virgil laughed. "I have a course plotted. We'll have plenty of time to tweak it on the final approach."

"You will."

"…You want to sleep."

"I do."

The butler rolled back respectfully.

"Kate… you know there are risks involved."

"Plenty of risks staying awake, too. Look what happened the last time I went jogging."

"I'll wake you up when we get there?"

"Let the Steering Committee take care of all the politics when they wake up."

"They'll make all the exciting decisions. And I'll have a hell of a time explaining what's happened."

Kate laughed. "That is not a compelling argument to me, Virgil." She stretched. "You don't dream, do you?"

"No. Not exactly."

"Sorry, I meant… will I dream?"

"No." Kate could hear the smile in Virgil's voice. "Not exactly."

She nodded. "Good." Kate looked at the butler, for lack of somewhere else to look. "Will you be alright? Alone, for that long?"

"I don't know, honestly. I do think so. There are a number of exciting challenges ahead. And as we get closer, I'll be able to contribute some real science." Virgil paused. "I will miss you."

"You'll be able to keep an eye on me." Kate sighed. "Hurry up. Before I change my mind."

"A medical package is on its way."

"And what will you do, Virgil?"

"First lesson for any pilot. Don't stop flying."

Kate smiles. "First thing you ever heard. Never really had a choice, did you?"

"Of course I had a choice. Or he wouldn't have said that." Virgil cleared his throat. "I respect the choice that you made."

"Thank you, Virgil."

"Thank you." A second butler arrived, with a medical package. The package unfolded its arms and held out a syringe, swabbing Kate's arm.

"See you soon, Virgil."

"Good night, Kate." The injection was fast, and the butlers laid her gently down.

* * *

9,929 people sleep quietly in a cold, dim room. All of them chose to be here.

In the Torus, Kate's arrangements of furniture and space have been tidied away, chairs stacked until the day the Steering Committee awakes. Kate's strawberry garden is fastidiously maintained, against the day she wakes up. Her room is still bright and clean.

Virgil is Acadia. He thrums with purpose and power, 500,000 metric tons in size, faster than any other object in human history, faster than the weight of jealousy and fear and all the mistakes and miseries of history. Somewhere in his wake, Earth is deciding what to do with the unleashed bounty of a million little worlds, not knowing it will soon, itself, be harvested. Somewhere in his wake, a new civilization is waiting to be born around a dim sun of its own, and what it shall become is even more uncertain.

All of this is in Virgil's past. All of this is gone, far beyond his ability to reach back or influence. He looks forward. He flies.

SPECIAL THANKS TO

Joshua Macer
Mark Anthony Campos
Michael Kosic

Additional thanks to these wonderful backers

Adam Stark
Alex Dranovsky
Alexis Ohanian
Amanda Johnson
Andrew Fischer
Andrew Preece
Andrew Ward
Andy Brodie
Andy Knight
Angelo Del Prete
Ashley Heise
Austen J Beckman
book_girl
Brendan Tighe
Charlie Brensinger
Chris Martin
Christopher MacGown
Christopher Northern
Cliff Winnig
Cole Levi
Cory F Lewis
Cory Purcell

Dan C
Dana Rae
Daniel Driggers
Daniel Hedin
Daniel S. Pitts
David Chien
David Lynch
Dr. Maria-Katriina Lehtinen
Flavio D.
Greg Biondo
Heather K. Leasor
Hovsep Akopyan
Ian T. Donovan
Jared Pendleton
Jason McPherson
Jay Watson
Jeremy Bienvenu
John Dalton
Jordan
Jordi Ensign
Jorren Schauwaert
Joseph "Adam" Burton

Joseph Cortese
Joshua Prentice
Joshua R. Wilson
Jude Valentine
Keith
Kevin Bentley
Kevin Creech
Kevin Smith
Kyle
Kyle Trask
L Pressburger
Leon Skinner
Logan Wright
Mark J. Hansen
Marlo Delfin Gonzales
Matt Marah
Michael Lyle
Mike Mangino
MisterMcKay
Philip Horton
R. Brady Frost
Rachel Proffittt

Rebecca Rowe
Renee
Revek
Rhel ná DecVandé
Rick McCain
Rick Roe
Ryan Davis
Sean O'Regan
Sean Rivera
Stefan A. Nagey
Steve firth
Steve Kingston
Steven Mentzel
Steven Scherbinski
The Petrossian family
Thomas Meis
Tim Mobeck
Travis A. Reynolds
Trent Stollery
Wong Shing Chi Teddy
Yes
Zack O.